T0149008

THE
ANCHORESS OF
CHESTERFIELD

THE
ANCHORESS OF
CHESTERFIELD

CHRIS NICKSON

*To the church with its glorious crooked spire,
the original inspiration.
With gratitude to Waterstones in Chesterfield
for their support with this series.
For Chesterfield Museum, where the windlass sits:
it's helped my thoughts turn.*

First published 2020

The Mystery Press is an imprint of The History Press
97 St George's Place, Cheltenham,
Gloucestershire, GL50 3QB
www.thehistorypress.co.uk
© Chris Nickson, 2020

British Library Cataloguing in Publication Data.
A catalogue record for this book is available from the British Library.

ISBN 978 0 7509 9309 8

Typesetting and origination by The History Press
Printed and bound in Great Britain by TJ Books Limited

MIX
Paper from
responsible sources
FSC® C013056

CHAPTER ONE

Chesterfield, September 1370

John felt the axe bite into the wood, deep enough for it to stay. He straightened up and stretched, then wiped the sweat from his face with an old piece of linen. Chopping the branches from a fallen tree was labour to make the muscles ache and moan in protest.

It had come down during the night, blocking the road that led north from Chesterfield to Sheffield. At first light the town bailiffs were out knocking on the doors, begging all the craftsmen and labourers in town for their help. Everyone with tools and a strong back. John the Carpenter had been one of the first, bringing his mute assistant, Alan. Soon a dozen men and more were working on the tree with axes and saws. It was an old, thick elm that had rotted at its core until the weight became too much and it had toppled.

Now the trunk lay in sections the height of a man, each one pushed to the side of the road. The only task remaining was to strip the branches, and they were almost done with that. John told Alan to fetch them ale from the jug a kindly goodwife had left. Only six men were still working. Themselves, three foresters who seemed locked into their labour, never joking or gossiping, and a farmhand, a sullen man sent along by his master who kept pausing to grumble.

The sun sat high in the sky. But it was September now, with none of the fierce heat that had burned his skin all summer and turned it the colour of tanned leather. A pleasant day, with the high clouds flitting and dancing above the fields.

At least he'd be paid for this, John thought. Fourpence, a full day's wage. And there were one or two pieces of wood he might be able to scavenge and shape into things later, once business had ceased for the winter.

Truth be told, he was grateful for any money at all. It had been a meagre year. The only good thing was that the prayers of all in the town had been answered; no cases of plague in the heat of summer gave them all the hope that it might never return. He crossed himself at the thought.

For him, though, things had been hard. Two more joiners had moved to town and brought competition. Their work was rough and ready, they weren't proper craftsmen; still, they were able to handle most jobs that had been his. Men who charged less than he did and took much of his business. Incomers. Silently, he laughed at himself.

John had been here for ten years now. He was married, he had three children. Much of the time he felt part of the fabric of Chesterfield. Still, to some who'd been born and raised here, he was as much an outsider as someone who'd arrived just the week before. Another decade and he still wouldn't be a native to people like that.

He carefully pulled out his axe, wiped it with an oily rag and inspected the edge, running it along his thumb, before putting it back in the leather satchel. The tools he owned had once belonged to his father. They'd served the man well until he died in the Great Pestilence. God's blood, that was more than twenty years ago now. A lifetime and more.

The hammer, the saw, the awl and everything else had kept John alive as he wandered from place to place, growing from a boy to a young man and learning to harness his natural feel for wood. Life on the roads had taken him to York; for several years he'd honed his craft there, constantly employed in the frenzy of church building until circumstances forced him to leave. Only after that had he ended up in Chesterfield.

This was home now. He was settled, he'd lived here longer than anywhere else. To anyone looking at his life, he was a success. He'd become a family man with all the responsibilities that brought. He had his business as a carpenter, he owned two houses, he employed a young man. But he knew how readily appearances could deceive.

One of the properties, on Saltergate, had been in his wife Katherine's family; she was the oldest child, she'd inherited it when her mother died. The other, around the corner on Knifesmithgate, had belonged to Martha, the old woman who was friend to them both. She'd willed him her house when she died two years before. By then John and his family were already living there, caring for the woman in her old age. Martha had stood godmother to two of their children and they'd named their younger daughter after her; her memory would live on in his family.

Both houses desperately needed work. They'd been ignored for too long. John had done what he could, but so much was beyond him. The roof at Martha's old house leaked into the solar. It was going to need new slates before winter set in. If he left it for yet another year, the beams would begin to rot and it would be a much bigger, harder job. But a tiler would cost money he didn't have in his coffer.

He rented out the Saltergate house. The amount it brought barely covered all the never-ending list of repairs.

The constant worry about money grew more pressing every month. It kept him awake long into the night and gnawed at his heart. No peace. The other day he'd seen his reflection in a pond, shocked at the way his hair was turning grey and the lines that furrowed his face.

This year it was coming to a head. He was going to have to make a choice. Unless something happened and a fortune tumbled into his lap, he'd have no choice but to sell one of the houses. And he had no faith in miracles. Not for a man like him.

He loved Katherine's brother and sisters, but he was glad they were no longer part of the household. Fewer mouths to feed was a blessing when he had three children of his own. His brother-in-law Walter and his young bride were settled with her parents in Bolsover, while Katherine's two sisters were in service on a farm near Holymoorside.

He sighed and began the walk back towards Chesterfield. It wasn't far, no more than a few minutes away. The spire of the church soared high into the sky, visible for miles around, as clear and welcoming as any beacon.

He'd worked on that when he first arrived in the town. Only for a short time, though. After a few days John had found himself a suspect in a murder in the church tower, a stranger who needed to clear his name.

That had happened ten years ago. Where had the time gone? It happened when he first knew Katherine, before he'd become a husband and a father and all the things that had happened since. John felt the weight of his own history pressing down on his shoulders. What could he do except carry on? With God's blessing, everything would be fine. He had to believe that. They'd all survive and prosper in His grace.

'Who knows, maybe we'll have work waiting for us in town,' he told Alan, with the kind of hope he didn't feel.

The lad was twelve now, as much a natural as a carpenter as John had been himself. He carried his own leather satchel of tools that banged against his back as he walked. He was growing into a tall young man with broad shoulders, his hands rough and thick with calluses from the work they did. Alan was old enough and certainly skilled enough to strike out on his own. But he was mute and he didn't know how to write. His fingers were quick to make signs, but most people would never understand them. It was impossible for him to obtain work himself, and he needed to be with someone who wouldn't take advantage of him. Six years before, the boy had started out as John's apprentice and bit by bit the lad had learned everything he had to teach. Now he was... what could he call him, John wondered? An assistant? An equal? He clapped a hand down on the boy's shoulder and watched the tiny flakes of wood rise from his battered tunic.

The road was dusty; they'd had no rain for over a fortnight. A few horses and carts passed them, and he could hear the sounds of the weekday market on the north side of the church as they climbed the hill. A town of stone and slate, of timber and limewash. Beautiful, in its own coarse way. Home.

Not too much more than a week and the annual fair would begin. It would be eight days of feasting, noise and entertainment, with all manner of goods for sale. Music and players, tumblers and jugglers. It would all begin with a service and blessing in church on the day of the exaltation of the Holy Cross. Already he could sense the excitement around town. Every year it was exactly the same. The children caught it first, dancing through the days in anticipation, then the fever started to affect the adults.

For a brief while, Chesterfield would feel like the most important, magical place in the kingdom. People came from all over for the fair. Not just the North, nor even England, but everywhere. John had met many from beyond the borders: Welshmen, Irishmen, even a Dane once, with his happy, sing-song accent; a German and a man from the lowlands of Holland. An entire world came to Chesterfield, bringing things beyond the locals' imagination. Goods to buy, foods to taste. Minstrels and clowns to entertain. There would be merchants and goodwives shouting out their wares and displaying all the luxuries on offer. Everything from the ordinary to the exotic. His children were counting down the days. Foolishly, he'd promised Martha a length of ribbon from the fair. She'd remember, of course, but he had no idea how he'd be able to afford it for her. The worry of an empty scrip crowded his mind.

Before he went home he'd stop at the Guildhall and pick up his wage for today's work. Four good pennies to spend on food. Katherine would be glad to see that. The garden behind their house had been fruitful this year, but the season was coming to an end and it didn't offer them bread or milk or meat. Only the occasional hen that had grown too old to lay eggs.

He looked as Alan nudged him and pointed towards a man hurrying along with a forceful stride and a determined look in his eye. He was wearing a dark green woollen tunic bearing the coroner's badge, he had a sword hanging from his belt, and he was coming directly towards them.

Pray God the man wasn't seeking him. It couldn't be good news if someone like that wanted him. Either something awful had happened, or the coroner wanted his help. Six years had passed since the last time that had happened. That was when de Harville was still alive and held the office of King's Coroner. Katherine had always hated the idea of him working for the man. Three times it had happened, and he'd always undertaken the work reluctantly, but what choice did anyone have when a rich man in authority demanded his services? The last time he'd almost been killed. Enough, his wife insisted, and he'd been quick to agree.

Then de Harville died, and John was thankful that his successor, Sir Mark Strong, had chosen to go his own way. He had no desire to be tangled up in any of that again.

'Are you John the Carpenter?' the man asked as he came closer.

'I am.' He felt his heart sink.

'The coroner would like you to attend him.'

'Me?' John asked. 'Are you sure you have the right man? Why would he want me? I've never done any work for Coroner Strong.'

He knew the words were hopeless, but he had to say them, to try and ward all this off.

The man shrugged. He was well-muscled, with fair hair and a ruddy complexion, a pair of smiling blue eyes.

'Nay, Master, I'm not the one to ask. I'm just the messenger. All I do is what I'm told, and my order was to come and fetch you. I don't know what he wants. But I can tell you this: there's a body at Calow and he'd like you to see it. You're welcome to walk out with me if you choose.'

Calow? It was nothing more than a hamlet half a mile from the town. He could picture it in his mind: just three or four tumbledown little cottages and a tiny church with an anchoress's cell. What could have happened out there to draw the coroner's attention?

'Is it a murder?'

The man shook his head. 'Couldn't tell you, Master. He gave me my order, that's it.'

'Who is it?'

'I can't say that, either. Coroner Strong will tell you himself, Master.' His face flickered with impatience. 'We should set off.'

'Not yet,' John told him. He wasn't going without telling Katherine. She wouldn't be happy; she wouldn't want to see something like this bubbling to the surface once more.

She'd married a carpenter, not a man who investigated deaths, even if he had a talent for finding the awkward truths behind someone's passing.

As it was, she stared at him with growing anger as he told her. When he finished speaking she scooped up Martha and stalked through to the buttery without a word.

'What else can I do?' he asked as he followed her. 'I don't have a say in it. You know I can't refuse a coroner.'

Katherine turned. 'You'll do what you want, the same as ever.' Her voice was cold as winter ice. 'I know the coroner doesn't care that you have a living to make and a family to feed. But what about you, husband? Do you care?'

'You know the answer to that,' he told her. 'You know it just as well as I do. It's the only thing I *can* think about.'

She dropped her eyes and ran her fingers through their daughter's curls.

'They make me so angry, the way they feel they can treat us all like this, like we're nothing.'

'Look, let me go out and see,' he said. 'It might be nothing at all. We're standing here thinking it's murder and it could prove to be something different.'

'Of course.' She snorted. 'And if wishes were horses, all the beggars would be riding up and down the King's highway. We'd have a stable full of them in the garden.'

She was right. Imagining anything else was pointless. The coroner's man wouldn't be waiting impatiently in the September sun unless Strong suspected murder. He kissed Katherine, then Martha, and left. In the hall of the house, he picked up a jug of ale off the table and filled one of the clay cups, drinking it down in a single swallow. Out on Knifesmithgate John brushed tiny flecks of sawdust from his tunic and hose. He didn't look like a man of property at all. He looked to be exactly what he was – a carpenter trying to scrape a living. But at least he'd appear presentable to authority.

'I'm ready.'

'We should hurry,' the man told him. 'The coroner doesn't like to be kept waiting.'

John was determined to hold on to the tatters of his pride. He might be summoned, but he was his own man. Strong didn't possess him.

'Whose is the body?' he asked.

The man shook his head. 'I told you, it's not my place to say anything, Master. Coroner Strong said to bring you and nothing more. He wants you to make up your own mind, that's his plan.'

A suspicion of murder, then, but apparently no certainty. The coroner wanted another opinion. But why him? He'd find out when they arrived.

Side by side, they crossed the bridge over the Hipper, then turned along the path to Calow. It wasn't a road, just something slightly better than a track, wide enough for a single cart, the earth beaten down by feet and horses' hooves. Clouds passed overhead, then the sun appeared again; the September air remained pleasant. Out in the fields, men were guiding their teams of oxen, ploughing the stoops left from the wheat back into the ground. The harvest was done and it had been a good year. None would starve to death this winter. There would be grain for bread and food for the pot.

He followed the man as he bore off on a path that cut to the right. Well, well, John thought. It wasn't in Calow itself. They were walking towards the church. It stood on its own, perhaps a quarter of a mile beyond the hamlet. Far enough to seem distant, yet still within shouting distance. It was placed to serve all the tiny settlements close by – Duckmanton, Ingersall Green and the others.

Who was the victim? It couldn't be the priest. He only came for service on Sundays. That meant it had to be the anchoress herself.

Two men were gathered by the stone cell. John recognised Sir Mark Strong, the coroner, dressed in fine cloth so black it seemed to drown the light, and dark hose; he'd seen him often enough around Chesterfield, although they'd never had cause to speak. Next to him stood a man wearing a clerk's robes. Not a tonsured monk, but a layman with ink on his fingers and the type of squint that came from spending too long looking at words on paper and in books. Strong glanced up as they approached. His hair was short, cropped close to his skull, a bright silver-grey that caught the light.

'Are you the carpenter?' His voice was deep, coming from somewhere low in his chest. John felt as if the man was inspecting and assessing him.

John bowed his head. 'I am, Master.'

'I've been told that you used to help de Harville when he was the coroner.'

'That only happened very rarely, Master. And the last time was six years ago. As you must know.' Maybe that would be enough to convince the man he wasn't the one for this work.

Sir Mark frowned. He glanced at the clerk, who shrugged. 'But you were able to solve puzzles that defeated other men. You found out how people had died and if someone had killed them.'

'No, Master,' he replied, and watched the coroner's eyes widen in surprise. 'I had luck, and God's grace helped me.'

Strong waved the words away and gestured at the cell.

'Do you know who lived here?'

'Gertrude the anchoress.' Everyone for miles around knew about her. The goodwives all swore she was a holy woman. They'd walked out from Chesterfield to see her after she arrived, to inspect her and form their opinions. They'd been surprised to find such serenity and humility in someone so young.

The anchoress sought a life of prayer and contemplation. She lived in solitude, walled away, a religious recluse. Food was provided through an opening and she talked to those who came to visit and offer gifts in return for prayers and advice. But she could never walk with them. She'd chosen to make the small cell her world. A slit between it and the church allowed her to observe services and receive the sacrament.

Gertrude had only been there for twelve months; it seemed like nothing at all. Barely more than a girl, she'd taken the place of the previous anchoress who died of old age. And now her time had passed, too. John crossed himself.

'What killed her?' he asked.

'Go inside,' Strong ordered. 'Take a look. Tell me what you see. I've been in there and for the love of Our Lord, I can't find a cause.'

Someone had prised away some of the stones, making a space just large enough for a man to crawl through.

John had never come out here to see the anchoress for himself. Why would he, when she craved solitude and prayer? But even so, it was impossible to avoid the gossip about her that passed around Chesterfield. Her father was Lord l'Honfleur. A rich man who moved in royal circles. He had influence. He owned this manor of Calow, John knew that, and many others besides, probably far more than a poor man could count.

'Go on, tell me what you think,' Strong urged.

With a quizzical look, John squeezed himself through the small opening and into the cell. He squatted on his haunches, letting his eyes adjust to the gloom. He inhaled and the stench hit him. He could feel the bile rising in his stomach and willed it down. A rank perfume of old vomit and shit filled the air as it stifled and clung. Decay, putrefaction. Death. He breathed through his mouth, then his ears picked out the constant buzzing of flies, a low, insistent drone. Slowly, very slowly, his vision began to clear. The main room was so small it was oppressive. Perhaps six paces long by four wide and barely tall enough for a man to stretch. He picked out the opening into the church along one wall. A small room stood in the corner. He opened the door. A jakes, with a bucket and seat for the anchoress to relieve herself. He turned back to the room. A window to the outside world in one wall, its shutter partly open. John stood and drew the wood all the way back to let the light flood in. Suddenly everything stood out in sharp relief. The pools on the floor were crawling with thousands of insects. He tried to brush them away, but it was an impossible task; they returned as soon as his hand had passed.

A pallet sat in the corner, a rough-cut wooden frame topped with straw and a threadbare blanket. No comfort of any kind for the anchoress. There wasn't even any space for a fire or a brazier to keep herself warm. Winter would have been a brutal season in here. Even now this place carried a damp chill that seemed to ooze out of the stone. He took another shallow breath. The young woman was slumped against the wall, her eyes wide with agony and fear. Her hair was hidden by a wimple that had long since lost its whiteness. Her gown was expensive, made from finely woven wool, but it had been worn to a threadbare shine in patches. John knelt by her, tracing the pale flesh on her hands and face, then looking at her body. He half-turned the corpse. The coroner was right. There was no sign of a wound or an injury. No blood. He sniffed the corpse's mouth, but he couldn't pick up any scent of poison. There was no sign of it, he thought; no discolouration of her lips or fingernails.

Very strange. There was nothing at all to show the cause of her death. And certainly nothing to indicate it had been deliberate. No violence of any kind. But the pain that had contorted her face told its own story. Gertrude's death had been terrible. John traced the sign of the cross over his chest and studied the room once more.

A knife sat on a low wooden table, but the blade was too blunt to do any damage; it would barely be able to cut meat. The anchoress had knocked the plate from her final meal on to the floor. It covered the few scraps of food the insects hadn't already carried away. He brushed the remnants back on to the plate then crawled out into the light.

'Well?' the coroner asked. 'What did you see?' But John ignored his question. He was studying the food. The answer had to be in there. That had to have been what killed her. But what was it?

It took him a few moments. Then he understood. A faint memory grew sharper as it took on form in his mind. The pieces of mushroom had been cut very fine. Only the sickly yellow colour and the sheen on the cap gave it away.

'That,' John said. He pointed, careful not to touch.

Strong stared. At the plate first, then at him.

'Why? What is it?'

'People call it the death cap mushroom. That's what killed her.' Most people out here would have known about its danger and kept away from it, he thought. Unless they wanted to kill.

The coroner didn't look convinced. 'How can you be sure?'

'I know,' John replied, 'because I saw someone eat one once.'

It came roaring back into his head. He was just nine, orphaned for a twelvemonth by the plague and simply trying to stay alive as he travelled through a land that the pestilence had laid waste. He'd been with a small group of starving men, tramping their way along the road from Ripon to Knaresborough. They'd been going slowly. Half of them were too weak to walk more than a mile without resting. Their tunics and hose were all filthy, the soles of their shoes battered and worn all the way through by time on the highway. One of them, Seth, had spotted the mushrooms, deep in the cool shade of a tree where he was resting. So desperate for anything at all in his belly, he'd started to eat them before anyone could stop him.

John didn't understand. He couldn't. He was too young to know. He didn't see what the man had done that was so wrong. Seth was hungry, he'd seen food, he'd eaten it. John's father had never told him that some mushrooms were deadly. The plague had taken him before he could teach that lesson. Him and so many others. In the end, it was the hard, toothless man leading their party who explained it all to him.

They struck up a rough camp and waited for the death. Someone trapped a coney and they roasted it over the fire. He could still remember the warm grease running down his chin as he gratefully chewed a scrap of meat and sucked at the bones.

Seth took a day and a half to find God's peace. He was in pain the whole time, but there was nothing they could do to ease it, no plants that might take the agony away for a while. John could still hear the cries. Seth suffered, screaming into the air, his body beyond his control, even when there was nothing else left inside. The silence when his breathing stopped had brought a sweet relief, and then guilt. They buried him. A shallow grave was the best they could manage, piled high with stones to keep the animals away from the corpse.

'Are you positive?' Strong asked him now.

'Yes.' He had no doubt at all. It was one lesson he could never erase. 'It would have taken her a long time to die.'

'How long?' a voice asked.

John turned. He hadn't heard the man approach, coming around from the other side of the church. Lord l'Honfleur. Dame Gertrude's father. He wore his wealth very easily and naturally. A light silk surcote dyed a deep, rich blue, cut to fall flatteringly around his body. He was well-barbered, his cheeks clean and still pink from the razor, and his grey hair was cut short. He had a fighting man's padded jerkin that reached down to his thighs, and high, shiny boots of supple leather that sat snug against his calves, over blue hose.

'God speed, my lord,' John lowered his head. 'A day at least.'

'I see.'

The grief bowed the man down like a powerful weight he couldn't support.

'I'm sorry, my lord,' John said. 'May God's light be on her now.'

The man nodded absently and took a deep breath. He started to pace around, clenching his fists then opening them again.

'Why?' he asked. A small word, a simple question, but none of them could answer it. 'Why? Why would someone do that?'

John looked at the coroner, then said: 'I don't know, my lord.'

'She was always her mother's favourite.' L'Honfleur started to speak as if he hadn't heard him. He was tracing a path backwards through the years. 'Gertrude was the youngest, she was the one most like her.' He closed his eyes for a moment. When he opened them again, a tear began to roll down his cheek. He let it fall, not even aware it was there. 'After my wife died, Gertrude found comfort in prayer and the church. In the priest and the sister who was teaching her.' A brief, wistful smile of remembrance. He didn't want an answer; maybe it was enough for him to know they were there, that someone would hear what he needed to say. 'I was urged to make a good marriage for her. I was already discussing it with a family, but she begged me to let her become a nun. *Begged* me. Nine years old and the only thing she wanted was to leave this world behind her.' He shook his head in wonder. 'My wife had always been a friend to the convent. How could I refuse? The vocation was plain in her eyes. The need.' He took a few more paces. 'And then she craved more and more solitude. When the old anchoress died last year, she pleaded with the Mother Superior to let her take on this task.' He breathed very slowly and seemed to return to the present. He stood, legs slightly apart, shoulders back. 'Who are you, anyway?'

'John, my lord. John the Carpenter.'

L'Honfleur raised an eyebrow in surprise. 'What kind of carpenter knows about death?'

'He did some work for the old coroner,' Strong said. 'You remember him – de Harville.'

The man nodded. His eyes peered into John's face, examining it for truth and honesty. 'Yes, I think I recall your name now. You're the one who has the gift for finding murderers.'

'Not really, Master. And all that was a long time ago.' He stumbled over the words. The very last thing in the world that he wanted was to have l'Honfleur demanding his services.

'But you were able to identify the mushroom.'

'True enough, Master.' He could hardly deny that.

L'Honfleur sighed. 'Tell me this, Carpenter: do you believe my daughter's death was an accident?'

What kind of answer could he offer? A lie that might ease the man's heart? That wouldn't give the girl in the anchorite cell any justice. Once the truth eased out, and it surely would in time, would l'Honfleur come after him? Honesty was painful, but it was better. It could burn and cleanse. Anyone who gathered mushrooms should know to avoid the death cap.

'No, my lord,' John said after a moment, 'I don't think it was.' He hesitated, weighing his words as if they were gold. 'It's possible that someone made a mistake. But my belief is that this was done deliberately.'

Who would want to kill a young nun? How could she have done anyone any harm in such a short life, especially alone out here? He thought of the pain and fear crowded together on her face. What had she gone through, hour after hour, on her own? What reason could someone possess for doing that to her?

L'Honfleur began to pace once more, hands clasped behind his back. This time he walked all the way to the treeline before turning and coming back. Strong and his clerk remained silent, staring at the cell. John waited, silently cursing the coroner for demanding that he come out here.

'Carpenter,' l'Honfleur said when he returned, 'I want you to find the person who killed my daughter.'

'My lord—'John began. For the blessed love of God, not that.

The man rode roughshod over his protest. 'You've done it before. You used to have a reputation for it. You can't deny that.' His voice softened and there was a plea in his eyes. 'I'm asking you to do it again. For me.'

It might have sounded like a request, like begging, but it was an order. And one he dare not refuse, not when it came from a man with l'Honfleur's power. A word would be all it took to ruin a life.

He bowed his head. 'Yes, my lord.'

'Succeed and I'll pay you fifty pounds.'

John shook his head. He frowned in disbelief, in shock. He'd misheard. He must have. That or he'd slipped deep into a dream. Fifty pounds? *Fifty* pounds? It wasn't possible. No one would offer that much, certainly not to someone of his status.

It was more than he could dream of making in more than ten good years as a carpenter. Plenty of wealthy merchants with their servants and their beautiful clothes earned far less than fifty pounds in a year. It was enough to repair both his houses and leave ample to keep his family comfortable until he was old. He glanced at Strong and the clerk. Both of them were staring at l'Honfleur with their jaws wide.

'Fifty pounds, my lord?' John's voice was a croak. He was afraid to ask, in case the man realised his mistake and took back the offer.

'Fifty.' He nodded towards the other men. 'You have witnesses, Carpenter. I'm a man of my word. Fifty pounds if you find the killer by the time the fair starts. What do you say?'

'Yes, my lord.' He agreed. But there was never a choice, and l'Honfleur knew it as well as he did.

CHAPTER TWO

'You made the right decision, Carpenter.'

L'Honfleur had remained at the anchorite cell, making arrangements to have his daughter brought to the church for her burial. John and the coroner's clerk were trudging back to Chesterfield, while Strong rode alongside them, looking down on the world from the saddle of his horse.

'Did I have a choice, Master?'

'No, you didn't, and it would have been unwise to try and refuse. What do you know about him?'

'Very little.' What did he know about any man with titles and lands? About as much as he knew about the countries beyond the Middle Sea. The rich were there; they existed in a world far removed from his own. They had money. It built a wall around them, left them warm and kept everything at bay. They were the ones who ran the country, who looked after the grand affairs. But none of that really touched his life, or anyone he knew. He lived among the small people, running around like ants and trying to avoid being crushed under the soles of those who controlled everything.

'He's a very powerful man. Twelve manors across Derbyshire and Yorkshire.' The way Strong spoke, it was supposed to impress him. Instead it made the man seem like someone who could part with fifty pounds and never notice it had gone. 'A man who has the ear of Alice Perrers, the King's mistress.'

And what did that matter, unless it was some sort of threat? He hadn't wanted to do this, but with little choice, he'd agreed to look into Gertrude's death. The money was meant to tempt him and keep him going, and he knew that it would. Now he had to hope he succeeded and earned the reward. It was the only thing about the whole business that made sense to him.

'I shall need some help.'

'What do you want?' Strong asked. They'd crossed the bridge and were climbing up Soutergate towards the church with its towering spire.

'Men,' John told him. He was certain the coroner would agree; he'd want to please l'Honfleur.

'Let me know when you need them and how many. I'll make sure they're available.'

'And I'll need to be paid.'

'But my lord said…'

'That doesn't feed my family while I'm looking into this,' John insisted. 'I can't do my own work, so I need to earn.'

The coroner eyed him suspiciously. 'I thought you owned two houses.'

'I do.' There was no need to give the man the full truth; the rumours would simply fly all over Chesterfield. 'But when you hire a labourer, you pay him for his work.'

'Very well,' the man agreed with a grudging sigh. 'Four pennies a day. But he wants this complete by the time the fair starts, Carpenter. I hope you'll remember that.'

'I will, Master. All too well.'

• • •

John counted out his four pennies from the Guildhall on the table in the hall.

'I'm glad you remembered to collect your pay,' Katherine said. Her voice was chilly. 'Especially when you had more important things to do.' She bounced Martha on her knee, and the child smiled. That sweet, easy grin which caught his heart every time.

Juliana was off somewhere, probably playing with her friends in the churchyard, and Richard was likely asleep in the solar. Ever since his birth he'd been a weak, sickly child, so close to death a few times that the priest had administered the last rites. Rest seemed to help him, but they both knew he would probably leave this world before too long. The knowledge hurt; it was like a knife forcing its slow, agonising way into his heart. But it was God's will, something beyond his control. All he could do was accept it when it happened.

'You know I didn't have a choice. I had to go.'

Her eyes flashed. She wasn't giving an inch.

'And what else does the coroner want you to do?'

He hesitated before answering. 'Not him. My Lord l'Honfleur. They body belonged to his daughter Gertrude, the anchoress. He wants me to investigate her death.'

'No!' She slapped her palm down hard on the table and shouted the word loud enough for all of Chesterfield to hear. With Martha crying and squirming in her arms, she stalked off through the buttery, down to the end of the garden to stare at the wall.

John waited. But she didn't return. Instead, she stood by the apple tree, running her free hand along the bark. They'd picked the last of the fruit only a week before. Richard had felt strong enough that day to climb up in the branches and toss the apples down into a basket as they all laughed and sang. A day to cherish when times grew dark.

He went to her, stood behind her and placed his hands on her shoulders. Softly, he explained it all, his lips close to her ear. She wouldn't turn her head to look at him, gazing straight ahead as she stroked Martha's hair.

'The money will solve everything,' he told her.

'I daresay it will.' Her voice was withering, full of scorn. 'If you're alive to enjoy it. Have you forgotten what happened the last time you did all this? You came a hair away from death yourself, John. Do you remember that you promised me you'd never do it again?'

'I do,' he agreed. 'But I know those four coins I brought home today are almost all we possess. What else can I do?'

'Maybe work will pick up.'

Gently, he turned his wife until she was facing him.

'It's September. There won't be much more business this year. We both know how the roof leaks, that we need new slates. If I don't do this, we're going to have to sell one of the houses to be able to repair the other and stay alive.'

She knew it well enough. They'd talked about it time after time once their children were asleep. And he knew how much she hated the idea. She didn't want to believe it. Katherine had grown up in the house on Saltergate. All the warm memories of her childhood lay within its walls. And this place... it was still full of old Martha and the love she had for them.

'It's dangerous work, husband,' she said. 'That's what scares me.'

But her voice had softened; John knew she'd accept it. It was necessary. The reward... it would save them. It held out the promise of a good life.

'I'll be careful. I'll go to the church and swear on the Bible that I will.'

'You know I can't stand you doing this,' Katherine said, and he nodded.

'I don't like it, either.' He took hold of her hand and squeezed it lightly. 'I don't want to, but what else is there?

L'Honfleur has ordered me to look into it. I can't tell him no, can I? I don't have the power to refuse his commands.'

Katherine shook her head. Below her anger and pain, she understood the reality of life. 'Just be grateful he's willing to pay a fortune for it.'

'Fifty pounds…' She said nothing for a long time. 'Do you really think he'll part with the money?'

John thought about the look on the man's face. The sorrow, the anger, the longing.

'Yes,' he replied, 'I do. He seems as honest as anyone in his position. There are witnesses, too; the coroner and his clerk. And Strong is giving me fourpence a day while I work.'

'How much do you trust them all?'

Very little; that was the answer. Trust had no meaning at all. But he didn't say a word.

'If l'Honfleur pays, we'll be safe for years.'

'*If* he pays,' Katherine said. She frowned as she spoke. 'And what happens if you don't find the person who killed his daughter? Have you thought about that?'

Of course he had. It had begun to gnaw at the edges of his mind on the walk back from Calow. He hadn't lied to the coroner and l'Honfleur; John knew he'd been lucky before. But luck could easily stop smiling. It was a fickle mistress; it shifted its favours. And if luck wasn't with him… l'Honfleur had influence. He had money. If he was angry at the failure, he could do anything he chose and no one would ever question it. No talk of justice and law. A poor man's death would be nothing. No one with a voice would even care.

• • •

Strong lived just beyond West Bar, outside the town itself, in a house he'd had built shortly before John arrived in

Chesterfield. The timber frames were solid, standing square and true, the limewash freshly applied this summer. The windows sat sturdy in their frames, and the roof looked tight. Everything snug and neat. The work had been done by proper craftsmen, John thought. The place wasn't especially large, there was nothing about it that shouted out the status of the owner. But everything looked exact, with no ragged corners or edges. It was considered and careful, like the man himself.

Strong's father had been a merchant, selling wool from the hill farmers to the weavers up in York. The business continued after his death, run by a factor. Strong's only involvement was to take the profit and enjoy his hunting and hawking. And for the last six years, his position of King's Coroner in Chesterfield.

The servant who answered the door wore clean, dark hose and a green jacket decorated with the coroner's badge. He showed John through the screens and into the hall. Glazed windows faced west, trapping the afternoon sun and warming the room.

A high wall kept the garden private. There was a carefully-tended herb bed and a small orchard of trees – apple, plum, pear, all splayed out against the stone.

'Well, Carpenter, I'm glad you had the sense to take the offer.'

He hadn't heard the coroner come down the wooden stairs from the solar. For a large man, Strong was light and easy on his feet. He was at home, so he wore no weapon to knock against his thigh as he walked. There was no sign of the clerk.

'Was there ever any danger of anything else, Master?'

'No.' Sir Mark laughed, nodded, then poured himself a cup of wine from the jug on the table. He'd changed into a short, embroidered tunic with small pearl buttons, cinched tight at the waist with a leather belt. 'Still, as far as I'm concerned, you've already proved your worth. I suspected she'd been poisoned, but for the life of me I couldn't see what had done it. You spotted it straight away.'

'Thank you, Master.' No need to mention that the memory of seeing someone die that way would have him riding the night mare tonight when he settled in his bed. 'I didn't ask when we were out there: who was the first finder?'

'A traveller,' Strong replied and glanced away. 'A man.'

'Who?' He felt the coroner wasn't telling him the full truth.

'A friar on his way to Baslow. I talked to him myself.' He waved his hand in the air, as if brushing away a fly. 'Just another of God's innocents on the road. He answered my questions, he gave the girl her last rites, then I sent him on his way. He was horrified, kept reciting decades of the rosary. Whatever you want to think, I'm convinced he had nothing to do with this. He found the body, that was all.'

'Where did he raise the alarm?'

'In Calow. They sent him here to me.'

'I'd still like to talk to him, Master,' John said.

Strong shook his head. 'Don't waste your time. He's gone. There's no stain of guilt on him.' The man chuckled to ease the mood. 'I talked to one or two people after I came back to town. They told me you weren't always respectful to my predecessor.' There was a twinkle in his eyes and a light smile on his lips.

'Perhaps not,' John admitted after a moment.

'I knew de Harville. He could be a difficult man at times. But he had a good heart and he was full of honour in the end.'

'That he was, yes.' Strong was definitely trying to deflect the talk from the topic of the first finder. He'd leave that lie for now; he could always return to it later. 'What can you tell me about Gertrude, Master?'

'Nothing.' The man shrugged. 'I never met her, never went out to the anchorite cell to talk to her. The first time I saw her was today.' He exhaled slowly. 'You heard her father, Carpenter. That's as much as I know. He owns the manor at Calow, for whatever it's worth. Next to nothing, from the look of it. It seems like a poor place. I do know he originally built the cell there because his wife asked him to do it. There was a nun at the convent she supported who wanted a solitary life. When his daughter desired the same, how could he refuse her?'

'How long ago did Gertrude join the convent?'

'I have no idea. You'd need to ask him,' Strong said. He narrowed his eyes and calculated. 'His wife died a good while ago now, at least ten years. It may even be a fair bit longer.'

'He never remarried?'

'No. He didn't seem interested, although the family name will die out with him. He has two daughters. The other one is married. You heard him talk about the betrothal for Gertrude and how that changed when her mother died.'

He recalled every word l'Honfleur had spoken, all the fragments of his daughter's short life.

'I told you I'd need some help, Master.'

'I know, and I'll stand by my agreement. We're both here to serve my lord. I'm sure he will give you every assistance, too.' He gave a sly smile. 'You'll be a rich man if you solve this, Carpenter.'

'Something close,' John agreed. 'I'll definitely be someone who can pay his bills for once.'

• • •

The body had gone from the cell, more stones pulled from the outside wall to remove it. The whole thing would be torn down now, John imagined, and everything used elsewhere. L'Honfleur wouldn't want it to stand; it would bring too much pain to mind whenever he saw it. A month more and only the tiny church would remain; there would probably be no trace that the cell ever existed. The idea that an anchoress had ever lived there would become memory and legend.

For now, though, the raw stench of death was strong, with flies and insects crawling over the floor. He bent, peering closely at what was left in the vain hope that it might tell him something more. But if the scraps held any secrets, they were staying well-hidden. Finally, John stood and surveyed the countryside around the building. A single, large field rose along the hill towards the low horizon. It was divided into strips of an acre each to feed the families who lived in Calow. The cluster of four cottages that made up the hamlet stood close to the track from Chesterfield. There was nothing else nearby. Close to the top of the hill was the beginning of a forest that stretched off into the far distance. He followed the thin beaten path between the tall grass that led to the houses.

No voices, he'd noticed, and no sign of anyone working in the fields. But not silence. That didn't exist anywhere, he was certain of it. Even out here, the world was alive around him. The rustle of the wind through the leaves, birdsong on the air, the hum and buzz of insects as they flew around. From somewhere in the distance, the breeze carried the bleating of sheep and the lowing of the cattle. All of creation in one place. The noise of the country often surprised him. So loud that it was impossible for a man to think.

More than twenty years had passed since the pestilence swept through England. It arrived from nowhere. Some folk claimed it was the judgement of God for the sins of the people. John didn't know. Maybe that was truly what it had been. But it had killed half the people in the country.

He'd watched his own father die, his neighbours and relatives, until it seemed there was nothing left. If he'd stayed in his village of Leeds, he'd have starved. Hungry, looking for food, looking for life, he took to the roads to try and survive. That summer, and the one that followed, there hadn't been enough people to gather the harvest or milk all the cattle. The crops rotted in the field for want of labour. Wherever he went the countryside looked like a wasteland where nature was reclaiming everything it had once possessed before man arrived. That didn't seem like anything God would do to His people.

Now it was hard to believe that time had ever existed. The land was in excellent shape once more. All the fields were neatly laid out, the beasts cared for. But the order of life had changed. There were still masters and men; that would always be the way. But these days the ordinary men had more rights. Some little good had come from all those deaths, at least.

As he approached the small ville he could feel the sorrow hanging breathless and still over it. The place was subdued, as if the loss of Gertrude had been a personal blow. Perhaps that was how the villagers saw it. Having an anchorite, a holy woman, brought prestige to a place. It gave them a name, and it would have meant visitors, people bringing money as they sought advice and guidance from her. Because of Gertrude and her predecessor, people had heard of Calow. Without them, who could have ever noticed that it existed?

High clouds passed over the afternoon sun as he reached the houses, offering some shade on a bright autumn day. John knocked on one door and waited, hearing the shuffle of feet on the floor inside.

She was an old woman, with thin wisps of white hair gathered inside a grubby coif. Her face was red, the skin puffy, as if she'd been crying.

'Mistress,' he introduced himself with a small bow. 'My name is John. My Lord l'Honfleur has asked me to look into the death of his daughter.'

Curious, he thought, how easily the words rolled off his tongue.

'I'm Wilhelmina, Master. You'd better come in,' she said after a moment. 'It's a good job you're young. You'll have to stand. I only own one stool.'

She lowered herself on to the joint stool with a sigh. It was a widow's cottage. A single, small room, with a pallet bed against the wall and a fire burning low in the middle of the beaten earth floor. No rushes covered the dirt. Smoke gathered in the eaves, escaping through a single small hole in the tiles, up by the ridge. The air was thick enough to make his eyes sting; he tried to wipe away the tears that began to run down his cheeks. A pot of soup simmered on a tripod over the heat.

'Did you know her?' he asked.

'I did,' the goodwife sighed. 'We all did. You can see for yourself how few there are of us here. We're all going to miss her. She's a sad loss, may God rest her soul. So young and so devout. She prayed for the souls of every one of us of us here. Didn't matter that we had no money to ask her for a blessing. Who'll do that now, tell me that?'

No one, he thought. The death had brought a curse to the hamlet. There would never be another anchoress in Calow. But he kept his own counsel. Better to leave her question without an answer than tell her a truth that would destroy her hopes.

'Who took food to her?' John asked.

'Every one of us here. Not every day, because she liked to fast, she said it was good for her spirit.' The woman grimaced as she shifted her weight uncomfortably on the stool. 'She never went without. We emptied her bucket and took her food. You know an anchoress usually has a servant?'

John shook his head; he knew nothing about them.

'That's why they're rich women, Master. It takes money to live so simply, though who'd believe that? You need someone to look after you. But her father owns this manor. He paid us to take care of her. Pennies,' she said with a small smile, 'but it helps. And after we met her, it wasn't a task, it was an honour. She was a proper holy woman. Everyone knew. They'd come from all over to see her.' She smiled, filled with pride. 'A man travelled the roads from Oxford once. Gertrude was famous.' She considered her words for a moment. 'And she was very wise, so clever for someone so young. They'd come and bring her food and coins and ask her things.'

'What type of things?'

She shook her head. 'I don't know. I never heard and she wasn't likely to tell me, was she?'

'What about the coins?' He'd seen no trace of any in the cell.

'They were gifts for the convent. Someone would come with a bag and collect them.'

'When was the last time anyone from here went to see her?' John asked.

'It was three days ago,' the woman replied with a guilty look. 'I was supposed to go yesterday, but my ankle had swelled up and I couldn't walk proper, so I thought I'd leave it until today. It didn't seem to matter. Young Margery from down the lane said she heard that two men had stopped at the cell the day before, so we thought she'd be all right.'

Two days ago. It fitted. Very likely it was when she'd been given the food with the death cap mushroom.

'Two men?'

'That's what she told me. Round here we talked about Gertrude a lot.' She looked up at him. 'It's rare that anything happens in Calow. And she was one of us, you see. She was family. I know she was rich and she'd given herself to God. But she lived out here, same as the rest of us. We tried to look after her.'

Silence overtook her, and John knew what she was thinking. They'd tried to protect the anchoress from harm, but they hadn't succeeded. How could they?

'This woman, Margery,' he said. 'Would she be at home now?'

'Very likely,' Wilhelmina replied. 'And if she isn't, she doesn't go far. She can't, not with three little ones. They keep her busy. Her husband works in the fields. Why are you so interested, anyway? Is there something odd about the way she died? I know she was very young…'

'You haven't heard?' John asked in astonishment.

'Heard what?' The woman stared, confused.

'She was poisoned.'

A hesitation as she drew in a breath, then crossed herself twice.

'Oh, sweet Jesu, that poor, lovely girl. God rest her soul.' Tears trickled from her eyes. She didn't bother trying to rub them away, just let them fall. 'Who would want to poison a girl like her?'

'That's what her father wants me to discover.'

'Then may the Lord help you, Master. Sweet Jesu, sweet Jesu,' she muttered over and over.

'Margery,' he interrupted. 'You said she saw the men who came.'

'No.' The woman shook her head. 'She heard about it. I don't think she saw them herself. It might have been her husband who told her. He'd have been out working in the fields. He would have seen anyone who was coming or going. You can't help it out here. See for miles, you can.'

With so few people on the road around, any stranger would draw attention.

'I didn't see anyone in the fields as I came here,' he said.

'The men will be doing something for the bailiff,' she said. 'Probably coppicing up in the woods. It's the season for it. Or they might be up on the common land with the pigs.'

He was in no rush to leave, happy to let the woman talk about the people of Calow, to listen and to learn. There was young Agnes, her husband Hugo and their four children, Margery and her man and their brood, and Ralph, barely thirty but already widowed twice with two little ones he was paying Agnes to rear. By the time she finished, John felt as if he knew them all, that he was a part of the village.

Mostly, he wanted to hear her speak about Gertrude. There was genuine affection in her voice. Wilhelmina cherished the girl almost like the daughter she'd lost decades before and knew Gertrude in a way her father never could. She understood full well that the girl was different from everyone in the hamlet. A religious, from a wealthy family. But somehow there was a bond that was far greater than the divisions. Death happened. God took people when and how He chose, and often there was no reason for it that anyone here could see, beyond His will. You could mourn, but to be human meant you were going to die.

John had seen how bereft Wilhelmina had been when he told her about the poisoning. The tenderness she felt for the anchoress was very real; it touched him.

But she could tell him little that was useful about the woman who'd spent the last year living in the anchorite cell. Certainly nothing to help him discover her killers. He came blinking into the light, breathing deep to take in the fresh air after sitting in the tiny, smoky cottage.

CHAPTER THREE

In the distance, silhouetted against the ridge line, he could pick out the shapes of three men ambling down the hill towards Calow. The men of the ville, John thought. The ones he needed to see.

He waited, watching them, noticing the way their easy conversation stopped when they spotted him. As they approached, they spread apart, moving the saws and small axes off their shoulders. John held up his hands.

'Peace, Masters, peace, may God go with you.'

'And with you,' the oldest of them replied. He stopped ten yards away, a thickset man used to heavy, physical work. The others halted, too. John could feel them staring with suspicion.

'My name is John. I'm working for the coroner in Chesterfield.' Words to make the men uneasy.

'Who's died?' the leader asked after a moment. His eyes moved to the other men and back.

'Gertrude, Master. The anchoress.'

He waited as they crossed themselves.

'This death…' the man began.

'Was not natural.' There was no other way to say it. He could see the surprise and horror on their faces. 'She was found this morning. My Lord l'Honfleur has already been out here. I talked to Dame Wilhelmina; she said that Mistress Margery's husband might have seen two men by the cell recently.' John looked into the men's faces.

'That's me.' The man to the right took a pace forward. 'I'm Cedric. It was what, the day before yesterday? I'm sure it was. I was out in the fields when I saw them.' He nodded at the man in charge. 'Me and Ralph.'

'What did you see?'

'Very little.' It was Ralph who answered. 'We were a fair way off.' He pointed off into the distance. 'Over there. We were probably, what, half a mile away, trying to dig out a boggy area. It's best when it's been dry for a while.'

'But you definitely saw two men?'

'We saw two riders,' Cedric replied. He hesitated. 'We could see the dust from their horses. It's been dry.' John nodded. 'But we were working, didn't pay too much attention. They were riding towards the church. We were in the middle of some-thing, so we didn't see them stop there.' He looked towards Ralph, who shook his head. 'We didn't pay them too much mind, Master. No reason, see?'

'Can you tell me anything about these men? Was there anything you could see?'

He needed something. A place to begin.

'One of the men rode a piebald horse,' Ralph said. 'I pointed it out, do you remember? With a big patch of black on its back leg.'

'Yes.' The other man nodded. 'You did.'

Something, but hardly enough.

'What about the men?' John asked. 'Could you make out how they were dressed?'

Ralph shook his head, but Cedric said: 'I'm not sure, but I think they had red tunics. They were both wearing cloaks, but I thought I saw some red underneath. It was difficult to tell.'

'Bright red? Scarlet?'

'No, it was darker. Like my lord's livery…' He searched for the words. 'The colour of blood.'

L'Honfleur's own men? That didn't seem possible. All the questions, the objections tumbled through his mind.

'Are you sure?'

Cedric kept his gaze steady. 'I can only tell you what I thought I saw. We were far off, like Ralph said, and I only looked for a moment. No, I can't be certain, I'm sorry, Master. I wouldn't dare to take an oath on it.'

'That's fine. Anything you can tell me helps.'

He waited, hoping for more. Any scrap, however tiny. But they had nothing to add. That was everything.

The walk back to Chesterfield felt as if it took hours, the climb up Soutergate like trailing up a mountain. The promise of fifty pounds kept him moving. Enough to answer every worry he had, to let him enjoy life once more. But to earn it he had to find Gertrude's murderer.

Maybe it was that simple; maybe it was one of l'Honfleur's men. But the answer didn't sit easily in his gut. It didn't feel right. There was evil at work in this killing. Someone had been willing to let Gertrude suffer for hours on end. Anyone who could use a death cap mushroom to murder had lost their soul.

He wanted to go home. He was weary. His mouth was dry and his belly was empty. But he kept going through the town, beyond the empty marketplace with its stalls set up for the next morning, and out beyond West Bar to Strong's house.

The coroner listened as John recounted what he'd learned in Calow.

'My lord's own men?' he asked and frowned.

'Exactly what I was thinking, Master. We need to talk to him.'

Strong paced around the room. Outside the window, dusk was close, the shadows rising.

'Let me speak to him first,' he said.

'Yes, Master.' He was happy to give up that task. Let Strong break the news and have l'Honfleur's fury crash all around him.

'I'll see him in the morning. He has enough to attend to at the moment, preparing his daughter for burial.'

'What about me, Master? What should I do?'

'Nothing until I've talked to him. Just wait, Carpenter. Patience.'

• • •

Patience was a fine virtue for a man with money. But a poor man needed to earn, John thought as he walked along Beetwell Street with Alan. The carpentry job was simple enough, it wouldn't take more than a day. But it meant money in his scrip and food for his family while he wasn't investigating Gertrude's death.

Katherine gave him an appraising stare as he picked up the leather satchel of tools. She had the besom in her hand, sweeping the floor clean before putting down fresh rushes in the hall.

'They want me to wait,' he said. Martha ran towards him, arms stretched wide, hugging him round the legs. He'd spent time up in the solar with Richard. The boy was restless, moving on his mattress of straw. It pained him to see the lad this way, but there was little he could do. At this rate, they'd be grateful if he saw out the remainder of the year. It was just a matter of time. 'I might as well earn something for us until they want me again. Thomas needs a new bench built at the smithy.'

Straightforward work, but there was satisfaction in making every job the best that it could be. Wooden pegs, tapped in and soaked so they'd swell to make a tight, solid fit. Good iron nails to keep everything in place.

He was absorbed in the task, continuing as Alan went to eat his dinner. Small adjustments so that the last leg was completely square. He'd just finished when Coroner Strong stormed into the forge with two of his men trailing behind.

'What do you think you're doing, Carpenter?' His roar was loud enough to make Thomas and his apprentice stop and stare. 'I told you to wait. When I sent a messenger to your house, your wife said you were working.'

John stood, wiping his hands against his tunic.

'I am, Master. You can see that for yourself.' He gestured at the bench, complete and ready in the corner. 'A poor man works to earn the money to keep body and soul together.'

'I'm paying—'

'Not if I'm not doing any work for you, Master.' Let them find someone else. Let the fifty pounds slip away. He wasn't going to be humiliated like this. A craftsman deserved some dignity. He needed the money my lord offered, needed it desperately, but he wouldn't grovel to earn it.

Strong closed his mouth. His cheeks were still flushed red with anger. A tunic the colour of faded roses today, black hose and shoes. Every inch a rich man, someone with power.

'You know my lord's townhouse?' he said after a long silence.

'I do.'

'Go and see him there. He'll tell you what he wants you to do. I'll warn you, though, I told him you were attending to your own work.'

Strong stalked away, his men hurriedly following.

A few instructions to Alan. He could easily finish the job on his own and do it just as well as the man who'd taught him. They exchanged grins as John oiled his tools and put them back in the satchel.

He'd often passed l'Honfleur's Chesterfield house, a sprawling building on Glumangate, set between the High Street and Saltergate. The house itself wasn't large or overly grand; big enough for the master and his servants. But the kitchen stood apart at the back, built that way for safety in case of fire, and a large stable had been added at the very rear of the yard. The garden stretched out, ending in an orchard of apple trees placed to catch the sun.

He had to surrender his knife and tools to the servant. That was etiquette, he expected it, the same way he knew he'd have to wait for l'Honfleur to arrive.

The hall had glazed windows looking out on the garden, with bright, colourful hangings over the plaster. In the centre of the room, on raised flagstones, the fire burned low, just enough to take any edge from the air. The rushes on the floor were strewn with lavender and rose petals, the scents rising as he walked around.

He heard the ring of boot heels and turned to see l'Honfleur coming from the buttery, eyes dark and mouth set.

'The coroner ordered you to wait. Perhaps you're a man who doesn't know how to do what his betters tell him.'

'No, Master, but—'

'You have the chance to make a fortune, Carpenter. Men of your station would be happy to beg for the chance to make fifty pounds. Maybe you don't want it.'

John bowed his head. 'I do, my lord.'

Fury came off the man in waves. He wasn't going to be a man ready to hear reason and what life was like for those with no money.

'Why?' He smashed his fist down on the table, hard enough to make a pewter jug tremble, close to toppling. 'Why did you disobey?'

'A man needs to fill his time, my lord. I'm a carpenter, I have work. Instead of sitting at home, I could use the hours well.'

All the words were true, but it was truth bent so far it almost broke. Alan could have done the job at the smithy alone. L'Honfleur stayed silent for a long time. Too long, John thought, ready for a fresh blast of anger.

'In future, when you're told to wait, you wait.' He was in control of his voice again, calm, quiet. 'Sir Mark told me what you'd learned at Calow.'

'Yes, my lord.'

'You were told to wait so I could send a messenger out to my manor near Hathersage. My men all swear they hadn't seen my daughter. They hadn't travelled to Calow.'

'Do you believe them?'

'If I didn't, I'd have dismissed them long ago. And there are no piebald horses in my stables.'

'But the livery…' John began, then stopped. The men had admitted they couldn't be sure. The other possibility was that some of l'Honfleur's men might be lying. But where would they have found the horse?

'Someone in disguise?' l'Honfleur suggested. 'It's possible. We don't know.'

'Yes, my lord.' It brought up the question he needed to ask. But it was one the man wouldn't want to hear. If he had an answer to give, it would open wounds better left to scar over. 'Was there anyone who might want to kill your daughter, Master? Or harm you through her?'

'Gertrude?' he asked in disbelief. 'Of course not. She was young. She'd done nothing but good in the world. She prayed for people. For their illnesses, for their souls.' He turned his head to look at John, his eyes filled with sorrow and pain. 'Why would anyone want to hurt someone like that?'

The voice trailed to nothing. But there were more words to come. He simply had to find the place to begin.

L'Honfleur pointed out at the garden on the other side of the glass.

'You see that, Carpenter? The arrangement of everything? My wife began to plan it all after we moved in here. It was her joy. She wanted the herbs, the plants for medicines, the orchard there. Our daughters were three and five, and we thanked God for them.'

'Who is the other one?' John asked.

'Gwendolyn is the older one,' the man answered. 'She's married now. They live on a manor in Yorkshire, just outside Doncaster. Her husband inherited it when his father died. I've sent word to her of her sister's death.'

'Were they close?'

'No,' he answered with a sigh. 'I told you before, Gertrude was her mother's favourite. Mine too, may God forgive me for it. Do you have children, Carpenter?'

'Three of them, Master.'

'Then perhaps you understand. Whether we will it or not, there's always one who comes closer to your heart. When Gertrude was seven, my wife took ill. I brought in physicians to examine her. I tried everything they suggested. But none of it helped. She was wasting away. My wife had always been a devout woman. On our wedding day, she gave an endowment to a convent and she continued to support it. She was ill for a year, growing weaker and weaker by the day. I knew there was nothing I could do to help her, but I couldn't give up.' He stared at John with the empty gaze of a man who was lost in all he felt. 'You see that, don't you?'

'Yes, my lord.' His kept his voice hushed, hardly more than a whisper.

'When my wife died, we didn't know what to do. Gertrude took on my wife's mantle of religion. She wore it so well that it might have been made for her. The day she turned eleven, she told me she wanted to enter the convent. She had the calling, that was obvious to anyone. How could I refuse her?'

He didn't need an answer. He didn't need anything except the chance to remember.

'It was God's will. It had to be, and to refuse it would have been unnatural. It would have stained my wife's memory. Gertrude wanted to withdraw from the world. And as time passed, more and more she craved solitude and contemplation. To be alone with her thoughts and with God. When the old anchoress died after twenty years in the cell, Gertrude asked the Mother Superior if she might take her place.

'The abbess wrote to me,' l'Honfleur said. 'She said my daughter's calling was real and wanted to be sure I could support her as an anchoress. What could I do but agree? I'd have gladly paid for a servant, but there's nowhere in Calow she could stay. You've seen the place. I arranged with the women out there to make sure she was fed and her waste removed.' Another long hesitation. 'Since she died I keep wondering… if I'd said no, she'd still be alive. But would someone else be dead instead?'

'I don't know, Master.' It was the right answer to give now. But it wasn't the honest one and they both knew it.

L'Honfleur started to pace around the hall. His boots crushed the lavender in the rushes and the scent filled the air, as if spring had somehow crept into the room.

'You asked if anyone had a reason to hurt me through Gertrude.'

'Yes.'

'When she was very young, back in the days before my wife's illness started, we started talking to another family about a possible match between Gertrude and their son. They have a manor out past Cartledge. It abuts mine closer to Hathersage. Gertrude was probably seven or eight, and their boy was around the same age. We never discussed marriage that seriously. It was something that could wait until the children were a few years older. Then my wife became ill, and after that, my daughter found her vocation.' He held out his hands, helpless, and looked at them. 'This family… last autumn their son died. He was still unwed. Their other children all died before they could grow. There is no heir. I hear they have problems with money. I know the father feels I should have forced Gertrude to marry their boy.' A fleeting, cynical smile. 'I daresay he'd have found the dowry useful with his creditors. Is that enough reason to kill, do you think, Carpenter?'

'I couldn't say, my lord.'

'No. Of course, how could you?'

'What is their name?'

'Unthank,' the man answered. He placed a hand on John's arm. 'The father is a man of honour. He might be resentful, but I can't imagine he would do anything like this.'

Honour. A grand word that rolled so easily off the tongue, but it was as cheap as any other. From all he'd seen, as soon as desperation arrived, honour and truth and justice all fell away. Survival was all that mattered. Whether you owned a manor or just the clothes on your back, it was always the same.

Another family with wealth and power. Somewhere he'd never be able to dig out the truth, if there was anything to find.

'My lord…' John began, but l'Honfleur waved away his words.

'Don't say it, Carpenter. I can't believe Sir John Unthank would do anything like this. I've known him for decades. But they have servants. Ask them. The family will be gathering for the fair next week. They have a house here in Chesterfield. It stands on the road into town on the far side of the church.'

John knew it. A grand place on the brow of the hill, rebuilt just a few years earlier, the second and third storeys that jettied out one over the other, looming above the road, with the coat of arms painted in bold colours on the lintel. Glazed windows, the limewash renewed every three years to glow a glittering white.

'Yes, Master.' He'd have to worm his way in there. Go and ask if they needed any woodwork done. It was all he had for now.

On the way home, John stopped at the graveyard. No marker, but he knew exactly where old Martha was buried. He couldn't afford to pay a priest to say a mass for her soul, but he could stand here and offer up a prayer. For her place in eternity, but also that she might look down and give him a blessing, help him in all this. To succeed, to earn that fifty pounds, would make all the difference in his life. In Katherine's, too, and for Juliana and Richard and young Martha. His entire family.

Scaffolding had been erected at the side of the church; ash poles lashed together with strips of leather. He paused for a moment and watched a man climb, effortlessly swinging his way upwards to where the masons were working. They were using a windlass to pull up blocks of dressed stone to replace others that were beginning to crumble.

He sighed, envying a life that was so simple, doing the work and drawing the wages, with a barrel of ale to slake the thirst during the day.

But he'd chosen his life, John thought as he collected his tools. And no regrets for all he'd done. He had a beautiful wife and children. Perhaps he didn't have money, but he was blessed, nonetheless.

'Are you working again?' Katherine asked. 'Have they let you go?'

'Shouted at, then kept on.'

'Can you find whoever killed his daughter, husband?'

'I don't know.' He sighed. 'But I'm going to try. I have to. You see that, don't you? For us.' His voice faded for a heartbeat. 'And for her.'

She gave a reluctant nod. They didn't have many choices. But so few did in this world.

CHAPTER FOUR

A pair of dogs barked as he came through the arch and into the yard of the Unthank house. Two men were unloading a cart while the horse stood placidly in its traces.

A stout woman waited in the doorway to the kitchen, the wimple pinned so tight around her head that there was no danger of a single stray hair escaping. A chemise with a kirtle of homespun cloth covered her ample body. A ring of keys hung from her girdle. The housekeeper, he guessed, in charge until the owner and his wife arrived. She turned to look at him, and he could see her eyes assessing him in a single glance, then dismissing him.

He removed his hood, squeezing it between his hands.

'Mistress…' he began, but she cut him off.

'Dame Agatha to you,' she said, 'and you're the carpenter.'

He bowed. 'Yes. I'm John, Mistress.'

'I see your wife sometimes at the market by the church. What are you after?'

'To see if there's any work you need here.'

Agatha snorted. 'Times hard, are they? It can't be easy, keeping up two grand houses.'

He'd get nothing from her, he could already tell. But perhaps there would be others whose tongues might wag.

'They cost money.' He tried to grin and make light of it. 'And I have to earn it.'

'You'd best talk to Wilfred in the stables. If you can get on the good side of him. The master and his wife will be here in two days.' She nodded towards the cart. 'They're sending their goods and we have to prepare the house for them.'

All except her, John thought. Dame Agatha was quite content to stand in the warm September sun and watch.

'Thank you.'

Another bow and he hurried across the yard. The dirt was packed down hard, dust rising as he walked. In the stable the air was cooler, heavy with the scent of straw and dung. A man was counting the bales and marking them on a tally stick, turning as he heard the footsteps and frowning at the interruption.

He was powerfully built, with broad shoulders under his tunic, the sleeves pushed up to show thick, muscled arms. But he moved like a man bowed down by his size, awkward and lumbering. His eyes flashed.

'Who are you?'

'Master, Dame Agatha sent me over. I'm John the Carpenter. Maybe there are jobs in the house that need to be done before the owners arrive.'

'Who told you? Who sent you here?' His voice was an angry, suspicious bark.

'No one. I live in town and I pass here often, Master.' Better than a lie; let him make of it what he would.

'There's a pair of shutters hanging badly in the solar and the door to the buttery is too tight.' He thought for a moment. 'Two pennies if you repair them today.'

John patted his leather satchel. 'I can start now, Master.'

'Good.' But he'd already turned away, fingers moving as he re-counted the bales.

The shutters were a simple job, no more than a few quick minutes all told. But he tried to stretch it out, as servants carried in small chests from the cart. Just a chance to snatch a quick conversation.

• • •

The lad was a barrel of curiosity, asking endless questions, eager to do as little work as possible. He was probably fourteen or fifteen, still growing into his body, with a thicket of red hair that didn't want to be tamed, and a forest of freckles across his nose and cheeks.

It was easy enough to lead him on, to tease the knowledge out of him. He'd been in service with the Unthank family for five years, starting as a groom and now working in the kitchens. He knew the whole family and how the household ran.

He pursed his lips and frowned. 'No, there's no piebald horse, Master. The family doesn't own one. They haven't as long as I've been with them.'

None of the servants had been gone for a few hours lately, he said, except Dame Agatha and Master Wilfred, who'd brought the cart to Chesterfield last market day.

Innocent, John thought, as he tested the shutter, making sure it swung easily and closed smoothly.

In the buttery he removed the door and smoothed some wood from the bottom with a file. Straightforward, simple. Then he had to wait as Wilfred inspected the work before reluctantly reaching into his scrip and counting out the money.

Nothing. The Unthanks might resent l'Honfleur and his daughter, but it seemed that none of their servants had killed her.

• • •

'Are you satisfied they weren't involved in the death at all?' Strong asked. He strolled around the garden behind his house, looking at the twisted boughs of the apple and pear trees, rubbing a hand over a knot of wood as he spoke.

'As much as I can be, Master,' John replied.

'I'll tell my lord, but you'd better be absolutely certain.'

'I believe I am.' He'd considered it as he walked back through the town. The kitchen lad had convinced him. He was guileless, he couldn't have told a lie to save his life. There was nothing to defend, no reason for anything but God's truth.

'Then I'll make sure he knows.' He paused. 'There was another death today. Another murder, may the Lord rest him.' He crossed himself. 'Have you heard?'

John shook his head. He'd been too busy to listen to any gossip. Two killings in less than a handful of days? More than two years had passed since the last suspicious death. This was more than odd.

'Who was it?'

'A forager. An old man by the name of Oswald. He lived in Whittington. He'd been a labourer until he hurt his arm. He knew his herbs and plants, used to go out early to gather them and sell them to the people who have their stalls at the weekday market.'

'How did he die?' John asked.

'Stabbed. It seems he hadn't been dead more than an hour or two before he was discovered. The jury's already given a verdict of murder by persons unknown.'

'What about the body, Master?'

Sir Mark shook his head. 'Already in the ground. No reason to wait.' He cocked his head. 'Why?'

'A forager is the kind of man who would know about mushrooms that could kill.'

Strong grimaced. 'I never…' He banged a fist against the tree trunk in frustration. 'I should have realised.'

'Who was the first finder, Master?'

'Another old man, he lives next door to the one who died. He knew his friend always went out before it was light. He'd always bring back a little something tasty that he'd found. When he didn't appear, the neighbour went searching.'

'Did he have any enemies?'

Strong shook his head. 'Not according to his friend. He was just a harmless old man who was struggling to survive.'

'I want to see the finder, Master. Do you know if he heard anything? Saw anything? Men on horses?'

'Nothing that he told me. His name's Adam. Go and ask him questions with my blessing. If this is connected to Dame Gertrude's killing, we might be able to solve them both in a single swoop.'

It was too far to walk to Whittington and back today; he'd be travelling home in the pitch darkness. Tomorrow. It would be something to begin his day. Could the second murder be coincidence? That was possible; anything was possible. But everything in his senses screamed no. Not so soon after Gertrude's death, not a man with that kind of knowledge.

• • •

The ground still held a little of the day's warmth. John lay back and let Martha climb all over him. He lifted her up, the small body so light, then brought her back down as she giggled. He inhaled her smell, the scent of childhood and innocence. Juliana ran around him, singing out a rhyme in some game she'd devised.

And there, on the bench, his son Richard. Pale but smiling, a blanket wrapped around his shoulders, although the evening chill was nowhere near. Freshly washed linen was spread over the bushes as it dried. He heard Katherine in the kitchen, ladling out the pottage into bowls for them to eat.

If he could find the murderer and earn the fifty pounds, everything would change in their lives. In the meantime, he'd take the four pennies a day the coroner was paying him and be grateful; it meant food on the table for them all.

'Come on,' he said, setting Martha down on her feet and holding her until she was steady. 'Inside. It's time for supper.'

• • •

A mild morning. But the night had been warm enough for him to kick off the blanket and enjoy the pleasure of air against his body.

He'd set off just as the first band of lighter blue appeared on the eastern horizon. Still early enough to have the road to himself on the long hill up to Whittington.

By the time he reached the village, dawn had broken. Birds were singing, the lark and the sparrow, with blackbirds and magpies calling and fluttering round the trees.

People were up, smoke rising from the roofs. A man came out of his door carrying a long, sharp scythe. He gave John the directions he needed.

It was one of two cottages that lay side by side. They seemed to share a small yard and midden, and a jakes set far enough away that the smell couldn't travel.

On one of the buildings, the shutters were open to the day. On the other they remained closed. That must have been where Oswald the forager lived. Who'd be living there next, he wondered?

Adam was a small, spry man. Almost bald, his head shiny, eyes inquisitive, grey hair sprouting from his nostrils and his ears, and his eyebrows thick as a hedge. His tunic was neatly mended with small, even stitches, and his hose snug around his spindly legs. The shoes had been patched many times, squares of leather one over the other until it was impossible to see the original colour.

All very neat, but an air of sorrow hung around him. Hardly a surprise; the man had lost his closest friend.

'True enough, Master,' he said as they walked out to the forest that covered the hill going down to Unstone. 'We were both widowers, so we looked out for each other. I've always been good with my hands, and Oswald, he could come out of a wood with a feast. We helped each other and shared.'

'Who bought what he foraged?'

'People who sell at the market in Chesterfield,' – he made the town sound as if were in another county, not less than an hour's walk away – 'goodwives who have no time to go looking themselves, or no skill at finding.' Adam smiled. 'It was enough to keep going.' He stopped and craned his neck. 'Over there, do you see it? Where the grass has been flattened going off from the track.'

John followed the old man, coming into a small clearing between some young ash trees.

'He was here,' Adam said. 'Right there, Master.' He pointed at the ground.

John knelt and ran his fingers through the dirt. The earth was dry, but one patch of ground looked darker than the rest. Even as he looked around, he knew there would be nothing here to guide him. This was isolated. Far enough from the village that no cry would be heard. No one would see; even the track was hidden from view. Still, he'd seen the killing ground for himself now, he had the evidence of his own eyes, for whatever it was worth.

'Did anyone different come to visit Oswald in the last week or two?' John asked. 'Someone you haven't seen before, perhaps?' He made it sound like a light question, something asked in passing and of no account.

'No,' Adam replied. But his manner had changed. His body had stiffened and the expression sharpened on his face. 'I'd have seen if they had. If I hadn't been there, he'd have told me. His only visitors were his usual customers, Master.'

The man was talking too much, trying to fill the silence as if he had something to hide. That was interesting, but John wasn't going to press him on it yet. He'd pick his moment.

'Did he ever pick mushrooms?'

Adam shook his head. 'Only for us, Master. A handful of morels to add to a pottage. Nobody buys them. Why would they, when most people know what's edible and they can just come out and collect for themselves?'

'Yes.' But that sense was there again; old Adam was hiding something. He stood and they turned back towards the village. 'Tell me, do you have any idea who might have killed your friend?'

'No, Master, I don't. That's the honest truth, as I stand before God.'

Bold words for a man who might well be lying, John thought. Soon enough, Adam would probably need to confess to the priest and cleanse his soul.

'Then may he rest in the Lord's peace.' John crossed himself and started on the road back to town.

At the brook by the bottom of the hill, he cupped his hands and drank. The water was cold enough to sting his mouth, clear and sweet as he swallowed.

Someone had come to see Oswald the forager and paid him to find the death cap mushrooms that killed Gertrude. It made sense. Oswald had the knowledge and the skill.

Then they'd returned to murder him so he could never reveal the truth.

He had no proof. Nothing more than a feeling. But the pieces fitted together. And Adam was doing his best not to reveal something. Was he fearful, perhaps? That would be sensible. He'd seen what happened to his close friend. It was all too easy to cut another old man's throat or make him vanish in the woods. And with no one to search this time, the animals would eat his meat and bones, and no one would ever know what happened.

All John had was suspicion. Not a scrap of evidence. He'd press Adam on it once he knew a little more. But not yet.

Bramble bushes grew in the hedgerow and John picked the berries as he walked. Large and dark, with sweet juices. He should bring Juliana and Richard out here, let them gather their fill. The berries were good until Michaelmas, that was what the goodwives always said. He gathered a final handful and trudged on, nibbling as he walked.

He had pieces, fragments. A few sat well together, like Oswald and the death cap mushroom. Others, though… it was impossible to know yet. Too early for any accusations. But the coroner wanted answers before the fair began, and the sand kept trickling steadily through the hourglass. Time was against him.

• • •

'But you were certain the Unthanks had nothing to do with Dame Gertrude's death,' Strong said in exasperation.

'I know, Master. I still believe that. We need to be *sure*, though. I've been able to talk to the servants, but not the family. They could have employed somebody else.'

He was a carpenter. A nobody. The Unthank family had money and land, everything except a title. They'd never open their mouths to offer him the hour of day.

'Very well,' the man agreed with a grimace. 'But employing you is proving to be more trouble than it's worth. If you're so certain this old man knows something, why didn't you force it out of him?'

'Simple, Master. I have no proof,' John said. 'If he keeps denying it, there's nothing we can do. It's better to wait and have a wedge to ease the truth into the light.'

The coroner raised an eyebrow.

'Don't wait too long,' he ordered. 'I know someone who can fit into the Unthank house. I'll send him to you this afternoon.' He leaned an elbow on the table and rubbed his chin with his hand. 'Tell me, Carpenter, can you find the killer? And I pray the answer is yes, for my sake as well as yours.'

'I will,' John told him. He had strands of hope. A beginning that he could follow. 'I'd like to see my Lord l'Honfleur, too.'

'Again? Why?'

'An idea.'

'I'll talk to him and send word. Just don't dawdle, Carpenter. He wants answers. People are already starting to arrive for the fair.'

He knew that; he'd seen the carts on the road as he returned to Chesterfield. Out in the fields beyond the market square, streets of stalls were already beginning to take shape. The eight days that the fair lasted would be a boon, bringing in people and money. Every bed in the inns was already booked. They could fill each one four or five times over. People would be begging anywhere to sleep and offer good coin for a bench or a patch of floor.

'I'm sure it's busier than last year,' Katherine said as they settled to their dinner. Richard seemed a little stronger today, taking his place at the table. Juliana played with her food and Martha ate everything on her trencher; she never needed any encouragement. 'So many people in town and it's still a while before the fair begins.'

'We should take the children later,' John said. 'It won't be too busy yet.'

Suddenly the air was filled with chatter. He held up his hand and waited for silence.

'Later,' he repeated. He was about to say more when the thudding came on the door.

The young man standing there had a guileless look. He seemed barely older than Katherine's brother Walter. Certainly wealthier, though, and with the self-assurance money brought. In good silks and well-made woollen hose, with his shoes in a fashionable point, he introduced himself.

'I'm Jeffrey of Hardwick. The coroner said you might be able to use my services.'

The lad had a winning smile, full of charm, and was holding a hat between clean, soft hands. Not someone who'd ever done manual work for a living.

'You're welcome, Master. I'm John the Carpenter.' As soon as they were through the screens, his family was there, waiting and expectant. He named Jeffrey, who was immediately on his knees with the children, before standing and offering a courtly bow to Katherine.

'I'm honoured, good Dame,' he said as she blushed deep red.

John shooed them all away until he and Jeffrey were sitting at the table with a jug of ale and a pair of mazers that had belonged to old Martha.

'Did Sir Mark tell you what I need?'

'Someone who knows the Unthanks,' he replied with a bright smile. 'They're distant cousins of mine. I've been around them all my life.'

'I need information,' John said.

'I'm good at that.' The young man's expression became serious. 'I handle the business for my family's lands, the fleeces, the crops, the rents. God gave me a gift. My family uses it. Like you with wood, I imagine.'

'Yes,' he replied. 'Maybe it is.'

Jeffrey glanced around the room. 'I'd never imagined a trade would pay as well as this. The coroner said you own another house as well.'

'It's a long story. Would you be willing to find out information about the Unthanks?'

'Does this have to do with the killing of Gertrude?'

'It does.'

'Then I'll gladly do it. I'm related to her, too.' He gave a smile and shook his head. 'Another long story. It seems we both have them.'

John sketched out what he needed to learn. Jeffrey listened closely, asking questions to make points a little clearer. He had a sharp mind, quick to grasp ideas and see problems. By the time they'd finished, John was certain the lad would discover the truth and do it speedily.

'Time is vital,' he said.

The young man nodded. 'I should be able to find all this out in a day. I'll talk to my cousins. They'll all be coming in for the fair, anyway, and all the trading beforehand.'

As they parted at the door, Jeffrey smiled once more.

'Sir Mark said you wanted to see my lord. He has some time this afternoon.'

'I'm glad you told me.'

'I'll be back tomorrow morning, John, and tell you what I've learned.'

• • •

Today l'Honfleur was wearing an unfashionable burgundy houppelande trimmed around the neck with dark fur. He paced around the room, the lavender and rose scent rising from the rushes.

'Why?' he asked.

'My lord,' John said, 'I know the people on your manor claim they had nothing to do with your daughter's death. But the villagers in Calow said the riders might have been wearing your livery.'

'Exactly,' he said. 'They *might have been* wearing my livery. They don't know. They're not sure. It could have been anything. And I told you, I don't have a piebald horse in my stable.'

'Yes, my lord.' He'd thought this through; now he needed to convince the man. 'But Gertrude would have known your livery well, wouldn't she?' She'd have known it her whole life.

'Of course.'

'Do you think she would trust something that didn't look real?'

That was enough to make l'Honfleur pause.

'No, she'd know better that that. What about the men, though? She knows them all. And the horses? She'd recognise them.'

'It would be simple enough to leave the animals on the other side of the church. And the men could claim they were new in your service.'

L'Honfleur took two or three breaths before he replied. 'You're suggesting that two of my men lent their clothes to the people who killed my daughter.' His voice was bitter.

'I don't know, my lord. It's one possibility, that's all.'

'It's quite an accusation. How are you going to discover if it's true?'

'I need to be at your manor near Hathersage for a day or two.'

L'Honfleur raised his eyebrows. 'And what will you do there? A carpenter is hardly likely to be a welcome guest, is he? Or do you intend to tell them you're investigating my daughter's death?'

'Master, do you need any carpentry work at the manor?'

'Of course, there are always jobs to be done. The men do most of it themselves, the same as everywhere else.'

'Perhaps this time you decided to hire someone who can do the job properly.'

'Why do you feel you'll be able to worm out the truth? Assuming there's any to be found, of course.'

'My lord, you're willing to pay me fifty pounds to discover who was responsible. That means you must believe I can do it.'

'No, Carpenter. It means I'm desperate. Nothing more than that.'

'Then trust me, Master, please. We still have time before the fair.'

Silence filled the room as l'Honfleur stared out of the window and bit his lip. Eventually he turned.

'I don't like the idea that any of my men have betrayed me. I can't believe it of them. But you're right, we need to find out.' He sighed. 'Come here after dinner tomorrow. I'll give you a letter for the reeve at the manor, telling him what work I want you to do.'

'Please, my lord, don't tell him the real reason I'm there. No one should know. It needs to be between us.'

'Very well,' he agreed after a moment.

CHAPTER FIVE

'It'll only be for one night,' John said as they crossed the market square. 'Two at the most, I promise.' Juliana had run ahead to stand on the edge of the field where the stalls were going up.

Martha held his hand, dragging him along, and Richard walked solemnly beside Katherine.

'I know,' she answered. Her eyes gave a look that said enough, no more discussion about it now.

The air was filled with the scent of spices and cooking meat. Strange music played, an odd, hypnotic melody that seemed to slip in and out of tune, performed on a bagpipe. Juliana came running back, pointing in fear as a giant strode along. John laughed.

'It's just a man.' He ruffled her hair. 'He's walking on stilts, see? They're made of wood so he looks tall.'

Even with so few booths set up, it was still a spectacle to take the breath away. He let Juliana guide Martha around, keeping an eye on them both. After a few minutes Richard wandered quietly away.

He was alone with his wife, walking between the stalls. Pulled here and there by the music, the burbles of strange dialects and languages, the smells that caught his nose.

'You know, it surprises me every year,' he said with a voice full of wonder. 'There's so much here. It's as if everyone in the world has come to Chesterfield.'

But Katherine was distracted; she acted as if he hadn't spoken.

'Will the visit to the manor be dangerous?'

'Of course not,' John told her. 'They won't know why I'm there. I'll be another workman, doing a few jobs. Nothing more than that.'

The torches flaring in the dusk caught her eyes. They held a world of worry.

'It will be fine.' He squeezed her hand.

'Be careful what you say, husband.'

She was right. He'd do better to stay cautious and alert. He was going out there because he believed something was wrong. That someone on the manor had something to hide.

They'd be watching, on their guard.

Before bed, as the children slept, John sat in the hall and sharpened his knife on a whetstone. He didn't want to use it, to draw blood or to kill. Sometimes, though, life left no other choice.

• • •

Jeffrey of Hardwick was as good as his word. John and his family had barely finished breaking their fast than he was at the door, charming them all before he drew John aside into the garden.

'What have you learned about the Unthanks?'

'Enough to be sure they're not behind all this,' the young man answered. He stroked his chin as he walked around, bending to pluck a few blades of grass and chew on them. 'They still resent that the marriage never happened. But it was a long time ago now. Years. They have no love for my lord, they never will have—'

'But?' John asked.

'But they would never do anything like that to someone's child. They swear to it and I believe them. You'll need to look elsewhere.'

'Thank you, Master.' It confirmed what he believed, but it didn't make his job any easier.

'Not Master,' Jeffrey told him with a soft chuckle. 'No need for that. You're the man with two fine houses. I have nothing except what my family grants me. I should be the one calling you master.'

It was enough to make him smile.

• • •

He ate dinner before he left, a hurried farewell to his wife before scrambling out along the road to Cutthorpe. He carried the leather satchel on his shoulder and a small pack on his back with clean linen and his other pair of leggings. The air was fresh and clear, the sun showing off the brilliant purples and greens of the late heather. There were only a few other travellers on the road, every one of them heading to Chesterfield. Some led weary packhorses, others carried their goods on their backs, tradesmen or travellers. All of them in search of money.

John exchanged a few words as he passed. But none wanted to stop. They had their rhythm, they had their destination; it was better to keep on placing one foot in front of another.

He'd followed this road before, enough for it to feel familiar. It took him past Owler Bar and over the high track across the moors. There was little here beyond sheep and a few trees that had been stunted and blasted by the wind. His feet kicked up dust and his legs ached.

Finally, with Higger Tor close and the crags on the horizon, he turned and followed the path to the manor house, half a mile away. It was built of thick stone, with a slate roof. No defences against man, but who would ever attack here?

A stable, a barn, the kitchen tucked away in the garden. And the house itself; nothing especially grand or large. But serviceable against the weather, where the views on a day like this ranged to hills ten miles away and more. When the cloud came down it might seem to be the only place on earth.

John passed l'Honfleur's letter to the manor reeve, standing silent like a man in the presence of his superior.

The reeve read it twice before he bothered to look at him.

'We have men here who could do this work. Or there's someone in Hathersage, married to my wife's sister. Why would my lord send you?'

'I don't know, Master. He's seen my work in Chesterfield.' Easy to tell he wasn't going to be welcomed here. If the reeve resented him, so would everyone else on the manor.

The man snorted. He was large, with the red face and bulbous nose of a man who'd filched too much of his lord's wine.

'You'll have to find a bed in the hayloft, we don't have any room for people like you in the house.' He drew in breath and yelled: 'Hubert!' A few seconds passed with no response and he called the name once more.

Finally an old man arrived, his ruddy face hidden by a bushy white beard, dragging a lame leg as he walked. His tunic was spattered with dirt, the pipe of his hood drooped down his back, and his boots looked as though they'd not been cleaned since he bought them.

'Master,' he said.

'My lord has sent a carpenter from Chesterfield.' The words came out as a sneer. 'Show him what needs to be done. He'll eat with the men and sleep in the hayloft. You understand.'

Hubert bowed his head in acknowledgement and walked off, stopping after a few paces and staring at John.

'Come on.'

He hurried after the man; the reeve had already gone.

'Don't know nothing, that lad,' Hubert muttered. 'Been here half a year and reckons he has the measure of this place inside and out.'

'What do you need me to do?'

'Can't understand this land 'less you've been here ten year or more,' Hubert continued. 'Got four jobs for you. Start in the barn. You know my lord, do you?'

'Yes,' John answered, 'I do.' Hubert's mind seemed to jump like a flea. 'Why?'

'Always good to me. Didn't turn me off when I hurt my leg. That reeve, he'd see the back of me if he could. All he sees in this place is profit.'

Overall, the manor appeared in good order, everything tidy. In the barn, two of the stalls needed new boards and fresh wood across the bottom of the door. But inside, exactly as l'Honfleur had told him, there was no piebald horse. Just a roan, a gelding, and a foal that was close to grown, alongside the ox to pull the plough in the field. No horses out being ridden, according to Hubert. All the leather halters were well-soaped and supple. Maybe the reeve only cared about turning a profit, but he was certainly looking after things here.

Hubert stood and watched as John worked. Silent and vanishing into his thoughts. He'd talk, then the words would drift off into silence. But after a lifetime of living on the manor, he knew every inch of ground and all the men who worked here.

'Good men, are they?' John finished sawing the wood and checked once again that it was the right fit.

'Good enough,' the old man said grudgingly. 'Not like it were when I was young, though. Men would do anything for their lord then. Whatever he asked.'

'Are they loyal?' John asked as he nailed the final board in place, putting his weight against it to be sure it would hold firm. Hubert had given him the opening he needed for the questions.

'Them old ones were. Too many young 'uns these days. Look around and you can see them whispering in corners and turning away.'

'That's the stall finished. What's the next job?' He didn't want to force the conversation and leave Hubert with suspicions that might stick in his mind.

There was a task in the kitchen, then the remaining two in the buttery, working until the shadows were long and dusk was rising, thick and deep as velvet. John dropped in questions as he worked: how the manor ran, where the sheep roamed, more about the men.

By supper he knew more. Not everything, but enough to make him wonder about two of the young squires, a pair of brothers who were out here to learn their manners and weaponry from l'Honfleur.

'They reckon they're better than us and they make sure we all know it.' Hubert turned his head and spat into the dirt. 'You ever been treated like you were nothing?'

John gave a bitter laugh. 'Is there anyone who hasn't?'

'Aye, but them two… you'd think they owned the world. I know the manor their father has, too, up above Edale. All peat and rocks, it's hardly worth the bother. Won't bring either of them a living if they end up as old as Methuselah. But the way they act, you'd think they could buy and sell the likes of you and me.'

'They probably could.' He wiped down the tools with an oily rag, applying a fresh edge to the chisel with a whetstone before packing everything away in the leather satchel.

Supper was in the hall. No grand affair, nobody at the high table, just the workers from the manor who doled out pottage that had been cooking for days. The men looked warily at John, the way people always did with strangers. He spotted the squires, two young men with thick, fair hair, sitting together and leaning their heads towards each other as they talked. They were watching him.

John finished the meal without talking to a soul in the hall. They seemed to take pains to ignore him. Very likely the reeve had warned them away from him. Whenever he did try to speak to someone, the man simply turned his head and ignored him. It was as if they believed he couldn't be trusted, that they knew something about him. His eyes flickered around the faces in the hall. He hadn't seen any of them at l'Honfleur's house in Chesterfield. The fact that he was here investigating Gertrude's death was supposed to be secret. And yet… he wondered.

Outside, the night air was sweet and clear, the barn and the hayloft just ahead of him. Back in the hall, chatter had started. One of the men had begun to sing a song and others were laughing. It had all come to life as soon as he left.

Maybe it was nothing. Perhaps he was sensing things that weren't there. But as he climbed the ladder to the hayloft, ripples of fear cascaded through him. He wasn't safe in this place. It was out in the middle of nowhere. Someone could kill him and his body could readily disappear in all those miles of moorland. Maybe all the wolves of England were dead, the way people claimed, but there were plenty of other creatures who could do their damage. And none was more dangerous than man.

He pushed some horse blankets together to make a figure and spread the sheet over it before he picked out a dark corner for himself. The rough planks of the hayloft were hard against his bones. Never mind; he'd spend one uncomfortable night, but it was better to be safe and stay alive when his senses were pushing him to take care.

Well hidden, he blew out the rush light and settled down into a doze. His ears were cocked for any sound, the knife close by his hand in case of danger. And it would come, something told him that. It would come.

He jerked awake at each snuffling of the animals. Three times, four, listening just long enough to realise it was nothing.

And then again. Deep in the night, everything black around him. John raised his head and listened. Something was different. A smell in the air. Sweat, dirt, a very human scent. He closed his hand around the knife hilt, ready to move.

They were good. Almost silent. Not enough noise to wake someone who was sleeping soundly. Two of them, he decided; at first the sounds came from different parts of the barn, as if they were searching around.

The pair took their time. They were either cautious or confident, he wasn't sure which. Careful, John decided, after a rung of the ladder to the hayloft creaked, followed by a long, aching silence. Whatever they intended, it was serious. Deadly.

They were up in the hayloft with him. One of them was not even two feet away; John could have reached out and grabbed the man's ankle. Instead, he kept very still, barely daring to breathe in case they discovered him.

There must have been a signal of some kind. Suddenly they were plunging their daggers into the bundle of blankets in the straw. Time after time, a frenzy of stabbing. One of them hissed and they stopped, hurrying down the ladder and away. It was over so quickly that he wondered if he'd dreamed it all.

But everything had been utterly real.

John lay perfectly still. They wouldn't return. In his head he knew that, but his limbs refused to move. If he'd tried to stand, his legs wouldn't have supported him.

Sweet love of God, he'd been lucky. By rights he should be dead now and starting his long journey through Purgatory.

His senses had saved him before, but that was years earlier. Praise God that they still worked and he'd had the wit to listen to them. He let the night wash over his body, feeling the chilly sweat, the helpless quivering. They came and passed. Finally he could sit, hunched over, trembling and cold. More time passed and he was able to stand, careful to hold on to the posts for balance.

He was still alive, thanks be to God. But what good did that do him out in the moorland in the middle of the night and far from home? What could he do now? He could feel the way his heart was still hammering. The panic was there, clutching at his reason.

Part of him wanted to run away, to try and find his way back to Chesterfield. But if he set off in the pitch darkness, creeping out of the manor like a thief, he'd end up lost. He didn't know his way here. It was too easy to lose his footing and break an ankle or a leg.

Go at first light? Once the men discovered they hadn't killed him, they'd start hunting him, and there were precious few places to hide out there.

No. He stood and thought.

There was only one possibility. He had to appear when the men broke their fast, be there with all the other workers of the manor and try to act as if nothing had happened. He'd watch carefully to see who reacted when they saw his face. It had to be the brothers, the squires. He felt certain of that. Two of them, working so easily together, not even needing words to communicate – who else could it be? If he had any money, he'd have wagered it on that.

John didn't attempt to rest. Sleep wouldn't visit him again tonight. He wondered how many nights it would be until he could rest without the night mare riding through his mind, even in his own bed. He had time before dawn. He sat and thought, trying to work his way through this labyrinth of murder.

Some parts fitted together, but not enough to make a pattern. There was a trail to follow, starting with whoever had tried to murder him a few hours before. The men might be in l'Honfleur's house, but were they working for someone else? They had to be, but why? And above all, who? Discover the answer to that and he'd have the real murderer.

The first streaks of light crept over the horizon. He still felt uneasy but he forced himself to stand and move, to try to act as if no one had tried to stab him in a frenzy.

He walked around the manor, checking over the work he'd done yesterday. Hubert was by his side, prattling on about the way things had been when he was young. John made idle conversation, hearing about the sheep they kept and how many they lost to wild dogs, the price a fleece brought these days. He let the words run by him, constantly watching for the two squires.

By the time the bell sounded to draw them to the hall and eat, his belly was rumbling. He laughed at himself; stupid, the way a brush with death left him so hungry. He was the first man in, taking bread and cheese and ale and sitting at one end of the trestle.

He was there when the brothers arrived. They halted as soon as they saw him, eyes widening and mouths opening wide. Good, John thought, a shock for the pair of you. But he made sure his face showed nothing, giving a short nod in their direction as he ate.

More men were coming in, talking, keeping their distance from him, just as they had the day before. The brothers each downed a mug of ale and left.

John took his time. His work was done; all that remained was the walk back to Chesterfield. A fair day with thin, high clouds, not too hot. No sign of rain and he couldn't smell any on the air.

But two killers were around.

He let an hour ease by before he went to find the reeve. Hubert was talking to the man, gesturing and pointing. The reeve sent him away.

'What do you want?' he asked John when they were alone. 'Have you finished?'

'Has something happened?'

'The old man claims he saw the squires ride off together.' He shrugged. 'Says they packed what they brought and took off towards Hathersage like the devil was after them.'

'Have you sent a message to my lord?'

The reeve glared.

'Why would I do that? Because an old man who's only half here says he's seen something?' He turned his head and spat into the dirt. 'So they've ridden off. They've probably gone hawking. They don't answer to me. He won't thank me if I send to tell him that, will he?'

'He will if you tell him they tried to stab me in the night.'

'You?' The reeve laughed, a bellow that started in his stomach and erupted, full-throated and loud. 'You're worse than Hubert, and he has his mind in the skies. Christ's blood, man, why would they want to kill you? Is your work that bad?'

'My lord has hired me to investigate the murder of his daughter,' John told him. 'Somehow they know about that. They crept up to the hayloft in the middle of the night with their knives.'

The reeve shook his head.

'I don't believe you. You're a carpenter, not…' He couldn't find the words. 'If they tried to kill you, why isn't there a scratch on you?'

'I didn't sleep where they thought. Close enough to be hidden and to hear it all. They saw me still alive this morning. They've run off, and you need to send a message to my lord as quickly as possible.'

They stood facing each other. John could feel the reeve's anger and disbelief.

'No.'

'Don't you want the person who killed Gertrude found?' He didn't raise his voice; he stayed calm, composed.

'Don't be so stupid. Of course I do.'

'Those two were involved. My lord needs men hunting them.'

'They probably ran back to their father.'

'They should be easy to find, then.' John smiled. 'I'm telling you the truth. My oath on it.'

A moment passed, then the reeve exhaled loudly.

'If you're lying, my lord will flay you alive.'

'Every word is true.'

The man's face was grim. 'I'm not sure why, but I'm going to believe you. I'll send a man to Chesterfield. On horseback, before you say anything more. For your sake, I pray to God you're not lying.'

He stalked off, shouting for two of the men, and leaving John alone.

'Where did the squires sleep?' he asked when he found Hubert.

'Right there.' The old man pointed at an upstairs window, its shutters still closed. 'But they're gone.'

'I know. Thank you.'

The room was empty. They had no more luxury than any of the other servants. Two pallets for sleeping, a small chest standing open at the foot of each one. Nails hammered into the back of the door to hang surcotes and cloaks.

At first glance, everything had been stripped away. The chests were empty, no clothes anywhere. John plunged a hand into the straw of the pallets, spreading it, searching for anything that might have been hidden. The brothers had vanished in a rush. People in a hurry were often careless; they made mistakes. There might be something they'd forgotten.

Luck wasn't shining on him, John decided when he'd finished. He left the straw strewn across the boards on the floor. Nothing at all.

Still, it had been worth the time. If he hadn't looked, he'd never have known.

• • •

He had his bag of tools, the small pack strapped to his back, and a leather bottle of weak ale hanging from his belt, next to his scrip. His boots kicked up dust as he followed the track over the moor, back towards Cutthorpe.

There was nobody else out here. He had the land to himself, walking in the sunlight. High, thin clouds flickered across the sky, tempering the heat. The day felt still and calm. But still he kept looking around, checking in every direction. He felt uneasy, alone and helpless out here.

L'Honfleur should have received the message by now. He'd have a party beginning their search for the squires. Perhaps the reeve was right and they'd scurried off home, hoping that their father would offer them protection. But they were beyond anything he'd be able to do for them.

Were they the ones who'd taken Gertrude the meal that killed her? Yes, he was sure they were. But he'd know the full truth once they were caught. And what would happen then? My lord had the ear of important people at court. The King's mistress listened to him. And he would have a fury for justice forcing him on.

John had covered two miles when he saw the small cloud on the horizon. Dust; someone else was out travelling. But they were moving too quickly for a man on foot and there was more of it than a single man would raise.

He felt the chill rise up his spine. They were coming across the moorland, directly towards him.

He glanced around. Nothing but tussocks and clumps of grass. A few small folds in the ground, not a single one of them big enough to hide a man.

Move away from the path. That was the first thing. If he did that and stayed low, they wouldn't be able to see him. Get as far away from here as he could. There might be somewhere he could shelter out of sight.

Bent over, he began to run. But the weight of the tools, the pack and the bottle made it difficult. The satchel banged against his legs and his calves cramped.

John judged he'd covered half a mile when he stopped, gasping for breath. He knelt on the grass, staying low, raising his head just enough to follow the trail of dust. It was much closer now. Easy enough to make out a pair of riders swiftly covering the ground. He recognised the horses; he'd seen them in the barn at the manor the night before.

And the squires were riding them.

They were going towards the spot where he'd been. That was something. He had a small start on them. But he needed to move faster, to find somewhere they wouldn't discover when they looked.

A quick gulp of air and he was running again, trying to ignore the pain in his legs. Keep going, keep going. Far off, he could hear the rhythmic thump of hooves on the dirt.

He risked a glance over his shoulder. The squires were circling where he'd been, looking around, watching the ground and trying to track him.

Too close. They were far too close.

They had swords, they had fast mounts. As soon as they caught sight of him it would only take a minute at the gallop to reach him. When that happened, he was a dead man. All he had to defend himself was a knife.

No one would ever find his body out here. At best, someone might spot the buzzards and the carrion crows.

He ran. Breathing hard, bent double, he ran, arms out to keep his footing on the uneven ground as he tried to look ahead. There. Off to the right. A boulder laced with purple heather. The ground seemed to slip away behind it.

He crawled. He scrabbled, panting, checking behind. They still hadn't seen him. If this gap was large enough...

CHAPTER SIX

John slid down the earth and the thin scree of pebbles. His hose snagged and tore on the branch of a gorse bush. He pulled himself loose, aware of moments passing as his fingers frantically worked at the threads. Fifteen feet to the base of a slim ravine. A tiny stream burbled along the bottom, barely covering the rocks.

But it was flat enough for him to run. Still awkward, too easy to slip and turn an ankle, but he needed distance. He needed it quickly. A final glance back, seeing nothing, and he was moving.

The ravine twisted hither and yon. It was impossible to see far ahead. He'd covered a fair distance when he saw the roots of a tree growing out from the side of the hill. The space beneath them looked as if it ran deep and dark. There might be enough room for him to crawl through and push himself out of sight.

In there, no one would be able spot him from the edge of the ravine. He went as far as he could, feeling the cool earth, the tang of soil. John lay back, feeling his heart pounding, and took a drink from the leather bottle. For now, at least, he was safe.

A few minutes and he could hear the hooves and voices calling to each other.

'I don't see him,' one shouted. 'It doesn't look as if he's been down here.'

'We need to turn back,' the other said. The voice made him freeze. It sounded as if it was coming from right above his head. 'If l'Honfleur knows, he'll have men coming.'

For a moment, the sound of the horses as they cantered seemed too loud. Then it began to fade until he couldn't hear it at all. Still, John waited another five minutes before he crept out into the light and looked up, blinking at the brightness.

No sign of them.

Very cautiously, John climbed the slope. Gravel slid under his feet. He stopped, listening, waiting, then took hold of a bush and pulled himself high enough to glance over the rim of the spindly valley.

No sign of the horsemen. Just a faint plume of dust rising in the distance. A final push up, back to the moor, and he took another long drink of the ale as he sat.

They'd been close. And they might still decide to return.

John stood. It was time to move.

• • •

'How—' Katherine began, then caught full sight of his face. 'Sweet Jesu, what happened to you?'

He settled on the bench, grateful to be in the safety of his own home once more. He knew he was covered in dirt and scratches, but they didn't matter. He was here, he was alive and he was unhurt.

Martha was toddling around, gazing up and him with a broad, loving smile. He swept her up and cuddled her on his lap. John buried his nose in her hair and smelled the child's sweet innocence, drawing it deep into him. For the love of God, his daughter made it good to be alive.

Finally, he told Katherine. Everything, from the moment he arrived at the manor to hurrying through Cutthorpe on his way home, still scared that a pair of mounted devils were pursuing him. He closed his eyes and bounced Martha on his lap as he spoke.

His wife listened, letting the silence fill the hall after he finished.

'Husband… I know what he's promised.' Her voice was quiet and reasoned. She stared at him. 'I know what it can do for us. But please, listen to what you've just told me. Those men tried to kill you twice. God watched over you. I pray that He always will, but tell me, what if He doesn't? What's the point of the money if you're not here to enjoy everything it can do? I'll have no one, our children won't have a father.'

'If I don't do it, we'll have to sell one of the houses.'

'Then we'll sell it!' she shouted. But it was pain behind the words, not anger. 'I need you here with us. What would I do if you died?'

'I could die at any time,' John said quietly. 'Any of us could. That's God's will.'

She shook her head and a strand of hair fell clear of her wimple. 'But you keep tempting Him!'

'And each time, I pray He'll preserve me.' He stroked the soft skin of her cheek. 'That He'll keep us all.'

But there was Richard, the frail boy who probably wouldn't be too much longer for this earth…

'I need to speak to l'Honfleur,' he said. It was easier than having to think about all this to try and resolve it. 'He needs to know.'

• • •

The man held a wooden mazer that was decorated with fine, filigree lines of silver wire. He sipped at the wine it held as he listened.

'At least I know for certain who betrayed me now,' he said once John had finished. 'I sent a party out to hunt them as soon as I received the message.' He sounded bitter and cold. 'They know what to expect.' His eyes flickered. 'No mercy for men who do that.'

'My lord, if you keep them alive, we can discover who paid them and murdered your daughter.'

He nodded. 'I told my men to bring them here if they could. But if those brothers choose to fight, then they have orders to kill them.'

'I see.' Pointless deaths, he thought. More killing. If they were spared, the pair would quickly break under questioning. Then they'd learn everything they needed.

'You did well, Carpenter,' l'Honfleur said approvingly. 'Very quickly, too.'

'Thank you, Master.' No mention of the two instances when he'd come close to death in the last day. But why would a lord ever think of that? The only death that truly mattered to him was his daughter's.

'What will you do now?'

'I'll wait and see what your men can learn from the squires. That can tell me where to go next.'

L'Honfleur raised an eyebrow. 'What if they die without speaking? They might, you have to understand that, Carpenter. It would be a matter of honour.'

He said it as if it were an everyday fact. Honour? He felt he could spit the word. Honour wasn't trying to stab a man as he slept or chase him down when you were armed and on horseback. Or perhaps honour only applied if you were fighting a man of gentle breeding.

'Of course, my lord.' He bowed and left the house.

• • •

'You did very well.' At least the coroner sounded impressed. 'God's blood, man, how did you know not to sleep in the hay?'

'I can't put it into words. It was the feeling in the place, Master. I was certain something would happen.' He shrugged. 'I don't even know what it was. But I decided to be safe.'

Strong stared at him then nodded, a mix of astonishment and appreciation. He walked across to the window. New rushes covered the floor.

'You were lucky when they were chasing you, too.' He smiled. 'God must be watching over you in this, Carpenter.'

'Then I pray He continues.' John coughed. 'But if the squires die before they say anything, then I'm no closer to finding who ordered the killing, Master. I'll be back where I was before.'

'I know. So does my lord, believe me. He wants the answer to this more than the rest of us. He loved his daughter very deeply. She was his special child, far more than her sister. He saw his dead wife in her.'

'Then I don't understand. He's happy for these men to die without telling him everything they know.'

'He sees it as their choice to make. Their honour, if you like. That's always been an important idea to him.'

More important than his daughter's memory, John wondered? But his question went unspoken; it wouldn't change a thing.

• • •

What else could he do? Perhaps now was the proper time to take a walk back to Whittington. The old man there, Adam, knew more than he'd said; John had been certain when they'd met. It was time to press him and discover what it was. How far it might take him, though, and in which direction was a different matter altogether. Most likely it would confirm that the two squires had been Oswald's murderers. But maybe there would be something more he could tease from the man.

Tomorrow, he decided. Today he needed to feel ordinary, to revel in the simple joy in being alive.

He stopped at the house where Alan was putting in new glazed windows. He had the frames in place, pointing out the problems he'd encountered in that special sign language he and John had developed. The hard job was making sure they sat square in walls that were out of true. But he'd done well. The frames were complete, only the windows themselves to go, with the leaded glass already fitted in place. He tried moving a couple of them. Good and snug, but they'd still open easily. He'd make sure the lad received every penny of the money for this work. That was only fair; he'd done it all.

He wished he could have been here, working at Alan's side. But he'd committed himself to finding Gertrude's killer. So much depended on his success. And the truth was that Alan was very capable of handling any job that only needed one man. He'd served his time as John's apprentice. He'd absorbed all the skills and developed a few of his own.

• • •

At home, the family gathered around the table for supper. Juliana was full of talk about the fair, bubbling over with excitement as she talked about the people who'd arrived during the day, how their stalls were decorated, the long ballads and tunes the musicians were swapping with each other.

Her enthusiasm was exactly what he needed to lift his mood. A few minutes and he'd almost forgotten all that had happened. Soon Richard and Katherine were asking Juliana questions, the whole family caught up in the anticipation. The fair was no more than a few days away. By then, maybe he'd have money to treat them. And something better than a plain bean pottage to place on their trenchers. A little meat at least one day a week, a fish on a Friday. If God was good.

Martha had finished her food. She was full and she was sleepy. He gathered her into his arms and carried her into the solar, washing the day's dirt from her hands and face before taking off her gown and settling her under the blanket in her small bed.

'Tell me a story, Papa. Please.'

He began, the tale of a dog named Good Harry who could save his owner from every peril. But he hadn't even been talking for five minutes, wracking his head for ideas, before she was fast asleep.

• • •

It was a calm day with hardly any breeze to flutter the leaves in the trees. Very few clouds, and even this early in the morning the sun was beating down.

John left a trail of dust behind him on the long pull up to Whittington. Every hundred yards he glanced back over his shoulders, but no riders were following him here. If they had any sense, the brothers would be running for their lives. Here, at least, he felt a little safer.

Adam, the first finder of the forager's body, was outside his cottage, digging the autumn weeds from his garden before they could grow and strangle the late crops.

'Good day,' John called and doffed his cap. 'May God be with you this morning, Master.'

The old man stared at him with suspicion, not sure why John had returned.

'I have a few more questions.' He mopped his face on the sleeve of his tunic. 'It's a warm walk out here today.'

Still Adam said nothing, keeping a bland, empty expression on his face.

'You must miss Oswald. You'd been friends for so many years.'

'Aye, I do.' A wistful expression. 'The world's changed, young man. It used to be a place when a man might feel some safety.'

Safety, John thought? When the pestilence and drought stalked across the land? Where was the safety in that? But he swallowed the question; there was no need to argue the point. He'd come here to learn some truth, not to discuss life.

'Tell me, Master, did Oswald ever receive visits from a pair of men who might be squires?'

'Squires? No, Master.' Adam tried to sound perplexed by the idea. But his face had no talent for hiding the truth.

'Ah, I thought perhaps two men in the service of Lord l'Honfleur had been to see him. That was what I'd been told.'

A lie. But he'd be able to see its effect.

'Not that I know. I've no idea who'd tell you a thing like that. Adam never said anything about it to me.'

But he'd hesitated that moment too long.

'Are you sure, Master? Maybe you forgot, or you weren't listening when he told you.'

John kept staring at Adam. It let the old man realise that he knew the truth; he was offering him the chance to recover gracefully.

'I don't know.' His face reddened and he looked down at the ground. 'I suppose I might have been mistaken.'

'Did you ever see two men like that? Young, full of themselves, wearing my lord's tunic and badge?'

He shook his head. 'Not myself. But now I think about it, Oswald did mention once that he'd been talking with a pair of young men. I suppose it might have been them. I hadn't really considered it.'

'No matter.' John waved it away, giving the man a chance to finally tell him the truth. 'Can you recall what he told you, Master?'

The old man picked up a clay mug of weak ale and took a drink to wet his mouth.

'Not all of it. It didn't seem like much at the time. Just that the two young men had come looking for him when he was in the woods.'

'Whose livery did they wear?'

'It was my lord's.' He gave a wry, fleeting smile. 'It's impossible to live here and not recognise it. Oswald guessed who they must be from their age and the haughty way they carried themselves with him.'

'What did they want?'

'A few questions, he said. About different plants and the way they could heal or kill. They offered him money for his knowledge. He told them some things, and that was everything for that visit.'

John raised his head sharply. 'That visit? Do you mean there were others?'

'Aye, Master. One more. They came back about a week later. That was what Oswald told me,' he added. 'I never saw them for myself.'

Perhaps the part about not seeing them was true, John thought; maybe it was another lie. It didn't matter.

'What did they want the second time?'

'They brought some plants they wanted Oswald to identify. Things he'd told them about. They wanted to know if they'd picked the right things. They paid him again for his time.'

'Was there a mushroom?'

'Aye, Master, there was, and Oswald fretted over it after we heard what happened to Gertrude. One of the plants they brought was a death cap mushroom. But at the time he wasn't to know, was he?'

'No,' John agreed with a dip of his head. 'How could he?'

'That's what I said to him, Master, but the guilt weighed heavy on him.'

'Had Oswald told them what the mushroom could do?'

'Of course,' Adam replied in surprise. 'He was a forager. He knew the properties of every plant. He didn't want anyone to poison themselves with it. He didn't think they'd…'

No. But no one would imagine that.

'Once he found out what had happened, why didn't he tell someone?' John asked.

'When they were leaving the second time, the two men told him to keep the meetings to himself. If they heard of any stirring from him, they promised they'd come back and kill him and anyone he might care about.' He hung his head. 'I'm sorry, Master. But he was terrified. We both were.'

Too late for any blame or guilt. Gertrude was dead and so was the forager. But now the connection was certain. He could tell l'Honfleur that his squires had come up with the mushroom as the way to kill his daughter.

He had to hope that the hunting party brought the two young men back alive, to be questioned. There were so many things he needed to know. It might be his only chance to discover who was behind it all. How much had they done themselves? Had someone pushed or paid them to murder l'Honfleur's daughter? And if so, why?

'You must think we're weak old men, Master,' Adam said.

'I think fear is very human,' John told him. 'They came back to kill him and make sure he couldn't tell anyone about them.'

'They did.'

'Now you're scared they'll return for you, too.'

The old man nodded sadly.

'True enough, Master. I'm sorry. May God forgive me for my fear.'

'Have you told me all of it?'

'Everything. Let them come if they wish.'

'They're the hunted now, not the hunters.' As he rose, he patted the old man on the shoulder. 'The truth takes courage.'

'Too much of it sometimes,' Adam said.

'Talk to the priest. Make your confession. It will help.'

'I'll do that, Master.' He swallowed hard. 'What will my lord do when you tell him about me?'

'What's my guess, do you mean?' John answered. 'Nothing. It's all happened, we can't change anything. He's wise enough to understand that. He seems like a fair man.'

CHAPTER SEVEN

John found a spot by the side of the brook. He was shaded by a large willow, out of sight of anyone passing along the track. He'd been back to the place where Oswald the forager had been killed. All the grass had been trodden down and trampled until there was nothing to see. It was impossible to imagine the way the murder must have happened. On foot, though; that much was certain. In the middle of a wood, the squires wouldn't have been able to guide their horses anywhere close.

Even without any clue from there, he still had plenty to consider. Adam had said enough to make it certain that the squires were the killers. In all innocence, Oswald had told them about the mushroom.

John would tell the girl's father what he'd learned. But there were still too many questions to be answered. The squires were just two of the instruments being played here. And someone else was calling the tune.

Who?

He didn't know. He knew nothing about the brothers. They were from somewhere near Edale, that was what old Hubert at l'Honfleur's manor had said. He didn't know that area, he'd never been out there. Maybe there was something in the family, some link that had pushed them to it. He needed to talk to Jeffrey of Hardwick; the young man seemed to have a complete grasp of all the families at the tips of his fingers.

He wanted the squires dragged to my lord's house. But he had the gnawing feeling that once they were discovered, it would end in death. It seemed to be the way warriors proved themselves. No quarter. No life.

After an hour, John stirred and walked back to Chesterfield. It always lifted his heart to see the spire at the top of the hill, guiding him home again. It meant his wife and his children were close.

He was passing the churchyard when a voice hailed him. He spun around and saw the coroner. Today he was wearing parti-coloured hose in black and pale blue, a tunic in deep blue velvet and a silk surcote with a fur collar. Every inch a gentleman. They began to walk together.

'Good day, Master, may God save you.'

'And you, Carpenter. Have you heard the news?'

'News?' Maybe they'd caught the squires. He could allow himself to hope.

'My lord's men sent word this morning. They'd been tracking the pair who attacked you.'

'Did they find them?'.

'They did. Not far from Peveril Castle. They were somewhere near the top of Winnats Pass. I don't know all the details.'

John realised that he was holding his breath as he waited for the rest of the tale.

'The squires refused the chance to surrender and cast themselves on my lord's mercy. They chose to fight for their lives.'

From the expression on Strong's face, he could guess the ending.

'How long did they last?'

'I'm told they were brave enough, but they both died.'

'They were the ones who found the poisoned mushroom that killed Gertrude. They murdered the forager in Whittington, too.'

'Did they now?' The coroner frowned. 'You're certain of that?'

'The old man's neighbour just told me everything,' John answered. 'Oswald had explained to them about the death cap. He had no idea what they intended to do with it. They threatened him to keep him quiet, then murdered him to make sure he could never say a word.'

'I see.' The coroner exhaled slowly and shook his head. 'Then I can't find it in myself to feel any pity for them.'

'Indeed, Master; it would be a waste,' John agreed quickly. 'But they could have told us who was behind everything.' He explained his ideas as they stood in front of the empty marketplace. In the fields to the west, more traders were arriving and setting up their booths for the fair. Every avenue already looked crowded with people, and it was still days from starting. What would the town be like once the population streamed in from all the surrounding villages?

'You need to tell my lord what you've learned. Maybe one of the squires said something before he died.' He shrugged. 'I don't know, Carpenter.'

'Nor do I,' John said with a weary smile. 'That's the problem. Can you ask Jeffrey of Hardwick to call on me again?'

'I'll arrange it,' Strong promised.

• • •

'No,' l'Honfleur told him. He sat at the long table in his hall. Each day he looked a year older. His face seemed haggard, hollowed out, the skin paler than the day they'd met by the church in Calow. His hair hung lank, and his body appeared to have shrunk. He was a man surrounded by grief and death. 'According to my men, they didn't say a word. We sent their bodies over to the family in Edale for burial.'

It was what he'd expected. What he'd feared. But there was no harm in asking, just to be certain.

He should be glad they were both dead. They'd tried to kill him. They'd hunted him like a deer. But he couldn't help but wish they'd survived. Yet it was God's will that they hadn't.

Now he needed to find another road to the truth.

• • •

Martha and Juliana crowded around Jeffrey of Hardwick as if they'd known him for years instead of only having met him twice. In a moment he was on his knees with them, with no idea of dignity, enjoying the innocent pleasure of their laughter.

John couldn't help but grin. The young man had no sense of his station. He didn't care about it; he seemed to like life, to enjoy people, whatever their age. It was a rare quality. Katherine was smiling as she watched.

Finally he stood and shook himself like an animal as the children giggled.

'Please,' he told them, 'I have business with your father.'

'Come on,' Katherine ordered, holding out her hands and taking the girls into the garden.

Jeffrey brushed dust from the knees of his hose and took the mug of ale that John offered.

'You told the coroner you needed me again.'

'I want to find more information, if you can discover it. I'd like to know about those two squires that my lord's men killed yesterday.'

'I can tell you their names were Michael and Gabriel,' Jeffrey said. A sad smile. 'I know, naming them for the Archangels is a conceit, eh?'

John shrugged. 'Everyone needs a name. Did you know them?'

'No, we never met. They were probably friends of my brother. He's the one who'll inherit when my father dies.' His voice took on a wistful tone. 'I could ask him. There are one or two others.' Jeffrey's face brightened. 'This week everyone's coming here to be ready for the fair, so they'll all be in one place. What else do you want to know?'

John explained everything that had happened at l'Honfleur's manor and after, seeing the shock grow on the man's face.

'I don't know what to make of you,' Jeffrey said when he'd finished. 'Are you lucky or resourceful?'

'Lucky,' John answered. 'And I have an understanding wife who'd like this all to be done. So would I.'

Jeffrey nodded. 'Sir Mark told me what you've been promised if you find the killer. My lord can afford it, he wouldn't even notice fifty pounds. What do you want to know about Michael and Gabriel?'

'Whatever you can discover. Their friends, their family connections. I'm told their father's manor is poor. Does he owe money?'

'That should be easy enough. I know who to ask.' He swirled the ale in the mug then drank it down. 'I envy you, John.'

'Envy me?' He found that idea impossible to believe. Who could want his problems, he wondered, the constant worries about money? But the man sounded sincere. 'Why?'

'You have a family. Your children. I see the way Dame Katherine looks at you. You have a fortune right here. Most men would wish they had that.'

'Thank you,' John told him after a moment. It had been too long since he'd thought that way. He'd been swallowed up in the torments. All the problems that every day brought. He never stood back and looked at the pleasures, the joys in his life. Yet they were right here, plenty of them, in front of his eyes, if he'd only open them and look. Exactly as Jeffrey said.

'Thank you,' he repeated. Someone from the outside could see things more clearly. Someone who could see the beauty of the forest, not a man lost in the confusion of trees.

'It's true,' Jeffrey said as he stood. 'I'll come back with everything I can discover about the brothers.'

• • •

He was as good as his word. It was no more than two hours until he knocked at their door again. Juliana was helping Katherine gather together linen to be washed in the river, with Martha struggling to help. Richard... it was a bad day, he was in his bed. Katherine had given him a weak draught of poppy juice to help him rest. It was all they could do for him.

John sat on one side of the table, Jeffrey on the other, a jug of weak ale between them.

'Do you know Michael and Gabriel were twins?'

'No.' They had the look of brothers, but not the image of each other.

'They weren't identical,' Jeffrey said. 'But they always did everything together. Their father indulged them.' He pursed his lips. 'It's very likely why they died together.'

'Go on.'

'They're related to most of the families around here.' He paused for a moment, then added: 'I suppose that's true for almost every one of us. We marry each other, if the church allows and the relations aren't too near. You have to understand, John, we do it for land and power and money.'

'I know.' It kept them on top, kept them wealthy and in control.

'Sometimes I think you're the lucky ones – you can marry for love.'

'You don't have a wife?'

'She died giving birth. The child died with her.' Simple, bald words, but they said so much.

'I'm sorry. God save their souls.' What more could he say? But it explained why the man seemed comfortable around Katherine and the children. He ached to have a family of his own.

'Thank you.' A sigh. 'The twins' family are distant relations of l'Honfleur. Their father probably used that to place them with my lord. From what I've heard, they've been no better or worse than any other young men. They loved to drink and to fight. Plenty of high spirits.' He shrugged.

'How long had they been at the manor?'

'Six months. They'd been at others before that. They probably haven't spent much time with their father since they were seven or eight, and that's ten years ago.'

'They'll spend it all on their own manor now,' John said bleakly. A place they'd never leave.

Jeffrey nodded. 'They tried to kill you. They didn't even think twice about it. You should be glad they're dead.'

'An eye for an eye isn't always the best solution.' Certainly not when the corpses held answers, he thought.

'A man of the Christian testament,' Jeffrey said with a nod of his head.

'If you want to think of me that way. What else do you know about them? What obligations did they have? What's their father's manor like?'

'It's very poor. He owns two others that are better, but there's nothing he can do with much of the land above Edale. From what I've been told, it's all hills and peat, barely fit for sheep. But he's always been someone who thinks above his station. He likes the favour of great men.'

John stared into his face. 'Like my lord?'

'He *is* a great man, my friend. I know he spends much of his time here, and you can talk to him. But remember, the king's mistress will receive him, so will the great earls and the king.' He paused. 'You might think about that the next time you talk to him.'

L'Honfleur was a man of greater stature than he'd realised. The coroner had told him, but he'd only seen the grieving father. The gulf had been there between them from the moment my lord appeared in Calow. But there had been something beyond that. My lord he might be, but once he shed the fine clothes he was an ordinary man. Just one who could give a carpenter fifty pounds for discovering who murdered his daughter, he reflected.

'You make it sound like there's nothing that can help me.'

Jeffrey shrugged. 'That's what I've managed to find so far. There might be more if you want me to discover it.'

'I'd be grateful, Master.'

They grinned at each other. For a moment, the world seemed a lighter place. The mood flickered and passed.

'What are you going to do now, John?'

'Back to Calow,' he said. 'I want to talk to the people out there once again.'

'Didn't they tell you what they saw? That was what the coroner said.'

'They did. But given a little time, people often remember more, or their thoughts become clearer.'

'You're a curious man,' Jeffrey took a drink. 'Not like a carpenter at all.'

'Have you known many?'

'No, but you… understand this. The questions, the way you look at things.'

'Don't believe it. I'm a carpenter.' He showed the thick calluses on his hands and patted the old leather satchel of tools. 'I don't really understand anything but wood. And I'll be a carpenter again, once this is over.'

'Whatever I can do to help, let me know. I'm lodging with Dame Judith on Beetwell Street. Do you know her?'

'By sight.' Everyone knew the woman with the loud, braying voice and the curiosity about their affairs.

'Leave a message with her. She'll pass it to me. I'll try to find out more for you, too.'

• • •

Rain had passed during the night, leaving the long grass sodden. By the time he reached the turning towards Calow, John's boots were sodden. They'd dry; they always had before. His hose were damp and clinging to his legs. No matter.

Before going to the small village, he visited the church. The anchorite's cell had been tumbled. Only a few stones remained; people had already carried the rest away to repair their houses or barns. The poor never wasted anything.

In the church he knelt and said a prayer for Gertrude. He could still feel her here, almost hear her breathing. It would fade; a year from now only the local folk would be able to recall her clearly.

Dame Wilhelmina told him where to find the men. They were firing the stooks in the lord's fields, plumes of smoke rising into the sky to guide him. At the edge of the field, John stood and watched. The three men worked easily together, tasks they'd likely done together for years. Each one knew his part.

They stopped their labour as he approached, staring at him with a mix of suspicion and curiosity.

'Good day to you, Masters,' John said. 'I wish you God's peace.'

'And to you,' Hugo replied. 'You came asking questions after Gertrude died.'

'I did. I have a few more.' John held up his hand. 'Only one or two, not long enough to interrupt your work.' He turned to Ralph. 'You said you saw a piebald horse when the two men in livery came to see the anchoress.'

The man straightened his back. 'I did. I pointed out the patch of black.'

'Forgive me, but are you sure of it, Master? It was a fair distance.'

'I'm certain.' Ralph didn't hesitate. 'My eyes are good.'

'I have no doubt they are,' John agreed with a smile. 'Are you positive it was the same day?'

He'd come back to this point in his thoughts. It was one thing that had stood out. It didn't fit. If the horse was a piebald, then the squires hadn't delivered the food themselves. He'd told l'Honfleur all this. But the more he considered it, the more the idea became awkward and convoluted. Passing their livery to two other men who would have to return it? He couldn't find the sense in that. The squires knew about the death cap mushroom; he'd proved that. It seemed far more likely that they'd deliver the food themselves. The thing that made no sense was the piebald horse. Neither l'Honfleur nor the Unthanks owned one. That was why he'd come back here, to be certain.

'Not many people come by here on horseback,' the man said.

'Of course.' Maybe it had happened exactly as the man said and the mystery would remain.

'No, don't you remember, there was a rider the day before all that?' It was Cedric who spoke, reserved and thoughtful. 'You said something about his horse.'

'No, I didn't.'

'He's right.' Hugo folded his arms and stared at Ralph. '*That* was the horse you said was piebald. You wanted us to look, but we were busy digging out that tree stump. You were gawping like you'd never seen one of the beasts before.'

'No…' Ralph began, then his eyes widened and his voice trailed to silence as he realised they might be right. Shamefaced, he turned to John. 'Master, we'd been drinking the night before Gertrude…' he didn't want to say the word. 'It was the name day of Hugo's daughter. We celebrate things like that out here.'

He gazed at the expanse of fields as if he'd never seen them before and they were a thing of wonder.

'You might have been confused?' John said kindly.

'I might.' The man nodded. 'It happens sometimes after the drink.' He reddened. 'I get ideas in my head and nothing can shift them.'

'Then you might have been wrong about the piebald horse?'

'Aye, Master. I might. God's word,' he added hurriedly, 'I believed it when I said it. I wouldn't try to lie or send you after something else. I'd never do that to my lord.'

John believed him. He was scrambling around to apologise, and the amusement of his friends had turned to concern. Ralph might be taken before the coroner and even l'Honfleur. Who knew what men like that might do?

'At least we know now.' John smiled and rested his hand on Ralph's shoulder. 'I'm glad we reached the truth before any damage had been done.'

'Thank you, Master.' The relief spread across the man's face, and his companions looked a little easier.

'We all make mistakes.' He looked from one face to another and the last. 'But I do need to know, are you certain on this? Would you swear on it if we went into the church?'

'I would.' Ralph was the first to speak. 'I had it fixed in my head. But what Cedric said… he was right.'

John turned to the others. 'What about you?'

Hugo shook his head. 'Master, I never saw the horses either day. I daren't swear to something I didn't see with my own eyes.'

He understood; swearing on something, taking an oath, was a serious business. A man damned his soul for swearing falsely. If Ralph was willing to go that far, John would believe him.

At least he knew now. Another piece that fell into place. The squires had come and given Gertrude the dish with the death cap mushroom. The truth was simpler than any twisted explanation his mind could devise.

Once, long ago in York, he'd talked with a young priest as he mended a bench in one of the city's churches. He couldn't even remember the topic, only the words the priest had spoken in his grave voice: *the obvious explanation, the simple one, is usually correct.* It made sense to him then. It came into his mind again; it was still true.

One question resolved.

Something else lingered in his mind, from the day the coroner had summoned him out here to see the body.

The first finder.

A friar on his way to Baslow; that was what Strong had told him. One of God's innocents, those had been his words. But he hadn't wanted John to talk to the man. He'd pushed him in another direction.

At the time he'd wondered why. Now the question returned as he set off to walk to Baslow. It was far on the other side of Chesterfield. But the weather was warm, the sun darting in and out of high clouds. And he didn't know where else to take this.

Maybe Jeffrey would be able to bring him something. But for now, he'd try to find the friar.

CHAPTER EIGHT

Baslow hadn't grown since the last time he'd been there. The village was a series of cottages straggling along the road. A short way beyond, another road leading up to the moors crossed it, and a gibbet stood where they met. No body hung from the noose now, but it served as a stark reminder that justice was always waiting.

A branch hanging over the door marked the alehouse. John welcomed the chance to sit and rest his feet and ease his parched throat. It was a good place for gossip and questions. Sometimes a man could simply listen and learn a great deal. At times more than he might from asking questions.

Not today, though. An old man sat in a corner, more asleep than awake, while the alewife moved around in the back room, brewing a fresh batch of small beer.

She told him where the friar was staying, a small camp he'd set up close to the brook.

'There's not a drop of harm in him,' the woman said with a warm smile. 'He gives us the Lord's word. We listen and give him food and ale.'

'It seems like a fair exchange,' John told her.

'It is, Master. It is.'

The friar had cut himself a stick and had a line bobbing in the stream as John arrived. The man sat hunched over, staring intently at the water. A Carmelite, by the look of him.

He wore a patched brown habit, the white cloak rolled up behind him.

'God's peace to you,' John said.

The friar turned his head slowly, blinking as if he were coming out of a dream or a trance.

'May His peace rest in you, too.' He put up the makeshift rod; no catch on the end of it. 'It's good to sit here and contemplate the world.'

'And catch your supper?'

The man smiled. 'That, too, if God pleases. I'm Friar Gerald.'

'John the Carpenter. I've come from Chesterfield to find you, Father.'

'Oh?' Gerald tilted his head. 'Why might that be, Master?'

'You were in Calow, you went to visit the anchoress there.'

'May God rest her,' Gerald said and crossed himself.

'You were the first to find her.'

'I was.' He described the scene, growing more distressed as he talked, until John finally stopped him. Now he saw why the coroner had let the man leave. There was no cover on his emotions. The friar could no more lie than a bird could stop flying. It wasn't in him.

After he was calm, once Gerald had run through Latin prayers under his breath, John asked one last question.

'Is there anything you can remember that you might not have told the coroner? I know you were upset, and that you gave the good sister her last rites. You might have overlooked something.'

Very slowly, the friar shook his head.

'I told him all I saw. I'm sorry you've had a wasted journey.'

'Father, please, if there's anything you recall, it would help me find who was responsible. Someone murdered her. It wasn't an accident.'

The man was silent for a long time, then raised his head.

'I suspected there was no peace in it,' he said after a long time. 'There was a sense of evil around the cell. I could feel it.'

The man was talking now, thinking of the death.

'You looked through the opening in the wall. What did you see?'

'Gertrude.' The friar spoke hesitantly. 'She was sitting there, with her back against the wall and her eyes open. The flies were crawling over her. Have you seen the dead?'

'I have.'

'Then you know. You can tell.'

'Yes.' The friar was right. It wasn't just the way a corpse looked, it was the sense of something gone, that the soul had left.

'I prayed for her and ran off to those houses close by.'

'Calow,' John said.

'The women there sent me to Chesterfield. I asked for the coroner. He came back with me and brought some of his men. They broke down some of the wall to the cell. I went in and gave her the last rites.'

'What was the cell like inside?'

'It had the smell of death.' Friar Gerald's voice was flat and empty. 'It has its own scent.'

'I know,' John said. 'Was there anything you noticed in the cell?'

'I went to give her the rites,' the man answered. 'I didn't look at anything else. The poor woman needed to be shrived.' He cocked his head and looked at John. 'That was all.'

'Did the coroner make you pay a fine?' That was common for a first finder, to bind them close until the inquest.

'No.' He smiled. 'What would I use to pay it?' He held open his scrip. No glint of coins or anything valuable. He was a friar, a preacher who was meant to live on charity as he roamed. So many didn't, but it appeared this one really did that. Not one of God's innocents in quite the way Strong had said; the man's mind was clear and sharp enough. But he'd had nothing to do with Gertrude's death.

John rose and stretched.

'Thank you for talking to me, Father. I'm sorry to stir the memories.'

'I wish you joy in finding whoever would do that to a holy woman.'

'With the Lord's direction.'

A short blessing and he began the walk home. The air was still warm where the day's heat had clung, and by the time he saw the spire rising above Chesterfield, his feet were weary, feeling the miles he'd covered during the day. John wore good boots and sturdy hose, the clothing of a working man, but after so many hours of tramping, he was tired.

His thoughts were drifting, going over what the friar had told him and fitting it alongside everything else. At first he didn't see the man coming towards him. Even when he noticed the figure, he paid him no mind.

As he drew closer, the man reached to his belt and drew a knife. John felt the prickle of fear up his spine. He gave a quick glance over his shoulder. No one behind him. That was something. He'd only have to face a single opponent. But it meant that nobody else was in sight to stop things.

'God's peace to you,' he called. Still the man said nothing, but kept walking towards him, no expression on his face. Who was he? A thief? A robber? Or had he been sent to stop John finding Gertrude's killer?

He had no choice; he slipped his own knife from his belt, gripping the hilt tightly. The other man never slowed, never shifted his gaze.

He didn't want to fight. He'd never been one who relished anything like this. He'd seen too much death. All he wanted was to be home with his wife and family. But John had the sense that if he tried to run, the man would keep on coming, following at the same, steady pace, never wavering, never stopping, pursuing him all the way to Chesterfield. All the way to the grave. He was dressed in a tunic that was too heavy for the weather, stained on the sleeves, his hose loose on his legs.

And still he didn't speak, marching, growing closer and closer until he stopped, three yards away.

'If you want to fight, we'll fight,' John said. 'But tell me why?'

Not a word. He didn't appear like an outlaw or a bandit. He was more like an evil spirit, a demon, something not human. The man tried a feint to the left, hoping to catch John off his guard, then followed with a jab to the right. John didn't try to counter. For now, he was content to keep out of the way. The man was clumsy and slow. His eyes showed what he was going to do long before he did it, and he was wild in his efforts. The type who thought silence and movement were enough to intimidate an opponent. But even someone like that could be lucky. A wound from him could be as deadly as a well-placed cut from an assassin.

He made a few more swipes that only caught the air as John jumped back or twisted his body out of the way. The man was growing frustrated. Good. He made sudden moves, his face contorted in anger.

John watched and waited for the right time. He parried a blow, pushing back hard to test the man's strength. Powerful muscles; it was like hitting iron. Strength alone wasn't going to beat this one. He needed something better. Something inventive. Something cunning. And something that would leave the man no choice but to answer questions.

The chance came almost immediately. The man lunged, aiming for John's chest, but not even close as he skipped aside. It left him stretched too far, off balance and easy prey. It was a simple task for John to use the man's weight against him and send him sprawling onto his back on the dusty road.

The knife had tumbled from his hand. As he tried to reach for it, John's boot came down hard on his wrist.

'I've no desire to kill you, Master. But I have a blade and you don't. That gives me the right to ask you questions. What do you want with me?'

The man shook his head. No words, but a faint smirk on his face. John pushed down harder on the wrist, grinding it into the dirt until finally the expression changed to a grimace of pain.

'Are you going to tell me?'

Still no answer. The only sound came from the birds in the trees and the rustle of the breeze through the branches.

'No?'

Silence.

John couldn't take the man back to Chesterfield. He had nothing to bind him, and there were still a few miles to walk before they reached the town. The man wore no scrip; there was nothing to indicate who he might be.

'Why did you attack me?'

The man stared up at the clear sky. John reached down and sliced through the muscle at the back of his thigh. Even then, he didn't cry out, just clenched his jaws together and closed his eyes for a moment.

It was self-preservation. If he'd done nothing and left, the man would have stood up and kept coming. John wouldn't willingly take a man's life, but this would stop him following, keep him crippled for a few months. The man would still be alive, but he'd pay a price. He'd hobble for the rest of his life. That much was justice.

'Why?' he asked one last time, holding his blade by the man's throat. But there was nothing, no answer, and he knew he'd never have one if he asked until Doomsday. Finally, in disgust, he kicked the man's knife into the long grass by the side of the road and left him barely able to crawl away.

He was safe, he knew he was safe. But that didn't stop him glancing over his shoulder every hundred yards. It was all too easy to believe the man had some dark magic that would help him spring up again.

Foolish. In his head, he knew that. It was impossible. The man couldn't stand with an injury like that. But that didn't stop him turning his head and holding his breath. He hurried, pushed on by all the fear.

The squires and now this. Three attempts to murder him. To stop him. Someone feared him finding out the truth.

The man might have been an outlaw. There were plenty all over the country. Masterless men had been roaming ever since the Pestilence, looking for easy pickings and lone travellers. But he hadn't seemed like that. He was alone; robbers usually worked in packs.

The determination… that scared him more than anything. It wasn't human. It was… he didn't possess the words for it. It was an attack to kill. John knew that. It could have been him lying on the road.

Once he could see the spire standing in the distance his heartbeat slowed to normal and his breathing eased. Safety was close. A final glance behind him, then across the bridge over the Hipper and up Soutergate.

He wanted to sit in his own garden, to hold his wife close and give thanks. But first he had to do his duty.

Coroner Strong was sitting with his clerk, going over his accounts. His face darkened as he listened to John's reports.

He sent for the head of his guards, the one who'd first escorted John over to the church.

'You're sure you crippled the man who attacked you, Carpenter?' Strong asked.

'I know I did, Master.'

'Where did it happen?'

He told them everything he could remember. There were few landmarks, little to distinguish the place from anywhere else along the road.

'Take two men with you,' he told the guard. 'Search the area and bring him back here. If he's had the muscle cut, he can't have crawled far.'

'Yes, sir.'

The coroner turned to John. 'Do you think he was a robber or had someone sent him?'

'I don't know, Master.' That was the truth. The man had said nothing at all. It could be either one.

'You lead a charmed life, Carpenter. You go up against a man who wants to kill you and come back without a scratch after you cripple him.' He took a drink from the mazer of wine on the table. 'Yet you insist you're not a fighter.'

'I'm not, Master.'

Strong snorted. 'Then I'll take ten like you behind me in battle any day of the week.'

How could he reply to that? Was it a compliment or an insult?

'And you decided to return to Calow.'

'Yes, Master. The more I thought about everything, what they'd told me in Calow didn't fit with everything else. It was too… complicated. I didn't think the squires had brains that worked in those ways.'

A nod. 'It seems you're right. But it would have been easier if they'd remembered everything properly the first time.' He slammed his hand down on the table, but there was no force behind it. Exasperation, not anger.

'They were scared, Master. The people cared for Gertrude. They were confused, nothing more than that.'

'Maybe,' the coroner agreed after a while. 'And what are you going to do now, Carpenter?'

'Go home. Eat and drink and sleep and see my family.' An honest answer; it was all he wanted.

'And tomorrow?'

'I don't know yet.' He hadn't considered that far ahead. He didn't want to consider it until he was rested and able to think clearly.

'Go,' Strong said. 'You've earned it. Remember, though, it's not too long until the fair. My lord needs to know who wanted his daughter dead by then if you're going to collect fifty pounds.'

'I remember, Master. Believe me, I remember.'

How could he ever forget? It might as well have been carved into his skin.

CHAPTER NINE

He tried to make light of it, but Katherine read the truth in his eyes. She said nothing until the children were all asleep up in the solar.

She took a delicate sip from a mug of ale. 'You're a fool, husband.'

'For fighting?'

Katherine nodded. 'You could have run. Never taken out your knife at all.'

'He'd have kept coming.'

'And he wouldn't have caught you.'

'If someone had sent him, he'd still have been there tomorrow or the day after,' John said, but she stared at him.

'Perhaps you simply wanted to prove yourself, husband.'

'No.' He shook his head. 'I had no choice. Suddenly he was there on the path, coming towards me.'

'Was he an outlaw?'

'I don't know.' He shrugged. 'I keep thinking about it. He could have been anything at all. He wouldn't say. He never spoke a word, even when I cut his leg.'

'You think it's connected to Gertrude?'

'It might be.' He sighed as he looked at her. 'I wanted him to tell me, but he didn't say a word. It's all a guess, wife. But if it weren't, the coincidence would be strange. The coroner's sent men out to search for him.' He took hold of her hand.

'We might as well go to bed. We can talk all night and never find the truth.'

• • •

Strong's guards hadn't found the man.

'We were in the right place, I'd swear to it.' The head of the guards turned to John. 'It was just as you described, even that large oak on the hillside. We searched all around, a good half a mile in every direction, but we didn't see him.' He looked at the coroner. 'I swear it, Master. We did.'

Strong nodded and dismissed the man.

'You said you'd hamstrung him.'

'I did,' John said. 'I cut him. I saw the blood.'

The coroner glowered. 'But he still managed to get away.'

How could anyone do that? He must have crawled, on his hands and knees, for a mile or more. He'd have been in constant pain. It seemed impossible. But so much about the man who'd attacked him was unlikely. Otherworldly. Yet he was human; he'd bled when the knife sliced his flesh.

'I have no idea what else to say.' He could make no sense of it.

'What now, Carpenter? My lord will be asking when I see him this morning.'

'I don't know yet.' Last night he'd been too weary to think properly, falling into a welcome, dreamless sleep as soon as he pulled up the blanket. This morning he'd had little chance to dwell on it. Richard was unwell, and they'd had to decide if they could afford to send for the apothecary. It would take every spare farthing they had, and it would do no good. They'd already been told there was no cure. But they couldn't bear to see the boy in pain, and finally he'd gone through the streets to call on the man.

Gertrude's death hadn't come into his mind until he walked past West Bar on his way here.

'He won't like that. He's paying you to find his daughter's killer.'

No, John thought, l'Honfleur wasn't paying him anything at all. The coroner was paying him, four pennies a day. There would be no reward from my lord unless he succeeded.

And he truly didn't know. Everything he'd learned brought him back to the two squires. But they were both dead, and with them any chance of learning more.

'I'll find something, Master.'

• • •

There was a chill to the air, a note that autumn was close. Leaves were falling, along with the fruit of the horse chestnuts for children to break open and play with. The greens of summer were giving way to browns as the world edged towards winter.

John crossed the marketplace, reaching into his scrip in the faint hope there might be another coin hidden away, when a voice hailed him. He looked up sharply, seeing Jeffrey of Hardwick loping towards him with a smile on his face.

'You were miles away, John. That was the third time I shouted your name.'

'I'm sorry. I was distracted.'

'I saw the coroner last night. He told me what happened to you.'

'That was yesterday.' He didn't want to think about it again. Simply consign it to the past along with the curious, unlikely man who'd attacked him. 'I need something for today.'

Jeffrey's eyes twinkled. 'Perhaps you need someone to help you. I'm free all day, at least until our shipment of leather arrives, and no one seems certain when that will be.' He rubbed his hands together eagerly. 'What did you have in mind, Master?'

'Nothing yet.'

'Then we need to find something.' His enthusiasm was infectious, almost enough to make John forget that he didn't have any path to follow or that at home his son was dying by degrees.

In the alehouse on Low Pavement, Jeffrey took out the money and paid, not even noticing it. For a moment John resented him. But the man seemed so young, so eager. It wasn't his fault he came from a family where he didn't have to think hard about every penny.

'I heard about Calow and that priest who was the first finder. You were a busy man.'

'More than I'd like,' he agreed ruefully.

'I've never had someone try to kill me,' Jeffrey said. 'Nothing more than raised voices.'

'You don't want it,' John told him. 'Please believe me on that.'

'Oh, I do. I'm quite content to only use my knife for cutting the meat on my trencher.' A smile and a gentle laugh. 'What do you know, and how can you find out what you need?'

He was not weighed down by life and responsibilities that slowed and coloured his thoughts. Most of his ideas were no more than bubbles floating to the sky. But a few had substance. They sat and talked them through.

'My cousin the coroner wants me to help, and I'm glad to do anything I can. I know there are places you can't go, John.' He blushed at the truth of it. 'But I can, if you tell me what to ask.'

Long ago, when the coroner had been a man named de Harville and John had been pushed into looking at deaths, he'd had help from Katherine's brother, Walter. Now he was married, with a family of his own, and a business carrying messages and small parcels across the entire area, from Sheffield down to Ripley and across to Bakewell. Men and boys worked for him and he was becoming wealthy. But he worked so hard that most of the family never saw him. He'd bring his wife and children into town for the fair. Everyone would be here for that, Katherine's sisters, too; it was too important to miss. It would be good to see them all again.

When John investigated, Walter had been another pair of hands and a set of eyes. People said he was slow, but he'd never been that. He was sharp; he'd proved them all wrong.

Sitting here, talking to Jeffrey, he felt that he had someone to work with again. He wouldn't have to do it all himself.

'Won't your family resent you taking time to do this?'

Jeffrey shook his head. 'How could they? The coroner is kin, my lord is distant kin. I told you before, John, we're all related. What I'm doing here aids the family. You know I can help; I can talk to people you could never approach.'

John stayed quiet for a long time, swirling the ale in the mug. It was cloudy, maybe from the bottom of the batch.

'The father of the squires,' he said at last.

'He'll be mourning his sons,' Jeffrey answered. 'They were the only two boys he had.'

'Do you think he'd be willing to talk to you?'

Jeffrey grinned. 'He has a daughter of marriageable age. He'll be looking for suitors to wed her. My family has money…' He spread his hands on the table. He'd be welcome in the household.

'Out to Edale… it's a distance to walk.'

'I ride, Master.' He looked up at the sky to judge the time. 'Almost dinner. It's too late to go there and back before dark. But if I have an early start in the morning, I can bring you some answer by evening. Now, what do you want me to ask?'

• • •

He felt hopeful as he walked home for his dinner. Each moment brought less time to find the person behind Gertrude's murder, but Jeffrey's eagerness had infected him. The young man was filled with hope; he believed they'd be able to discover the answers.

'A good morning?' Katherine asked as she served up dinner. A bean pottage, with more vegetables added to the small cauldron over the fire. A poor man's meal and he was grateful for it. The girls ate, not even noticing what they were putting in their mouths.

'Yes,' he said. 'I think it was. Is Richard sleeping?'

'I went up and looked at him earlier. He was resting, he didn't look like he was in pain.'

The hurt was there behind her eyes. Lately it showed more and more; she couldn't hide the way she felt. But John knew that the sorrow showed on his face, too. He loved his son. When the boy was born, he'd felt such joy when the baby reached out and grasped his thumb. However much he cherished his daughters, it was nothing compared with that moment, the sweetest he'd ever known. But Richard was going, inch by inch. Soon enough his soul would be with God. No Purgatory, surely; he hadn't spent enough time on this earth to commit any sins.

He was going, and there was nothing they could do to stop it. They were powerless before heaven, the way they were powerless down here.

'God be praised,' he said, and crossed himself. Soon they'd be grieving for Richard. For now, though, he was grateful for every day the boy was still with them.

• • •

The light faded in the afternoon and the sky darkened from the west. An hour passed and the clouds grew thicker and thicker until the air felt moist and the first heavy drops of rain began to fall.

For an hour it came down heavily enough to bounce off the ground, drenching any man or beast caught out in the weather. John closed the shutters at the front of the house and stood at the back, staring at the garden. In the hall, the girls were using stones to draw on pieces of slate as Katherine watched them. Richard was still asleep upstairs.

There were people he wanted to see, but it would have to wait until tomorrow. By then this weather would have passed. The roads would still be mud, but they'd have drained enough to be passable.

'What are you thinking?'

He hadn't heard her approach. John put his arm around Katherine and pulled her close.

'About all the things I need to do.'

'Do you have a plan? This morning you looked lost.'

'I was,' he agreed with a sigh. 'But now there's a way forward.'

'And the man who attacked you?'

'I still don't know about him.' He'd probably never learn the truth.

'Yesterday…' she began with hesitation. 'I still believe what I said. But maybe not the way I said it.' She looked into his face as she spoke. He stroked her cheek, not knowing how to reply, not wanting to say anything; to do nothing more than to enjoy this moment together. But it couldn't last. Martha began to shout, complaining about her sister. With a sad, quick smile, Katherine put her fingers over his and pulled away. Not the softness of a gentlewoman's hands, but the redness and roughness of a life well-lived.

Night seemed to arrive early, but the rain finally passed. All that remained was the constant drip from the tiles to the ground. John examined the leak in the roof, placing a fresh wooden bucket to catch the water. It was already like this and the rains of autumn and winter hadn't arrived; a stark reminder that the house needed plenty of attention. And money. If he couldn't earn the fifty pounds that l'Honfleur was dangling in front of him, he'd have no choice but to sell one of the houses he owned before the bad weather came.

• • •

Bernard the scrivener always seemed like a happy man, ready with a joke and a laugh. He was different, using the quill with his left hand instead of his right, and made fun of himself for it. He was a sinister man, he laughed, the devil's own helper. He'd been a novice in holy orders until he discovered he preferred women and drink to the sacred life. Still, he put his learning to use; there were always men who needed letters written.

He was working at his desk by the window, sharpening the tip of his quill with the short knife he kept in his right hand, then inspecting it before dipping it back into the ink.

'God's peace to you,' John said as he entered.

'And to you, too, Carpenter,' Bernard replied with a broad grin. 'I haven't seen you in a while.' He winced as he straightened his back on the stool. 'Although I hear you have a new job these days.'

'For a short while. Please God, I'll be back working with wood soon enough.'

'You're not a man who sends letters, John, and the coroner has a clerk who'd write one for you if you needed it.' He smiled. 'That means you're here to ask me some questions.'

'You should be the one in my shoes.'

Bernard grinned and shook his head. 'I prefer sitting on my arse in a warm room. Words will do for me.'

'Have you written any letters that might concern my Lord l'Honfleur or his family at all?'

'No. Families like that, there's always someone who can write, probably two of three of them.' He raised an eyebrow. 'Sometimes even the women learn. And if there's nothing else, they'll all have their own clerks to handle everything relating to their estates and their wealth.' He sighed. 'I'd love to have a rich client, but it won't ever happen.'

John nodded. It had seemed like a good idea when he left the house this morning. Bernard knew his business. This was another road that went nowhere. If anyone had been sending notes and messages, he hadn't been the one writing them. He'd trudged along streets heavy with mud for no reason at all.

'I'll wish you a good day.'

'There was something,' Bernard said. 'Somewhere around a fortnight ago a man came in to ask how much I charged to write a letter, and whether I could arrange for delivery to Edale.'

Edale. That was where the father of the squires held his manor.

'I recommended your Walter to take it there. But once he heard my fee he started grumbling and wanted to haggle me down. A man has to live.'

He knew it all too well. He'd walked away from jobs before when a householder tried to bargain away his profit. For now, though, it was the destination that set him thinking.

'Did he say who he wanted to send the letter to in Edale?'

'No. We never got that far.'

He'd never been to the place, but he knew Edale was small; very few people there would know how to read, let alone write.

'No indication who would receive the letter?'

'No. I'm sorry, John.'

'What was the man like?'

'I haven't seen him before.' Bernard narrowed his eyes, trying to see the man in his mind. 'Good clothes, a silk surcote and a velvet tunic. They weren't new, but they were well made, I remember that.'

'How old was he?'

'Thirty, perhaps,' Bernard answered after thinking. 'But a worn thirty, a man weighed down by cares. I had the sense he'd possessed money once, but he didn't now.'

'Yet he was still willing to spend some of it to have you write a letter.'

Bernard chuckled. 'He just wasn't willing to spend enough.'

Perhaps it hadn't been such a wasted visit, after all. Jeffrey would be back from Edale by evening; he'd be able to tell him about the place. That might help.

• • •

By the time the sun was setting, he'd been back to Whittington to see old Adam once more, then across to Calow to talk to the men again. Fruitless journeys. He'd never really expected much, but he had no other ideas, and something else might have sprung from their memories. In the end, though, he walked home weary and with no more knowledge.

As he opened the door of the house on Knifesmithgate, he saw lights glowing beyond the screens and the sounds of excited voices. His girls, laughing. He stopped for just a moment, long enough to take in the pleasure of it.

Jeffrey was there, silhouetted in the rushlights, little gifts for the children in front of him. A tiny square of marchpane for each of them, carved into the shape of an animal. A bear, a dog, a rooster. He was teaching them a game with a pack of playing cards. Even Richard was there, a blanket around his shoulders, smiling as he paid attention.

Katherine stood at the entrance to the buttery. She had her arms folded, looking happy as she watched it all. The children deserved small presents; he just wished he had the money to indulge them that way.

Jeffrey noticed him and stood, suddenly embarrassed.

'John, I was just…' he gestured.

'You carry on.' He ruffled Richard's hair, pleased to see the boy look up and give a warm smile. 'I need ale and something to eat.' Jeffrey had a mug and empty plate in front of him.

A nod and he returned to dealing the cards. Another few moments and the girls were giggling again.

'He came a little while ago,' Katherine said. 'I told him I didn't know when you'd return, but he asked if he could wait.'

'I like him,' John told her. 'He's always welcome here. And the children seem to feel the same way.'

CHAPTER TEN

The night garden was filled with scents. The dark loam of the earth, the perfumes of the flowers. They became so much stronger after the light fell, John thought as he sat with a mug of ale. He could hear the movement of small creatures through the long grass, and caught the flit of a bat from the corner of his eye.

'You had a long ride today,' he said.

'Not so far,' Jeffrey said as he shifted on the bench. 'The problem is that I haven't been on a horse over rough ground for a while. I can still feel it.'

'Is it bad out here?'

'That Edale manor can't bring in much of an income,' Jeffrey said. 'There's hardly anything they can farm and most of it's too steep and rocky for sheep. The land rises up directly behind the hamlet.'

'It must be a sad house, with the sons both dead.'

'It is,' he agreed. 'It is, although they know what happened. My lord made certain of that when his men returned the bodies.'

'Did you find anything worthwhile?'

'Nothing that might help you find a murderer.'

'It sounds as if your day wasn't well spent.'

'I don't know,' Jeffrey said with a sigh. 'Whatever made the squires kill Gertrude, I don't believe anyone at the manor knew about it. There's too much sadness out there, John.'

'What's the village like?'

'It's small, hardly worth calling a village. There's no more than a tiny cluster of houses. The manor house is about a mile away along the valley. Why?'

John told him what he'd learned from Bernard the scribe.

'From the places I saw, I can't imagine anyone outside the manor can read,' Jeffrey answered slowly. 'And most of those on the manor probably can't read, either. The family, maybe the reeve. Your scrivener, he has no idea who wanted to send a letter?'

'He claimed he'd never seen him before.'

'A mystery. It doesn't mean it's related to this, but the description doesn't fit anyone I know.'

'No,' John agreed. 'But given when it happened, it would be a strange coincidence if it wasn't.'

'Maybe.' Jeffrey stood and stretched and gave a small groan of pain. There was a wry touch to his voice as he spoke. 'I'm going to my bed. I ache in places I didn't even know I possessed.'

John raised his cup in a toast. 'Then I hope your pain is mild. Thank you for your help today.'

'You can have more of it tomorrow,' he replied and took a step before rubbing his thigh. 'If I can walk by then.' He sighed. 'I need to spend more time on horseback.'

• • •

Alone, John sat, feeling the coolness gather around him. No light showed through the shutter of the solar; Katherine would be asleep. He tried to fit today's knowledge into what he already knew about the killing. But it added nothing at all. One question was still unanswered – who was meant to receive the letter which was never written? Perhaps he would never know.

Time was passing. Another few days and there would be the parade and service in the church to mark the start of this year's fair. If that happened and he hadn't found the murderer, he'd lose the chance of the fifty pounds that could change his life. He couldn't let that happen. He couldn't *afford* to let it happen. There had to be something he could use to pry it all open.

He wasn't sure how long he'd been sitting there, lost in his thoughts and trying to see a way forward. The light touch on his shoulder made him reach for the knife on his belt.

'Shhh,' Katherine whispered. 'It's only me.'

He reached out and gathered her close. Her body was warm and John realised how cold he was out here.

'Jeffrey needs to marry again and become a father,' she said. 'The children adore him.'

'I think he'd like that. Let's hope God is kind to him this time.'

'You should come to bed. You won't solve anything sitting on your own.'

'I know.' Suddenly he felt weary, as if all those hours had been toppling over on him. 'Maybe the answer will come in a dream.'

• • •

There was sleep, but no dream he could recall once he opened his eyes, and still no answers at all. He was the first to rise, washing and scrubbing at his teeth before he pulled on his clothes. In the buttery he took bread and cheese, sliding them into his scrip before he left the house.

A morning of high, pale clouds, and an edge to the air. Autumn was here, and his tunic was more threadbare than it had been a year before. He pulled up the hood and fastened his leather jerkin over the top. Better, but he'd suffer in the bitter days of winter. He needed a new tunic, something padded to keep him warm on those days he worked outside.

He had time to see Alan before the lad started making the new feed bins for the stables at the inn. Thomas the ostler wanted them lined with tin to keep out the rats. It was a good idea, although Alan was less sure. In a quick series of gestures, he showed the problem. The metal was too soft; the rats would soon gnaw through it. A waste of good tin and the expense of the labour. Something harder might work; sheets of iron, perhaps. But that would take time to forge.

But when he told the man, Thomas shook his head.

'We'll go with tin,' he said, and gestured to a pile in the corner, covered with sacking. 'I've bought it, I'll not see it go to waste.'

'He's paying the bill,' John explained to Alan with a shrug. 'I agree with you that he's wrong, but give him what he wants.'

• • •

They met on Low Pavement. Jeffrey was walking awkwardly, with bowed legs, looking as if each step brought him pain.

'God's peace on you,' John said. 'And some balm for your aches, too.'

'That will teach me to think I can still ride for miles.' A rueful smile. 'Hopefully I'll remember the lesson. Walking might help. As much as anything can right now. After I left your house last night, I took myself to the alehouse,' Jeffrey continued as they browsed through the weekday market near the church. Cheeses and potatoes, carrots fresh from the ground, butter from the churn, onions and dry wild garlic.

'A sore head as well as a raw body?' John grinned at him.

'No, no, just a single mug of ale, I swear. But I did learn something useful. One of the cousins of the Unthank family was there. Happy to be out for the evening.'

'And did he like to talk?'

'To talk, flirt with the girls, play dice… last night Cuthbert couldn't get enough of life.' He gave a broad smile. 'We all need times like that.'

'What did he have to say that was useful?'

'A rumour about Gertrude's sister.'

John had forgotten that the dead woman had a sister. She'd been mentioned a few times in passing, but nothing more than that. He'd never given the woman any thought.

'What about her?'

'If Cuthbert Unthank is right – and for the love of Jesu, it would be the first time in his life – Lady Gwendolyn and her husband are desperate for money,' Jeffrey said.

'Plenty of people have nothing,' John said. They'd strolled further, around the side of the church. He craned his neck to stare up at the scaffolding at the workers on the roof, and for a moment he envied them the order of their lives.

'I know.' Jeffrey's voice grew serious. 'But most people don't spend their way through dowries and marriage settlements.'

'No.' It was a world John would never be a part of, one he'd never understand. The way the wealthy and the powerful lived their lives and arranged their marriages made no sense to him. Where was the passion, where was the joy? It all seemed to be duty, keeping a name going, building estates. 'Does it mean much?'

'I don't know.' Jeffrey pushed his lips together. 'I heard my Lord l'Honfleur was generous with her, but I was younger when it all happened. I had no interest in how much it was.'

'Some people are spendthrifts.' He'd seen that often enough in his life.

'Cuthbert said they've asked the husband's father for more money.'

John sighed. 'It's helpful if there's someone they can ask. Most people don't have anyone to turn to when they have nothing. But I'm not sure how this helps us.'

Jeffrey shrugged. 'It probably doesn't. It might be nothing more than gossip. But it has to do with the family, so I thought you'd want to know.'

'Thank you.' As they walked, he tried to fit the information into the puzzle of murder. But there was nowhere for it; it didn't have a place there. Gertrude had a very different life from her sister. A much smaller life and a briefer one.

'I wouldn't give the idea too much time,' Jeffrey told him. 'Remember, there's not much love lost between the Unthanks and the l'Honfleur family. They might be spreading rumours and causing mischief.'

'Maybe so.' Some delighted in trouble and in grudges. From all he could see, this had nothing to do with the anchoress; it was better to put it out of his mind. 'We're missing something.'

'What, though?' Jeffrey asked. 'What else is there?'

'If we knew that, we'd have the answer to the problem.' John was about to say more when someone shouted his name. He turned. It was the captain of the coroner's men, running along Low Pavement and waving his arms as people stopped to stare at him.

'Carpenter!' He panted out the word, bending over with his hands on his knees, breathing hard. 'My master wants you.'

'What is it?' He glanced at Jeffrey. The young man gave a quick shake of his head and quietly slid away; this wasn't his business.

'I've been looking all over Chesterfield for you. Your wife didn't know where you'd gone.' He said it like an admonishment. 'A body.' The man took a deep breath. 'Come on, Master.'

John followed as the guard cut through the tiny streets of the Shambles. He was a big man, a hand on the hilt of his sword as he ordered people aside in the name of the coroner.

They took the road past the church, down the hill and along the Tapton road that led to Brimington.

'Where are we going?'

'Not far now, Master.' He kept his quick pace to where the road turned, then stopped. 'Down the hillside, Master, down by the water. A pair of serfs from the manor found him this morning.'

A group of men had gathered at the bottom of the slope. He could pick out Strong, but he didn't know any of the others. A man's body lay twisted on the ground, half in the water, his face turned away.

'Who died?' John asked, but the guard just shook his head and gestured down the hill.

'Go and see, Master.'

The earth was dry, the dirt and pebbles shifted and vanished under his feet as John made his way from tree to tree, holding on to stop himself tumbling down to the bottom. It was steep, so easy to lose footing. Had that happened to the dead man, he wondered?

'Carpenter.' The coroner's voice was grim. 'Take a look at this.'

He stood aside, the other men moving with him. John squatted and examined the body. The angle of the head gave the cause of death: his neck was broken. Only a single glance at the face; a young man who'd been fair-looking when he was alive. But this wasn't anyone he knew. Good clothes, a dark green velvet tunic, fine woollen hose and boots of smooth, rich leather that reached to his ankles. A man of some wealth. But the tunic and the hose were ripped, the leather of the boots scuffed. He turned over the corpse's hand. No real cuts, no recent dirt under the fingernails. The smooth skin of someone who'd never known manual labour.

John stood again and looked back up towards the road. From here he could trace the man's path, the scratches and gouges in the ground as he fell. Or perhaps he'd been pushed.

But there was nothing to show why Strong needed him out here.

'Do you know who it is?' the coroner asked.

'No, Master.'

'His name's Cuthbert Unthank.'

CHAPTER ELEVEN

That wasn't possible. Last night Jeffrey of Hardwick had been talking to the man. For a fleeting moment, John wondered if Jeffrey had killed him. No, he wasn't the type, and he was too clever. If he'd been responsible for this, he'd never have mentioned talking to Unthank the night before.

'A broken neck,' John said. But that was obvious to everyone looking at the body.

'Before he fell down here or as he tumbled?' the coroner asked. 'Maybe after he landed?'

'Before he left the road.' He showed Strong the hands. 'If he'd still been alive, he'd have been grabbing for everything to stop himself. There would have been plenty of cuts. You see here? There's no sign of that. Even if it had happened while he fell, there'd be something to see beforehand.'

The coroner nodded. 'Very observant, Carpenter. He's been dead for several hours. What was he doing out here? The family's Chesterfield home isn't in this direction.'

John didn't reply. He had no answer, and the question wasn't meant for him. And he had something else to think about: should he tell them about Jeffrey being with Unthank?

He had no choice. One way or another, it would come out. If he didn't say anything, who could tell what the reaction might be? Jeffrey was innocent, he was sure of that. If not, he was the best dissembler John had ever met.

He drew the coroner aside, explaining what he knew. There were only two things: the fact that Jeffrey and Unthank had been drinking together, and what Cuthbert Unthank had said about Gertrude's sister.

Strong frowned as he listened, glancing back at the body by the stream as if it might have suddenly slithered away. He beckoned one of the guards and whispered in his ear, watching as the man scrambled awkwardly back up the hillside.

'Strange how his name comes up and the next day he's dead,' the coroner said.

'I've found that there's no such thing as coincidence,' John agreed. He studied the body more closely. This would be the only chance he'd have. Very soon the corpse would be gone.

The man's scrip was still there, attached to his belt; this hadn't been a robbery. Inside, there were a few coins, a comb carved from bone, and a few scraps of paper. He patted at the man's clothing. Nothing hidden away. His knife was still in its sheath. John took it out, testing the edge. Quite blunt. He held it up to the light. A few scraps of meat from where Unthank had cut his dinner. No blood, no sign it had been used in anger.

He couldn't tell how the man's neck had been broken. But who could? He'd never heard of anyone with the skills to discern that. All the other injuries had come from the fall down the hillside.

'Do you see anything else?' Strong asked.

'No.'

'Could he have been drunk and fallen?'

'It's possible, but I don't believe so.' The road was wide enough. No reason for Unthank to be at the edge, even if he'd been drinking.

'My men are searching for Jeffrey. I told them to have him at my house in an hour. I'd like you there, Carpenter.'

It was neatly phrased. A request, although there was no possibility of refusal.

'Yes, Master.'

'I'll want your evidence as to what he told you.' He stared at the dead face. 'But I don't see how this relates to the death of Gertrude.'

'Nor do I, Master,' John agreed. 'But I'm certain it does.'

• • •

Jeffrey of Hardwick stood calmly and completely at ease in the hall of the coroner's house. He wasn't tied, he'd been treated with deference. A guard lingered by the door, but he didn't seem alert or aware of any danger.

Sir Mark Strong sat at the table, his clerk close by, writing out the questions and answers. John stood in the corner, out of the way. He'd speak if the coroner spoke to him, otherwise he'd stay silent, listening.

Jeffrey didn't need any help. He replied readily, pleasantly, recounting the time he'd spent with Unthank, recalling their conversation.

'Where did you leave him?'

'Outside the alehouse on Low Pavement. We'd both been drinking, but neither of us were drunk.'

'What time was that?'

'Not late,' Jeffrey answered. 'My landlady was still up when I returned to my lodgings and she likes an early bed.'

That brought smiles.

'How did Unthank seem?'

'The way he usually was. He'd always been a morose man, a little bitter and given to gossip.' He paused. 'I'm sorry to see him dead, Master, but I had nothing to do with it and I don't know who might have killed him.'

The coroner glanced at John and raised an eyebrow. A quick nod in return.

'When you parted, did he say where he was going?'

Jeffrey turned his head sharply, smiling as he saw the carpenter.

'No. I thought he'd be going home.'

'Did he talk to anyone else? Any friends who came over and said hello?'

'He flirted and chattered, but no real conversation with anyone else when I was with him. It was just the two of us.'

The coroner had no other questions to ask. Jeffrey was telling the truth, he was certain of that.

'Master, if there's anything I can do to help find the person who did it—'

'Talk to the carpenter,' Strong said. 'That's all. You're free to go.'

'Well?' Sir Mark asked when they were alone. He poured himself a mazer of wine and began to drink.

'We're no further on. Jeffrey is innocent.'

Strong nodded. 'Use his help.'

'I have. I like him. And now he has even more reason to be involved. He'll want to clear his name.'

'I saw my lord before anyone reported Cuthbert Unthank's death. He wants to know what progress you've made.'

John drew in a breath. 'What did you tell him, Master?'

'That you were learning more, but you didn't seem to know yet who was behind his daughter's killing.' A pause. 'He reminded me that the fair opens in a few days.'

He knew. He couldn't forget the fact. Every minute it was drawing closer and he was still flailing.

'Thank you, Master.'

• • •

It was late morning already, time for dinner. The hours had slipped by. Outside the coroner's house, John looked around. Jeffrey of Hardwick was sitting on a wall, smiling like a man without a care in the world.

'Come home and eat with us.' They didn't have much, but they could tease out another portion of pottage. Katherine and the children liked Jeffrey; he'd be a welcome guest.

'I can't, but I thank you. My father wants to see me at the warehouse so we can check some of the invoices.' He rolled his eyes. 'He wants me to take more responsibility, but whenever I do, he tries to stop me every step of the way.'

'Being questioned didn't worry you?'

'Why? I didn't kill Cuthbert. I don't know who did. If I'd suspected anyone, I'd have said.' He sighed. 'I can't believe we were talking just before he was killed. He was a good man, John. You might have liked him.'

He'd never have had the chance to find out if that was true. The Unthanks were a different class. Cuthbert Unthank wouldn't have mixed with a carpenter. John smiled.

'I'm sorry for your loss. May God keep him.'

'Give me an hour. I'll be able to satisfy my father by then. I suppose I have a good reason to find whoever killed him.'

'You do,' John agreed. 'We can meet in the church porch.'

• • •

He was early, talking to the men working on the church. Masons and tilers, men whose trades took them from place to place, wherever there was work. He'd once been that way himself, but he didn't miss it. He no longer envied them their freedom. Instead, he felt complete here, settled, with a family.

Yet there was still pleasure in hearing them talk about the problems with the job, the things that still needed to be done to the building. They talked easily, full of humour and the kind of camaraderie that only came from a group of men working and staying together.

By the time Jeffrey arrived, looking haggard and careworn, the men were drifting back to their work and clambering up the scaffolding to the roof.

'That would terrify me,' Jeffrey said as he watched them.

'A few times and you don't even think about it. It's wonderful to look out and see so far.'

'You've been up there?'

'I worked on the tower. The master carpenter was murdered and people suspected me because I'd just arrived.'

'I didn't know… I'm sorry.'

'No need. It was ten years ago now, and it changed my life for the better. You don't look too happy.'

'Someone told my father I was with Cuthbert before he was killed. He thinks I've brought the family into disrepute since I'm involved in it all.'

John clapped him on the shoulder. 'Then we'd better discover who's responsible. We both have an interest.'

The young man pursed his lips. 'Are you sure it's connected to Gertrude's death?'

'Yes,' he said after a small moment. He couldn't see *how*, but he knew it inside. It felt right, it had to be that way. 'I want to take another look at where it happened. Maybe you'll see something I didn't spot.'

But there was nothing left. The coroner and his men had been all over the road above the stream. They'd obliterated any marks or signs that might have been left. Searching farther didn't help.

'We don't know how many were with him,' Jeffrey said as he shook his head in frustration.

'Unthank looked quite big.'

'He was. But he was slow and awkward. He was never a fighter, although his father once wanted to make one of him. He never had the skills or the desire for it. He'd have been happiest raising sheep, I think. He liked the countryside.'

But he'd never have the chance now. His poor corpse was probably being lowered into the ground as they searched out here.

Finally, though, there was something. Jeffrey was halfway down the slope, tracing the path Unthank's body had taken as it fell. He looked in the bushes in the vain hope that something might have fallen, something to point them in a direction.

'Here,' he called out, and held up a scrap of vellum.

John was down in the riverbed, checking that nothing had been tossed away from the corpse as it landed. He scrambled up the hillside, feet slipping, reaching out for saplings and tree trunks to give him purchase.

'What is it?'

'I can't tell how many times it's been written on and scraped down,' Jeffrey said. The scrap was the size of his thumb. It had caught on a mayflower tree, snagged on one of the thorns. Something had been scratched on it, two words written in ink from the oak gall.

'What does it say?'

'*Cui bono*. It's Latin. It means who benefits from something. A Roman consul called Lucius Cassius first said it.' He beamed, happy to remember something his tutor had probably beaten into him.

'I don't understand.'

'Who profits from something. Who gains? It's one of the basic questions of law.'

Now it made sense. A few tiny scratches on a piece of sheepskin that said so much. Who profited from Cuthbert Unthank's death? Who gained by killing Gertrude? He tried to think. He knew nothing about Unthank. But Gertrude was an anchoress, a nun. She possessed nothing; poverty was her choice. What could she have to leave anyone? No one could benefit from that.

'*Cui bono.*' His mouth hesitated over the words, drawing them out and examining them. A foreign tongue, the language of the Church and the courts, of the educated and the wealthy. He'd never heard the words before. But the question was good. He should have asked it from the beginning.

Now he had to find an answer.

'Who profits from Cuthbert Unthank being dead?' John asked as they walked back to Chesterfield. Their tunics and hose were smeared with dirt from climbing up and down the hillside, but they'd found something.

'I don't know.' Jeffrey stared at the tiny piece of parchment once again. 'His branch of the family isn't wealthy. They have enough money for themselves, but that's all. And I don't think they've ever done anything wrong.'

'That leaves us with nothing. How can we be sure that even came from him?'

'He could read and write and he spoke a little Latin. How many around here could say the same?'

Precious few; it was a convincing argument. But all it meant was that the words were teasing them. How could anyone profit from the death of a young man or an anchoress nun? Anyone religious had renounced the world.

That was the idea, at least. Yet he'd seen bishops weighed down under their jewels and rich clothes in York. They had their houses filled with servants and their coffers stuffed with coins. But most in holy orders were good people.

All he knew about Unthank were the few things Jeffrey had told him. It was a shaded picture, he realised that. But unless he had a fortune or was heir to one, there was little to make anyone kill him.

An argument that turned violent? That was possible. Jealousy over a girl? It could have been. But Jeffrey shook his head at both ideas.

'Cuthbert wasn't going to inherit, and he was never especially interested in a girl in all the years I knew him. He flirted, but it was all in fun. Nothing more. He didn't go wenching, never made remarks the way men usually do. No, I don't believe it's that. And why would he be out on the Tapton road after dark? His home is in the opposite direction, and he wasn't drunk enough to wander that far away.'

'Maybe he went to another alehouse after he left you.'

Jeffrey shook his head. 'He had precious little money left.'

That made sense; there had only been a couple of small coins in the man's scrip when John searched it.

'What, then? How could anyone gain by his death?'

'I don't know,' Jeffrey answered in a voice filled with sorrow. 'I truly don't.'

They talked for an hour, pushing ideas back and forth as they leaned on the wall around the churchyard. Men shouted and sang as they worked on the building. The weekday market was over, traders packing up what was left and leaving. People passed. He knew many of them, giving brief bows and smiles. He was part of this place. Most of the people accepted him.

Any murder tore at the fabric of a community. The killing of Gertrude had ripped it open. And now there were the deaths of two other innocents, Cuthbert and the forager. Add to that the bodies of the squires. Too many, far too many. The bill was too high.

'What are you thinking?' Jeffrey asked.

'I'm trying to find something that connects all the people who've died. Did Cuthbert ever have anything to do with Gertrude?'

'No, she was his cousin. As I said, he had no particular interest in women at all.'

The other deaths all appeared to be linked, a chain went from one to another. But this stood apart, with no obvious reason or rhyme behind it. Perhaps it had nothing to do with the rest. More likely they simply hadn't discovered what connected it yet.

'Do you know any friends of his?'

'One or two. They'll be in town for the fair.'

'Talk to them. Ask some questions and see what they have to say about him.'

'So soon after his death?'

'Yes, he'll be in their minds. Leave it and their thoughts will fade.'

With a nod, Jeffrey stood. 'What about you?'

John shook his head. 'Master, I wish I knew. I really do.'

· · ·

Who might have answers? He wracked his brain to come up with a name but there was no one. Dame Gertrude, the squires, Unthank, they all came from a different class. The solution to all this lay with them, he was sure of that. But men like him were barred entry.

Standing at l'Honfleur's door, he wasn't certain why he'd come. There was little to tell. Maybe the man would have something to spark an idea.

But he wasn't at home. He'd gone hunting, and would spend the night at his manor near Hathersage.

He scuffled his way back to Knifesmithgate, kicking at pebbles and trying to think. He'd almost reached his door when the sound of running feet made him turn. The head of the coroner's guard coming, waving at him.

'What is it?' John asked.

'He wants you.'

He felt the dread rising through his body. 'Is someone else dead?'

'Not this time, thanks be to God.'

They hurried through the streets, walking quickly, not speaking, out past West Bar to the coroner's house. They entered, passed the screens, and he saw Sir Mark Strong pacing over the rushes. He held a mug of ale, his mouth set and firm, his face dark as thunder.

'Carpenter. I've had a messenger from my lord.'

He didn't say anything, just waited silently for an explanation.

'He went hunting this morning with a small party. They were out on the moor, near his manor. Someone attacked them.'

CHAPTER TWELVE

'What? Attacked?' At first he couldn't believe it. Who would dare to do something like that?

'No one was hurt. Someone firing arrows. But two of the horses were hit.'

'Did they—'

Strong shook his head.

'By the time they managed to organise a chase, the man had vanished. My lord sent someone to ask for a few of my men to help in the search. But I thought you should know.'

Attacking a lord… how could anyone attempt that? Why? Was it desperation?

'Is he coming back here?'

'He's staying at the manor, exactly as he planned,' the coroner said. 'Returning to Chesterfield would look like he was running away.'

Of course. Honour. L'Honfleur would be safer in Chesterfield than out on the moors. But he had to show his men that he was strong.

Who would have tried to kill him? Had it been a real attempt? A skilled archer should be able to hit his target at a good distance. Maybe that hadn't been the intention. Not to assassinate, but to scare.

He stopped himself before he could speak. He didn't know, he hadn't been there. He had no idea how far away the archer had been. Everything was a guess.

'Don't tell anyone,' Strong said. 'I know people will hear, but later rather than sooner.'

'Yes, Master.'

'Who did this is involved in everything else. I want him found.'

It was a dismissal. Outside, as clouds started to gather over the peaks to the west, he stood and thought, then began to walk.

• • •

'No, Master, no one's brought a horse here today.' The man leaned on his shovel, turned his head and spat. 'No one's taken one out, either.' He shrugged and looked around. 'No business at all.'

It was hardly a surprise. He looked around the stables. It was dirty, stinking of dung. Even to his eyes, the horses in the stalls looked ungroomed, with a touch of wildness in their eyes.

Two men had taken horses from the second stable. But they were regular customers, on their way up to Sheffield and then to York; they made the journey every month. None had brought one in.

There was one more place, just beyond the bridge over the Hipper.

'A man hired a black gelding this morning,' the ostler said. 'Due back tomorrow, and if he doesn't bring it, I'll see him hanged for a horse thief.'

'Who took it?'

'I've not seen him before. He told me his name was Edward from Wingerworth and that he needed to get to Glossop.' The man shrugged. 'He had the money.'

'What did he look like?'

'A light green tunic and hood, black hose.' He shrugged again. 'Not as tall as you. Dark hair, I think. I didn't look closely.'

'Was he carrying a bow?'

'He was. Why?'

It might not be the same man; so many knew how to use the bow. But a feeling bubbled inside him that this was who he sought.

'When he comes back tomorrow, keep him talking and send someone for the coroner.'

The man frowned. 'The coroner? Why? Who are you?'

'I'll have the captain of his guard come and tell you, to make it official.'

'You do that,' the man agreed warily. 'I don't have any idea who you are.'

'That's fair,' John agreed. 'You need a reason to believe me.'

• • •

The eyes of the coroner's captain lit up when John told him.

'That's good thinking,' he said.

'It's pure luck, nothing more.'

'More than that,' he began, but John shook his head.

'Go and talk to him. Tell him you need to know as soon as the man returns the horse.'

'I will.' A slow, satisfied smile formed on his mouth. 'Tomorrow we'll have him.'

It was something to give them hope. But it would only happen if the man returned his horse. If he was cautious, he wouldn't do that; he'd keep clear of Chesterfield.

Why go after l'Honfleur? And why now? It seemed to be a stupid move. Killing a lord would bring the royal gaze; no one could escape that. He'd be hunted down.

Was it to sow confusion? What good would that do? He didn't understand, he didn't know enough to make sense of it.

• • •

At home, he played with Martha, then told Richard a story, something he spun from a tale he'd heard once in York. He didn't possess a teller's gift, he couldn't weave a tight web of words, but it was gratifying to see his son so rapt as he lay in bed. It might take away his pain for a little while.

When he came down from the solar, Jeffrey was sitting at the table in the hall, cradling a mug of ale and talking softly to Katherine. Her eyes seemed to sparkle as she listened to the young man, the way they'd once glistened for him, and he felt a twinge of resentment. But it was only natural – the attention of a handsome young man would make her feel alive again.

For a moment he stood and watched them. Then Jeffrey turned his head and his expression became serious.

'The coroner told me what happened.'

John explained what he'd discovered.

He frowned. 'That description is too vague.'

'I know, but it's all we have. What about Unthank's friends? Have you seen any of them yet?'

'Two,' he said. 'And neither of them can imagine who'd want to kill him. He was very temperate in his ways, no one could recall him being in a fight.'

'They don't have any names for us?'

Jeffrey shook his head. 'None.'

'Every way we turn, we end up nowhere.'

'This attack,' Jeffrey asked slowly. 'What do you make of it?'

'I don't know.'

'It seems…' the young man began, then stopped.

'Seems what?'

'If they wanted to stop things, the person to go after would be you.'

'I know.' He'd thought about it. 'Believe me, I know. It's not a comforting thought.'

'Then why didn't you tell me, husband?' Katherine asked. Her expression was brittle, her voice full of accusation.

'There's been nothing to tell. And I don't believe there will be.'

She frowned. 'Why?'

'They'd have done something by now if that was what they wanted. Is that what you mean?' Jeffrey said slowly.

'Exactly. Perhaps they feel they don't have to worry about me finding the truth.' He put his hand over his wife's and smiled at her. He wanted to reassure her. 'That's why I didn't say anything; there was nothing to tell.'

Reluctantly, she nodded, then slipped away. Silence filled the room.

'She's never liked me working for the coroner,' John said. 'She hated it when the old one was still alive, and now…'

'She's scared for you.'

'Of course she is. But she also knows how desperately we need the money l'Honfleur will pay if I solve this in time.' He sighed and ran his palms down his cheeks.

'Tell me something. If you had to sell one of the houses, which would it be?'

'The one on Saltergate.'

Jeffrey looked thoughtful. 'If you decide to sell it, will you tell me?'

'You? Are you looking to buy?'

He nodded. 'I think it's time. I like my lodgings, but when I marry, I'll need a house, especially once there are children.'

'It's a good place for that. Katherine and her sisters and brother grew up there. I had no idea you were close to marrying.'

'My family have been plotting since my wife died. The daughter of a landowner from somewhere near Buxton.' He shrugged. 'I've met her a few times. I think we'll be able to make a match of it.'

'But not love?'

He pursed his lips and frowned. 'No, not love. Duty. You lose your life to it.' He slapped his palm down on the table and gave a weak smile. 'Enough about that. Let's see if we can understand who's behind these deaths and earn you that fifty pounds.'

The man wasn't unhappy, John thought. It was more that he was resigned to the idea of marrying someone who didn't have his heart. But Jeffrey was right; money meant duty, and your life stopped being your own at a young age. Perhaps they could be envied for their comforts, but there was little about the lives of the rich that he wished for himself.

'Yes,' he agreed.

It was someone who knew the family who was behind the murders. It had to be; no one else would have a reason for wishing Gertrude dead. Someone with a grudge?

Jeffrey frowned. 'I can't think of anyone. L'Honfleur has always had the reputation of being a fair master.'

'Before he died, Cuthbert Unthank was telling you about Gertrude's sister.'

Jeffrey snorted. 'Lady Gwendolyn and her spendthrift man. I know I passed it on, but what he told me wasn't much of a secret. I first heard it months ago.'

'It's still a possibility.'

'No, I honestly don't believe it. My lord told them he wouldn't give them more money and threatened to cut Gwendolyn out of his will if she kept asking him.'

'Who else is there in the family?'

'No one, not with Gertrude dead. Nephews and nieces.'

John paced around the hall, stopping to pick up his mug and take a sip of ale.

'How long ago did l'Honfleur make the threat to Gwendolyn?'

'I'm not sure. Two months, maybe three.'

'Well before Gertrude's death.'

'It was,' Jeffrey replied, and his eyes widened as he understood the implication. 'No, I don't believe that. I can't say I trust her, but she would never have arranged her own sister's death. Who could do that?'

'If you can imagine it, someone will do it. I agree it's not likely—'

'Her own sister?' Jeffrey interjected in disbelief.

'—but it's possible. We have to think about it.' He stared at Jeffrey. 'That means you'll have to be the one to look into it.'

No one of that class would be willing to answer questions from a carpenter, no matter who was employing him.

'If you want.' Jeffrey looked uncomfortable at the idea. 'I should tell you, I knew Gwendolyn before she married. After my wife had died.'

'Surely that will help.'

He shook his head. 'She wasn't always chaste in her friendships.' His face reddened and he stared down at the rushes on the floor.

'Would she talk to you?'

'I don't know. Honestly, John, I don't. I wouldn't even know what to ask her. She and her husband aren't likely to admit to murder, are they?'

'Then we need to think of some questions.'

'You have the brain, Master,' Jeffrey said with a brief bow. 'I'm just the hand that carries out your wishes.'

They walked halfway to Unstone and back as they tried to come up with questions that might offer the hint of proof they could take to l'Honfleur. Without that, anything they said would be rumour and accusation.

'Do you believe it will work?' Jeffrey asked.

'It might,' he said. 'We should pray that it does. Do you believe Gwendolyn will talk to you?'

'The God's truth, John, I don't know. She might, as long as her husband is in the room. For the sake of propriety.'

'Of course.'

'Anything they tell me, they can always deny it later.'

'I realise that.' Words only possessed value if there were plenty to hear them and agree what was said. But something, some tiny nudge along the way, would help. 'You don't have to do it.'

'I promised you I would,' Jeffrey said, but there was no pleasure on his face. 'I'm a man of my word. I know they're in town for the fair, I caught a glimpse of them this morning.' He sighed. 'What you need to understand is that their idea of poor is very different to yours. They have money to live on. They're comfortable enough. They'll never starve, they won't be turned out on to the street for want of a farthing. It means they can't afford luxuries. The truffles they particularly like or a tun of the Gascon wine. That's what they consider poor.'

A different world to any he could ever understand. One that was far outside his knowledge. He knew why Jeffrey was telling him all this. It was to try and give him some insight into the way these people looked at life. Perhaps it helped, but more than anything, it left him tangled up in anger and sorrow. He'd only known ordinary people, poor people; he still did, those who hovered between life and death because they didn't have coins in their scrip or a roof over their heads. That was poverty and desperation.

But would Gwendolyn and her husband kill for more money? Maybe so. Greed could push people to do awful things.

'Come on,' John said. 'Let's sit for a while and have a mug of ale. It might make us feel better.'

'Not now. I'd rather find Gwendolyn and have this done.' He gave a wan smile. 'Duty.'

'You know where to find me.'

• • •

It was late evening when Jeffrey tapped on the door. The children were already asleep, the usual snuffling and sniffling coming from the solar. Katherine was sewing, lowering the hem of Juliana's dress; she seemed to grow an inch a month at the moment.

She stopped with her needle in mid-air as she heard the noise.

John kept his knife in his hand, letting it slip back into its sheath as he recognised the face.

'You promised me a mug of ale a few hours ago. Is it too late?'

'Come in. Come in.'

Katherine's face brightened to see him as she set her mending aside, and she blushed as he bowed to her.

'I had to return after they came back from a day's hawking,' Jeffrey began. 'Then Gwendolyn made me wait while she attended to this and that. A reminder that we'd once known each other.' Small patches of red grew on his cheeks. 'Her maid and her husband were both there.'

'Did you ask the questions we'd prepared?'

He nodded. 'They denied everything.'

'Of course.' John nodded.

'But none of the other questions tripped them up, either. They both kept to the same tale – all the stories about them not having money were rumours, nothing more than that.'

He shook his head. 'They did everything except offer me the chance to inspect their accounts.'

'Do you believe them?'

He stayed silent for a long time, rubbing the back of his neck and staring at the floor.

'I don't know,' he replied finally. 'I don't have the right skills to tell the truth from a lie. Give me figures on a page and I'd be able to tell you if someone is being honest. But when people speak… no, not even when they look in my eyes.'

'Then I'll have to talk to my lord in the morning.'

'He's due back early, he has business that needs attention, I'm told.'

John had hoped for some evidence to present, at least some clarity. How could you tell a man that one of his daughters might have plotted the murder of her sister?' 'I still don't see *why*, though. Or why they'd try to kill him.'

'*If* they did,' Jeffrey cautioned. 'Don't go accusing anyone. Not yet. Not until we know more.' His voice lowered to a warning. 'That's dangerous.'

'I'll be very careful in how I speak.'

• • •

Yet it was impossible to watch his words enough. He saw l'Honfleur's face darken as he went through the ideas. When John hesitated, uncertain if the man wanted to hear more, l'Honfleur waved for him to continue. By the time he finished, the man was staring out of the window at the garden. It was growing barer with each day, leaves tumbling to cover the grass.

While he'd been gone, the old rushes had been replaced, with sprigs of thyme in with the fresh ones covering the floor.

'Tell me, Carpenter,' he asked eventually, 'do you believe they did it?'

'I honestly don't know, Master. I didn't speak to your daughter or her husband. I've never seen them.'

'Who talked to them?'

'Jeffrey of Hardwick.'

L'Honfleur nodded slowly. 'He's a good man. He used to know my daughter, I'm sure he told you. I've heard the rumours, just like everyone else. But I know that Gwendolyn hasn't approached me again to ask for more money.' His tone became harder and more strident. 'And I know she would never have tried to hurt Gertrude. They weren't close, but they were still sisters.'

'Yes, my lord.' One more question to ask; he had no choice, he needed to know. 'I heard about the attack on you yesterday.'

'God be praised, no one was hurt, but two of the horses were hit. Good beasts, too. We haven't found the people who did it yet. But if you want to imply Gwendolyn is responsible for that, you'd do well to hold your tongue, Carpenter.'

'Yes, my lord.'

'Is there anything else?'

He explained about the horseman with the bow. On the way to the house, he'd stopped at the stable, but the man hadn't returned the animal and the ostler was becoming worried.

'I see. I'll have the coroner handle that. It's best you leave. I have more important business than gossip about my family.' As John reached the door, l'Honfleur called out once more: 'The fair starts very soon. You have until then to earn your fifty pounds.'

As if he could forget. It echoed through his body with every single beat of his heart.

• • •

'What did he say?' Jeffrey was waiting, pacing anxiously up and down on the street. He looked even more worried when John finished talking. 'He's telling us not to pursue that?'

'That's the way it appears. Why? Last night you didn't know what to think.'

'I'm still confused. I won't make any bones about that,' Jeffrey agreed. 'But when I was trying to fall asleep, I kept going over everything they said to me. I can't explain it, but there was something that kept troubling me.'

'What?'

'I don't know,' he answered in frustration. 'I had a feeling that there were pieces of the truth missing.'

'You mean they were lying?'

'Perhaps. I can't be sure. I've told you before, I don't have your way with people.'

'They would never have been willing to speak to me,' John reminded him.

'True,' he agreed. 'But what do we do now?'

'Can you look into the things they told you about their money? Very carefully and very quietly. But quickly, too.'

'I can try,' Jeffrey replied. 'We're lucky people are gathering for the fair. I'll be able to ask a few discreet questions.'

'As soon as you can.'

'What about you?'

That was a good question. So much of this took place in the kind of realm where he would never be allowed.

'I'll see if I can learn anything from Lady Gwendolyn's servants. They always know more than people think. Where are they staying?'

'They have a house on the road to Newbold. Do you know where it turns to the left?'

'I do.' John had once known someone who lived there, the widow of the master carpenter who'd been killed just after he arrived in Chesterfield.

'About a quarter of a mile further along there's a house that stands back along a drive. That's theirs.'

He could picture it in his mind. He'd passed the place many times, sometimes seeing people working in the garden. But he'd never been curious who owned it, and the name would never have meant anything to him before all this.

CHAPTER THIRTEEN

Ten years of being known in town as a carpenter possessed some advantages. Even if he'd never spoken to the servants in the house owned by Lady Gwendolyn and Sir Roland, they recognised his face and didn't turn him off as a stranger and a beggar. He carried his tools in the leather satchel, and a worker took him to see the steward.

'Do you need any jobs done, Master?' John asked. The man had a long, sharp nose and small, button eyes; far from handsome, but he had power in the household and revelled in it.

'No,' he said at first. A short, abrupt answer. He turned away, then back again. 'Yes, I suppose there is something you could look at. Tell me how much you'll charge to mend it.' He raised his voice. 'Elspeth, come and show him the window frame that's rotting in the kitchen.'

She had a shy smile, a woman about the same age as Katherine, but with a face that looked beaten down by life and service. The woman kept her shoulders stooped, as if she constantly expected people to shout at her. Maybe they did. There was no warm feeling in this house; he had the sense that the place ran on fear and anger.

'Where is it?' John asked as she led him down a corridor, past the buttery. The house was larger than he'd imagined. A covered path connected to the kitchen in the garden. Far enough away in case of fire, yet still protected as servants carried in the dishes.

The kitchen was sagging. Any fool could see it. One corner had sunk a good two inches into the ground. The post might be rotten and crumbling, or the ground could be giving way. Without a proper examination, he couldn't tell.

'This is the window the steward mentioned, Master.'

The whole frame felt soft under his fingers. The shutters closed when he moved them, but there was too much play. He'd need to replace every scrap of it with good, weathered oak that would last. The plaster all around crumbled as he rubbed it. But the entire kitchen needed to be rebuilt.

'How long has it been like this?' he asked the woman.

'The cook started complaining two years ago,' Elspeth answered. 'But no one thought it was worth the worry or the expense.'

'It would have been easier to do back then,' he told her with a smile. 'Cheaper, too.' She'd given him the opening he needed. 'There must be plenty of money in a house this size.'

She shook her head. 'They're always arguing about it.' As soon as she spoke, she put a hand over her mouth. 'Please, I didn't mean to say that. Don't tell anyone, I'll lose my position here.'

'I won't say a word, Mistress,' he promised. 'What are they like, the master and Lady Gertrude?'

She glanced around, enough to be certain no one could hear them. She'd spilled one secret, now she seemed willing to give him the rest, John thought. God be praised for that, it made this visit worthwhile.

'They go at each other hammer and tongs about money. Every day. You met the steward, he handles the house and their manors. They're all ill-kept places. Just look for yourself,

Master. It needs money, but they won't spend it because they don't have it.'

'Do they treat you well?'

Elspeth shook her head 'They give more attention and care to their horses. The steward beats us if we don't do our work fast enough.'

'You could leave.'

'How?' She stared at him, helpless. 'They own land. My Lord l'Honfleur is the lady's father and she keeps reminding us of the fact. Who'd employ us if they said we were troublemakers?'

The plight of the poor, he thought. He might not have money, but at least he was his own master; his future didn't depend on the graces of a family. Even as the thought came, he shook his head. Stupid. He was here because he wanted to earn the money from my lord, and trusted that he'd be a man of his word and pay.

'Lady Gwendolyn's sister was killed lately, wasn't she?'

'They talk about that, too. But they keep the doors closed and their voices low when they do it.'

Well, well. As the conversation continued, he examined the kitchen. Elspeth didn't know too much and didn't understand what it might mean. She didn't like her master or mistress, but she didn't see them as murderers. By the time she finished, John had heard all she had to say on the matter. She turned to him, red-faced.

'Please, Master, don't say a word to them. I try to be a good Christian woman, but it all overwhelms me sometimes.'

'The only things you told me involved the damage to the window,' he assured her, and Elspeth's grateful smile was all the reward he needed.

She vanished as he waited for the steward. From somewhere in the solar he heard a woman's voice raised in anger, but he couldn't make out the words. The noise subsided and, shortly after, the steward entered. The man looked flustered and uncomfortable. He listened as John explained the work that needed to be done, grimacing at the list.

'How much, Carpenter?'

The steward blanched as he heard the amount.

'Do you think I'm a fool?'

'No, Master, and that's an honest price. It's good, solid work that will last.'

'There are people who will do it for less.'

'I daresay there are,' he agreed, seeing the surprise in the man's eyes. 'And they'll have to do it all over again in twelve months or two years. This will last you two decades or more. Good wood and proper craft. But I'll tell you this, too, Master, and not because I want more work. Anything I do on that window will only serve you so far. The whole kitchen needs attention. New plaster, and you must have seen the corner that's sinking.'

'No doubt you could take care of that, too.' His voice was withering.

'I could. But you asked about one job and I've given you a price on that.'

'That's not a price,' the steward told him. 'That's lining your pocket.'

'If that's how you feel. Master, I'll wish you good day. May God be with you.'

He walked down the road back to Chesterfield with his jaw clenched. He was angry at being dismissed for a charlatan, for rising to the steward's bait. Finally he stopped and laughed at himself. He hadn't wanted the job. Asking about work had only ever been a pretext – why should it bother him?

Still he'd learned enough to leave him suspicious of Sir Roland and Lady Gwendolyn. Was it enough to go back to l'Honfleur and try to change his mind? Could you ever alter a man's attitude when it came to his own family, the children he'd raised? Would he listen if someone came and tried to turn his mind against Juliana or Richard or Martha? Of course not. He'd defend them.

But not all children turned out so well.

His feet took him to the coroner's house, but the man wasn't expected back until dinner. Another hour. At least it gave him time to think about what he needed to say and the best words to use. Jeffrey might praise his way with people, but John wasn't a man of words; he never had been. Survival was always more urgent than speaking. Perhaps that was the reason he'd always worked well with young Alan; the lad had learned to communicate without his voice.

At home he drank a mug of small beer to take the edge from his thirst. Too much talking this morning, too many things to consider. Martha came to him, wanting to play, and the distraction was welcome. He drew in Juliana and eventually left his daughters together, stopping to kiss his wife before he returned to the coroner's house.

'You look like you're carrying the weight of the world on your shoulders, husband,' she said with a loving smile.

'Sometimes I feel like it.' He sighed. 'Maybe it'll ease after I talk to Strong.'

'Do you believe that?'

'I hope so.' John pulled Katherine close. Her hair was neatly hidden, pinned under the wimple, and she smelled of the autumn, fresh and bright. 'I should go and talk to him before his dinner.'

• • •

But the man was already eating by the time he arrived, pork and stewed apples piled on his trencher. A pair of dogs sat at his feet, watching carefully for scraps. Strong listened as he cut his meat, chewing slowly and tossing the gristle down into the rushes for the animals.

Outside the glazed window, John could see the breeze stirring the leaves that had fallen on the grass.

'I went to the stable,' Sir Mark said. 'That man still hasn't returned the horse. If he's not back by dark, the ostler will swear a complaint.'

There could be an honest reason why the man hadn't returned, but he doubted it. At least they knew.

'He's gone.'

'I believe you're right.'

'Jeffrey talked to Lady Gwendolyn, and I went out to the house and listened to the servants.' He told the coroner everything he'd learned.

'You have your doubts about the couple,' the man said when John had finished.

'Many of them, Master.'

'And you feel my lord won't want to know because Lady Gwendolyn is his daughter.'

'I do.'

Sir Mark used a fingernail to push at a piece of meat caught between two teeth.

'I'm not sure I agree, Carpenter. I've known him a long time. Believe me, he has few illusions about her. Even fewer about Roland, that man she married. He always was a wastrel, never settled to a thing in his life.'

'Then why won't he listen?'

Strong rounded on John. 'Because no father wants to hear that one of his daughters was responsible for the death of the other. Especially from someone else. He had two children. He has one now. If Gwendolyn really is behind this, she'll die and he'll have no one at all. Stop and think about that.'

It was true enough. To consider the possibility meant he could lose his whole family. Everything. But it might not be true, all the suspicions might come to nothing.

'I have to keep on looking,' John said. 'If he wants the truth.'

'Deep down, he does. Even if it will wound him. He needs to know,' the coroner agreed. 'But he might fight it.'

'What about you, Master?' He took a deep breath. 'Will you back me?'

'What do you want?' Strong asked after a long moment.

'To take my side if my lord tries to stop me.'

'If you can find the evidence, then yes, I'll back you.' Strong paused. 'If you find enough of it, he'll believe you. I'm sure of that, Carpenter.'

That was all he could ask, all he could hope. He left feeling brighter. A little further out from town, all the vendors and entertainers were preparing for the fair. The field was fully laid out into streets now, all of them noisy and colourful, filled with different accents and tongues, enough to take away the breath. But there would be time for that when he found Gertrude's murderer. He turned away and as he walked through the market square, he saw Jeffrey.

'You look like a man who's lost his last farthing through a hole in his scrip.'

The young man shook his head. 'Not at all. Just wandering in my thoughts.' He gave a bittersweet smile. 'What about you, did you come up with anything?'

'Rumours and shadows,' John said once he'd explained. 'But they're all worth following.'

'If we can. I had a word with Roland and Gwendolyn's man of business.'

'What did he have to say?'

'He wasn't about to let too much slip. Have you eaten?'

He hadn't; he'd left home before dinner and Strong would never ask him to share a table. At the thought of food, his stomach began to gurgle.

'Come on,' Jeffrey said, jingling coins. 'A pie from the cook-shop and we'll talk.'

The food went down well, he couldn't deny it. Meat of some kind, still hot, plenty of thick gravy, and pastry that flaked on his tongue. They ate in silence, enjoying every last bite. When he was a single man, John had often eaten like this. Now it felt like a rare, guilty treat, something to keep hidden from his family as they had their bowls of bean pottage.

'Their man of business…' John began as he wiped crumbs from his mouth with the sleeve of his tunic.

'I'm not a fool,' Jeffrey said. 'I'm not about to press someone like that for too many details. I know him, I've had dealings with him. He's an upright man, very honourable.'

'Go on.'

'I could see the look in his eyes as soon as I mentioned Roland and Gwendolyn. He became worried and anxious.'

'How much did he tell you?'

'Very little,' Jeffrey said. 'But there was enough, with his hints and silences, for me to think that they owe a great deal of money.'

'How can you tell, if he didn't say so?' He didn't understand. 'And what does it mean, that they owe so much?'

'You know I work with figures. When I speak to someone else who does the same, I can learn things from everything they say and don't say. Isn't it the same in your business?'

'No.' Wood was straightforward. It might hold its secrets, but it never lied or misdirected. And there were few untruths carpenters could tell about their trade. What they made stood there for everyone to see.

'Ah.' Jeffrey nodded, as if he'd expected a different answer. 'Well, you can make figures lie, as long you know what to do. But there are limits. From what I can tell, Sir Roland and Lady Gwendolyn have reached them.'

'And the money they owe?'

'It won't vanish.' He shrugged. 'With so little coming in, they'll need to borrow more and more. They'll have nothing left to leave their children, if they ever have any. No dowry for a daughter. Their lives will be completely controlled by the moneylenders.'

'But they'll still live well, you told me that.'

He nodded. 'Well enough, yes.'

'None of this proves anything, does it? What you've learned, what I saw at the house. There's nothing we can point to and say it makes them guilty.'

'No,' Jeffrey agreed. 'But it all mounts up.'

'That's not enough. I need proof to take to my Lord l'Honfleur. She's his daughter, he's not going to accept anything less.'

•••

'Maybe she doesn't have anything to do with it,' Katherine said after he told her all they'd learned.

He turned his head sharply. 'Why would you think that?'

She spread more flour so the dough wouldn't stick to the wood, and continued kneading the bread. No rich man's white loaf for them; instead they had the coarse dark grain, the same as most people.

'You have a collection of rumours, you have this and that. But there nothing to say they're guilty, is there?'

'No,' John admitted.

'Maybe the reason is that they have nothing to do with it.' She held up a finger. 'I'm not saying it is that way, but it's possible. And the more you pursue this without looking elsewhere, the less chance of you finding other things.'

'But—' he began, then stopped himself. 'You're right.'

'You know I don't want you to be a part of this at all.'

'I didn't have a choice. You saw that.'

She dipped her head in agreement. 'Then you need to look at everything with open eyes. You have the idea of this couple fixed in your mind.'

'You know why, I've told you.'

'Yes,' she agreed, and slammed the dough down heavily on the wood. 'But that doesn't mean you're right. Keep looking around, husband. It's not just you; it's Jeffrey, too. You think you're both so clever, but you're like a pair of boys.'

Were they? He didn't think so. But maybe she was right. Katherine could stand on the outside, looking in. He needed to think. Time was slipping away from him if he was going to find a true solution before the fair began. He didn't want to watch the money slip through his fingers because he'd been fixed on the wrong thing.

'Take a walk,' she told him. 'Consider it all.' She stared at him. 'But do it honestly. You know I'm saying it because I love you.'

'I do.' He kissed her gently, wiping a smudge of flour from her cheek. 'I love you, too. You keep my feet on the ground.'

• • •

He walked and wondered. Very carefully, he separated facts from ideas, what he knew from what he hoped or imagined.

Katherine was right. He was too willing to believe Gwendolyn was guilty, to build suspicion into fact.

But it left another question. What else was there? Who else might have had the power and the connections to arrange and desire Gertrude's death? Try as he might, John couldn't think of another name.

He needed to look again. To ask more questions.

• • •

The labourers at the church were finishing for the day as he passed. They climbed down the scaffolding, young men full of laughter and high spirits, hardly needing to look where they put their feet. They were sure about themselves and life. Noise followed them along the street and into the alehouse of Low Pavement.

John waited, allowing time for them to be served and to settle before he entered. The day was dying and the shadows were long. All the old men gathered together near the back of the room, crowded around a table. John bought his mug of ale and joined them, greeting with a nod or a single word.

He listened to the idle chatter for a few minutes.

'What do you think about the death of Gertrude?' he asked.

'Thought you were the one looking into it,' one man said with a harsh laugh. 'In't that right? You should be the one telling us.'

'I'm curious to hear what you say. You've lived here a long time—'

'All my life.'

'—and you know the people. You must have ideas.'

'What he means is he doesn't have a clue.' More laughter. The words were closer to the bone than they imagined.

He simply smiled. 'Tell me. I want to know. If I had any money, I'd buy you drinks.'

It was desperation. He knew it; behind the laughter, the men at the table probably knew it, too. But they might have some ideas. They knew Chesterfield and the people who lived here.

'Who would want to kill the anchoress?' John asked.

'No one,' a man answered, serious now. He leaned forward with his elbows resting on the table. More hair grew from his ears and nostrils than on his head, and the white stubble was thick on his cheeks. 'There's not a soul in this town who'd want to hurt a girl like her.'

'Someone did.'

'Wouldn't be one of us,' another said. 'My wife went out to see her and get her blessing. Holy, that was what she said, and all the others who saw her said the same thing.'

He looked from one face to the next, all around the table. Every one of them nodded in agreement. 'Then who would want her dead?'

'Rich folk,' a voice said. 'Has to be. A poor man isn't going to gain from it, is he? We all liked her. Didn't you ever go out there, Carpenter? You or your wife, get her to pray for that son of yours?'

John shook his head. The idea of having Gertrude pray for Richard's health had never even come into his mind. He didn't believe it could change anything; God had already set that course. But it might have made the path easier, and there were always miracles. He dragged himself back to the conversation.

'Family.'

'Don't be so stupid. Why would her own family do anything to her?'

'I'm not saying they did. The carpenter's asking who killed her. I'm giving a possibility, that's all. From all I've heard…'

the man glanced around to be sure nobody was watching, and lowered his voice to a hoarse whisper '...her father has been ruthless with a few of his enemies in the past.'

'You don't know what you're talking about,' someone else replied with a shake of his head. 'He doted on that girl. He had since she was tiny.'

'Maybe she did something wrong.'

'How's she going to do that? Come on, tell me. She's been out living in the anchorite cell for a year. What could she do that was wrong?'

'I don't know, do I? It's not my family.'

The conversation continued, waves of it, but after a while he stopped listening. The talk was going round and round, saying nothing at all. The men didn't know anything, but they were enjoying the speculation as they drank. It gave them something different to think about, to stir up old rumours and gossip. John had hoped there might be some incident they'd remember, a little fact lost in time. But it seemed there was nothing at all. He listened politely for a few minutes, then took his leave.

Full dark had fallen, most people were at home, eating their suppers and preparing for bed. Noises came, the soft whinny of a horse in a stable, a raised voice in an argument behind the shutters of a house, but so much of the town was silent.

He knew the way back to Knifesmithgate. He could tell just where he was by the feel and the smell of a street. Up above, thousands upon thousands of stars shone, more than any man could begin to count. A perfect display of God's power, the beauty of a universe. He stood and looked at them for a moment, lost among them and wondering what each little piece of light up there contained.

CHAPTER FOURTEEN

Finally, he started to walk again. But something was wrong. He wasn't alone. There was nothing he could hear, and nothing he could see in the blackness. He could only feel it. Someone was there. He slipped his knife from its sheath and listened closely, hardly daring to breathe.

John sensed the attack; he couldn't see it. Movement that made the air flutter against his cheek. It was enough of a warning that he could throw himself to one side, landing in a crouch, and hearing a grunt of frustration.

How many of them? One? Two? It couldn't be more than that, they'd be making noise and getting in each other's way. Most likely a man on his own.

Staying low, he moved to his left, listening for the smallest sound. There. The man hadn't moved. John picked up a few pebbles from the road and tossed them behind his attacker. An old trick, but it worked. He heard a sudden sound as the man turned, trying to discover who might be there.

It was a chance, the best one he was likely to have. John lunged forward. But a guess. He still couldn't see him, couldn't even make out a darker shape against the blackness of the night. He had to hope.

The point of his knife touched something. It ripped through cloth and into flesh. The man cried out, then quickly stifled it into silence.

John pulled back, freeing his blade. What had he hit? Much too high for the leg or the belly. Not the chest; he'd have touched hard bone. It must have been the man's arm. Deep enough to hurt him and make it useless.

He could hear the man's breathing now, a low, harsh wheeze. He could *smell* the thick, foul stench of him. A moment's hesitation, then the man was skittering away, running down the street.

For a moment, John thought about following. Catch the man and bring him before the coroner. Strong would make him talk and find out who'd employed him. Then the idea passed.

If he'd been younger, if he hadn't had a wife and family, John would have done it. He'd have plunged after the man without a thought. But his responsibilities stopped him. Chesterfield wasn't that large. It shouldn't be difficult to find a man with a knife wound to his arm.

He was breathing hard as he turned for home. Suddenly, all the fear hit him. He'd hardly done a thing, but he was drained, so frightened he could barely move. The attacker wasn't a robber who'd gone after his purse. He was too sharp, too silent for that. He was a man who was paid to kill. With just a little more luck he'd have succeeded.

The squires, the stranger he'd encountered on the way back from Baslow, the attack on l'Honfleur when he was hunting and now this. A shiver ran through him. In his mind he knew he was probably safe, but he still kept the knife in his hand until he'd locked and barred the front door of his house behind him.

The place was quiet and dark, everyone already asleep. Better that way; he didn't have to explain anything. No need to use his tinder box to start a flame in one of the rushlights; he knew the hall well enough to reach for the jug and a mug of ale. Sitting quietly on the bench, he let it all play through again in his mind.

There were three questions, he decided as his thoughts calmed. First, who'd done it? He didn't know. But in the morning he'd tell the coroner; his men could begin searching for someone with a wound to his arm. Second was why? That was easy: he must be coming closer to the person behind Gertrude's murder. It was the only explanation. And third, how? That wasn't so simple. His attacker had been good, used to following in the dark. Someone trained for it. An assassin.

• • •

The day was still young when a servant wearing the coroner's green livery and badge showed him through to the hall. Strong sat at the table, reading through papers. He had bread and cheese and ale at his side as he worked. The clerk hovered close by, but was dismissed as soon as Strong saw John.

'You look like a man who hasn't slept, Carpenter. Is something troubling you?'

'Plenty, Master.'

He ran through all that had happened the night before. The coroner was right, he'd barely managed a moment's rest. As soon as he closed his eyes it had been there. He'd slipped out early, while everyone still slept. He could start things happening, and it meant a little longer until he had to explain the attack to Katherine.

'You're certain you hurt him?'

'Yes, Master. There were still a few flecks of blood on my knife when I looked this morning.'

A nod of understanding. The coroner stroked his chin as he thought.

'Who were you talking to in the alehouse?'

'A table of old men. People who've lived here all their lives.'

'Why?' he asked, his voice full of curiosity.

'They'd know about the old resentments and enmities, and who might want to hurt my lord and his family.'

'Did anyone overhear your conversation?'

'Master, I don't know. It was busy, quite loud… I wasn't watching.'

'When did you know someone was following you?'

'I'm not sure. I sensed him.'

'Sensed him?' The coroner cocked his head to one side. 'How?'

'I just knew he was there.' He tried to find the right words. 'I felt him.'

'Were you ever a soldier?'

John's eyes widened, astonished at the question. 'Me? No, Master, never.'

'I've known soldiers say that,' Strong told him. 'They claim they develop a feeling. It can keep them alive in battle.' He shook his head in disbelief. 'You're a strange man for a carpenter.'

'I told you before, Master: I'm lucky, that's all.'

'You're certainly right about that. You're alive and you're unhurt. That's what matters. Are you sure you wounded this man in his arm?'

'It seemed like it.' John replied. But the hesitation was there in his voice.

'You're not sure.'

'It was dark, Master. Black. I couldn't see where my blow landed.'

The coroner held up a hand to stop him.

'I'm not criticising you, Carpenter. I just want to be certain. But my men will keep their eyes open and they'll question anyone suspicious. I strongly doubt we have any assassins in town, though,' he added with a smile. 'We're small. This isn't London or York.'

'He knew what he was doing.'

'We'll find out when we catch him. Did you learn anything worthwhile from your old men?'

He shook his head. 'Nothing at all. Not even much old gossip.'

'Then you'd better find something if you're going to earn that fifty pounds.'

'I know,' he agreed. 'I know.'

'One last thing, Carpenter. The man who rented the horse from the ostler. He's still not returned it. Now's it's theft. He'll hang when we catch him.'

• • •

Sooner or later he had to tell Katherine. He'd put it off, but now the coroner knew, the news would break across Chesterfield like a wave. It was inevitable. Like any town, it thrived on news and gossip, turning it over and over, examining every shred of it. She needed to hear it from him.

She was on her knees in the garden, taking up the last of the carrots. Martha was scrabbling in the dirt, loving every moment. Richard sat on a bench close to the back wall, in the warmth of the sunlight.

Katherine kept working as he spoke, digging up each purple carrot and wiping the dirt from it before cutting off the green top with a deft flick of her knife. When he'd finished she turned her head towards him.

'You won this time.' There was no bitterness or anger in her voice, only a world of sorrow. 'What happens the next time, or the one after that? You won't know, you'll be dead. I'll be the one here with the children. What will l'Honfleur or Strong do for them? Tell me that, husband.'

He knew the answer just as well as she did.

'It means I'm on the right path.'

'And you don't know exactly which path it is.' Her eyes flashed. 'You said that yourself.'

'I have until the fair begins.'

'No. You have to stay alive,' she reminded him. 'I love you with all my heart, but remember: luck can run out.'

He reached out, taking hold of her hand and pulling her to her feet. Martha stopped playing to watch as John held his wife close, hugging her hard. He could feel the warmth of her skin, the rough material of her gown, the pleasure of her flesh beneath the clothes.

'I will be careful,' he promised.

'How many times have you said that before? It's promise after promise and you always break it. Until this began, I honestly believed I could trust you again. But listen to yourself: all you do is play with words. And you play with us.'

'I promise.'

Katherine pushed herself back and glared at him. 'How many times have people tried to kill you since you began work on this? Go on, husband, how many?'

'Four.'

'Four.' She repeated the word as she stared into his eyes. 'And do you think there'll be more? No, don't look away. Be honest with me for once.'

'Yes,' he admitted after a long silence. 'Someone might try again. That's the truth. All of it.'

'Is it worth your life?' Her voice was quiet, but somehow it had more power than a scream.

'Of course it's not. But this is our chance at something better. If I earn that money, we can live without always worrying about the next farthing. Not just me and you, but the children, too. They won't always be scraping and shifting for money. But,' John added as she began to open her mouth, 'do you think I ever had any choice in it? The coroner sent a man to fetch me at the start. Do you remember that? My Lord l'Honfleur took over and told me what he wanted me to do. You know how powerful he is. When have I ever had the chance to walk away? You can blame me if you like. But please remember that none of this was my doing.' He squeezed her hand lightly and gave a sad smile. 'Please.'

'I know. I know all that. But how do you think I feel? Every time you go out, I pray and hope that you'll come home safely this time. They're the same worries I used to have years ago when you did this. I thought they'd gone, but they're worse than ever now.' She bowed her head and tucked a few strands of hair back into her wimple.

'We have more to lose,' he said. 'I understand that. You know why I'm doing this; I just told you. I wish I didn't have to; I'd rather be working with Alan and building something.' He thought of the leather satchel sitting in the hall and the tools inside, the most familiar things in his life, extensions of his hands. 'But it is what it is. I can't change that and neither can you. We can't wish it away.'

'Then what are we going to do, husband?'

'Keep on,' he told her. He wanted to believe in prayer. He knew that she did, without question. 'And pray. I couldn't have avoided what happened last night. The other times... perhaps I can be more careful.'

'But careful won't bring an answer, will it?'

John pursed his lips. 'No,' he said, 'probably not.'

Slowly, she moved away, reaching out a hand to take hold of Martha, and walked back into the house. The hem of her homespun gown trailed in the dirt. From the way she moved her head and the set of her shoulders, John could tell that she was crying. His heart ached. He'd tried to explain, to make her understand. No matter which way he turned, he couldn't win.

'Papa.' Richard's voice jerked him back into the day. He took a seat on the bench next to his son.

'What is it?'

'Why do you make her cry?' The boy wasn't resentful. He was curious, wanting to know.

'I don't do it deliberately. Sometimes… sometimes I disappoint her.'

'Why?'

He tried to find the words to satisfy. But they weren't there, they were jumbled and lost in his head.

'Because sometimes I can't be a good enough man.' He patted Richard on the thigh. The lad was so thin, he looked so weary and fragile. The hose sagged on his legs, and his jacket had to be cinched tight with a belt. Even the hood, a cheerful red, seemed too big for his head. 'Maybe you will be when you grow up.' The boy wouldn't be alive then. There wasn't a miracle big enough in the world to keep him here that long.

• • •

'My cousin the coroner told me.'

He'd been leaning on the wall around the churchyard, staring at nothing and letting his thoughts drift, seeing where they led him. John didn't hear Jeffrey of Hardwick come close until he was standing two feet away.

'Have they found anyone yet?'

'No, but maybe they will. You weren't hurt at all?'

He stood upright and held out his arms. The jacket was dusty, mended so many times that it was more thread than cloth, and his hose and boots were old. But there was no blood.

'Not a scratch.'

'How did you know he was there?' Jeffrey asked.

'I just knew.' He couldn't begin to give reasons for a feeling.

'And you caught him?'

'Caught? No. I stabbed him. I was lucky, that's all.'

But Jeffrey looked as if he didn't believe that.

'You were good,' he said. 'Dangerous. That means they'll think twice before sending anyone after you.'

'They?' John asked.

'Whoever is behind all this.'

'Do you still think it's Roland and Gwendolyn?'

He shrugged. 'It might be. Truth to tell, John, I don't know anymore. That's an answer that seems to follow, but... killing her sister, attacking her father. Would anyone really do that?'

'People have. Isn't there a story in the Bible about one brother killing another?'

'Cain and Abel.'

'And some brothers selling another into slavery?'

'They may be—'

'People do worse things than we can believe. That's my point.'

'How do we find out?'

John shook his head. They were quickly running out of time. The fair would start soon. 'I wish I knew. We need a way to shake things up.'

'There is one,' Jeffrey said eventually.

'How?'

'We pass the word that I've found some evidence and I'm going to give it to my lord.'

'No. Why would you let word slip out before you told him? I can't imagine anyone falling for that.'

'People believe what they want to believe. Give them some hope they can stop things before the truth comes out and they'll be running to keep me quiet.'

'And you don't know how to defend yourself. You told me that.'

'I'm a man of numbers, not the sword,' Jeffrey admitted with a smile.

'Then we can't put you at risk.'

He straightened his back. 'Isn't it my choice? I'm old enough to make that decision. Wise enough, too. Some people think so, at least.'

'Katherine and the children like you. They'd never forgive me if I let something happen.'

'I'm flattered to hear that someone would miss me. But tell me, John, do you think they'll give me any peace if I encourage you to risk your life? That's what you're thinking, isn't it? I can see it in your eyes. You want to make yourself the bait.'

'Yes.' It was true enough; the thought had probably shown on his face. 'But I know how to use a knife.'

'There has to be a better way, my friend. A safer way.'

'How?'

Jeffrey gave a slow shake of his head. 'I don't know that yet.'

'The fair starts very soon. My lord needs this solved by then.'

'I haven't forgotten. If I could, I'd solve it with a snap of my fingers and put the money in your hand. We're two men with brains. We have to think…'

CHAPTER FIFTEEN

A shout made them turn. The head of the coroner's men, holding his scabbard as he tried to run. Red-faced and waving, attempting to draw their attention.

'I've been looking all over Chesterfield for you, Master. Your wife didn't know where you'd gone.'

'What's happened?' John asked.

'You saw old Adam out at Whittington, didn't you?'

He felt a chill run through his body. Was he dead as well?

'Yes,' he replied.

'Sir Mark would like you out there as soon as you can. You know where to go?'

'I do.' He nodded as the man loped away, still panting heavily.

'I'll come with you,' Jeffrey said.

'There's no need,' John told him. 'The dead never look handsome.'

'I've seen bodies before.'

They kept a quick pace, even on the sharp rise up to the village. The house lay a little farther away. Its neighbour, where Oswald the forager had lived until he was murdered, already looked neglected and abandoned. Soon this would be exactly the same.

The coroner was in the garden behind the rough cottage. Whatever Adam had grown had all been harvested and the earth dug over. He was sprawled across the ground, a hoe on the path where it had fallen from his right hand.

No doubt about what had killed him. The blood from the wound to his neck had soaked into the ground, a wide, dark patch. There'd have been no chance to save him.

Strong stood close to the body and next to him, a woman John had never seen before. She looked to be close to forty, her face lined and craggy, staring down.

'What do you think, Carpenter?' Strong asked, and the woman lifted her head. Her eyes were blue; they seemed to pierce his skin, trying to see what lay beneath. Her hair was carefully gathered under her wimple. Not even a strand showed to give away the colour. A homespun, undyed kirtle over her smock. Rough hands with short nails. Except for her gaze, she could be any woman in any village around here.

'You can see it for yourself, Master.'

'This is Dame Eleanor,' the coroner told him. 'Adam's daughter. She came to look in on him. He'd been growing forgetful since his friend's death and she was worried.'

'Mistress,' John said with a small bow. 'You found him like this?'

'Yes.' Her voice was a tight croak, scarcely able to form the word. 'Yes.'

'How long ago?'

She blinked and glanced around, as if the house or the garden or the trees might be able to tell her.

'It must have been near dinner,' Strong said. 'She asked someone to come for me. After I took a look at the body I ordered one of my men to find you.'

Afternoon now. With dinner at ten or eleven in the morning, that seemed right. He squatted and lifted the old man's arm. The skin felt hard and waxy, the muscles and joints were stiff. He'd been dead for some hours, well before the woman discovered him. It had probably happened early in the morning. It was just luck that Adam had been found at all.

'Mistress,' John said softly, 'forgive me. I know it's difficult, but I need to ask you some questions.'

She stared at the coroner for a moment, then nodded her agreement.

'Did you come to see him every day?'

'No.' The harshness remained in her voice. She coughed and it eased. 'No. It was every two or three days. He said he didn't want anyone fussing over him, he could look after himself, although it wasn't true.'

'When were you last here?'

'The day before yesterday.' She wiped at a tear that had started to trickle from her eye.

'I'm sorry, Mistress,' John said. 'I know this must be hard for you. Did your father say anything about seeing any strangers near the house?'

'No, nothing at all. He told me he'd talked to you, but that was a few days ago. Not another soul that he mentioned.'

'You haven't seen anyone.'

'I live on the far side of the hill, Master.' She pointed her hand towards the distance. 'I wouldn't see anyone around here.'

John thought for a moment, then glanced at the coroner. Strong nodded, placed a hand on Eleanor's elbow and gently led her away, speaking softly.

Good. It gave him time and room to examine everything. So much of the ground had been trampled and churned by the coroner's men that it wasn't likely to tell him much. But there might still be one or two hints he could find.

'What can I do?' Jeffrey asked.

'Take a look in the house. See if there's anything he could have dug up and put in there. Whatever catches your eye.'

The garden ended in a tangle of grass and weeds that gave on to woods. John stood, eyes searching. As he saw a path pushed through it all, he smiled to himself. Had the killer arrived that way? Or was that how he'd escaped?

The trail was easy enough to follow, through the undergrowth and the trees to a clearing. The imprint of horseshoes was still clear in the dirt and the dust. A track passed close by and he began to follow it, until he saw where it joined the road, just below Whittington village.

At least he'd learned something.

Jeffrey was waiting in the garden, saying nothing as John checked the body's hands, especially the fingernails.

'What are you looking for?'

'I'm trying to see if there's any skin under there. He might have fought with his attacker and scratched him. But there's only dirt from where he was working.' He looked up and sighed. 'What did you find?'

'Some carrots and greens on the table,' Jeffrey said. 'They're fresh. I'd guess that he picked them and came back out to hoe the ground. Look at the rest of the garden, everything's neat.'

That was true; he hadn't even noticed it. Every strip and bed and border perfectly aligned. The few plants still in the ground grew in straight lines. Adam had been a precise man in his gardening.

'His attacker must have been waiting for him when he came back out.' He explained about the clearing and the track. 'We need to ask if anyone in the village saw a rider. Any stranger at all.'

There was one last thing to do. He grimaced as he took hold of the body and rolled it slightly. Where it lay, the ground was damp, the dew on the plants. Elsewhere, it had burned off in the sun. Adam had been killed early.

The coroner was still with Dame Eleanor. He excused himself to hear what the two men had discovered, nodding his approval.

'You go and ask your questions. One of my men will escort her home. Is there anything else you need here?'

'No, Master.'

'Very good. I'll be around the village for another hour if you learn anything important.'

• • •

The goodwives had more questions than he did. They wanted to know every little detail, something to chew over like gristle. John watched their faces as he spoke, as eager as hungry children being fed sweets.

But they had little to offer in return. None of them had seen a rider early that morning. One woman believed she might have heard a horse, but that was all.

'It's quiet here,' one of the women told him. 'The only traffic is to Chesterfield, Master. We used to have a few who'd come and buy from Oswald the forager, but he's dead now.' She crossed herself.

He believed them. They'd have noticed any horseman. But it meant that the killer knew the ground all about the village: where to turn off the track, where to leave the horse and find his way through to Adam's house.

'Who'd have that knowledge?' he asked Jeffrey as they strode down the hill, heading back towards Chesterfield.

But they couldn't find an answer.

It was the shank of the afternoon, the warmth gathering on the ground. Yet there was a hint of change in the air, that the weather would soon be turning its face to winter.

'What can we do now?' Jeffrey asked.

'We think. Have you watched anyone play chess?'

'I can play the game. Not well,' he admitted, 'but I know how.'

'And how many moves ahead do you look?'

'Not enough,' Jeffrey said. 'That's why I always lose.'

'Someone here keeps thinking five or six moves into the future. I don't think poor Adam knew more than he'd already told me. But killing him makes certain he can never be a witness in court. And the whole thing was very carefully done. It was planned.'

Careful, yes, but perhaps not careful enough. Someone had thought of Adam long after the fact, a loose thread to be cut. John ran his tongue around the inside of his mouth.

'Why now?' he asked.

'Why kill him now, you mean?' Jeffrey looked at him.

'Yes. It's been a few days since Oswald was killed and Adam gave his information.'

'Maybe it's what you said, making sure there's no one to offer evidence.'

'Maybe that's all it is.' But the idea niggled and worried at him.

• • •

There was pottage in the pot, warm and filling, with a few scraps of bacon hidden among the beans and the vegetables. Enough to feed Jeffrey, too, who spooned the food into his mouth with thanks as Katherine and the children sat close. He'd interrupted the story he was telling Richard and Juliana to eat, giving a vow that he'd finish once the food was gone.

He was true to his word. When he put down the bowl and the spoon, he followed them up to the solar, sitting and finishing his tale in a low voice. Martha was already up there, asleep.

John cleared away the dishes and watched as Katherine scoured and rinsed them clean.

'He needs children of his own.'

'I told you that the other day,' she reminded him with a gentle smile.

'You did.' He lifted the back of her wimple and kissed the nape of her neck. 'He has a sharp mind.'

'Clever, kind, and plenty of money,' she said. 'I'm surprised his family never arranged a marriage.'

'There is someone. He told me. But I think he's in no hurry after losing his wife.'

Katherine turned her head, eager to hear more.

'That's all I know.'

'Men! You don't have any curiosity.' She paused and stacked the bowls on a shelf. 'I heard there was another body in Whittington.'

'The old man who lived next door to the forager. The pair of them had been friends for years.'

'How many now?'

'Four. Six if you include the two squires. Too many.'

'Do you know who's behind it all yet?'

'There's one small possibility.' He poured himself a cup of weak ale, took a sip and swirled it in the mug. 'But I still don't see how we can prove it.'

'Then what will you do?'

He sighed. 'Admit defeat when the fair begins and make plans to sell the house on Saltergate.'

She dried her hands on a square of rough cloth and he held her close. Defeat. It was an awful word. He'd told her the truth, but until the time it happened, it was better to banish the thought from his mind.

• • •

As he stepped out on to Knifesmithgate and closed the door behind him, John was all too aware of time passing. He felt it in his belly, a tightness that gripped at him. A breeze that scattered the falling leaves along the street. Autumn already. A group of children scavenged horse chestnuts, good for food and for playing. He had a faint flash of memory, of his father pushing a needle through one of the nuts and tying a piece of twine. A conker so John could compete against the other boys. A moment and it had gone again, blown away by the breeze.

As he crossed the marketplace towards West Bar and the coroner's house, he saw a group on horseback. A man and a woman, plumed like peacocks. She rode side-saddle, her horse walking slowly, pointing out this and that to the man. Behind them, a pair of bored, armed retainers. Swords in their sheaths, bows slung across their back. Hired men, not servants; he'd seen them escorting other people.

The woman had a hard face, the type who looked as if she gazed at the world and always found it wanting. Glittering eyes and a pinched, sour mouth. Everything neat, good clothes and a wimple of brilliant white to cover her hair. The man with her appeared cowed, as if she always dominated him and he'd given in to it.

A strange pair. He'd never seen them before, he knew that; they were a couple who would have stuck in his mind.

'Did you see them?' Strong asked. The rushes in his hall has been replaced; the new ones had handfuls of rosemary, the scent tricking the thoughts back to summer as he crossed the floor.

'Who, Master?'

'Sir Roland and Lady Gwendolyn. They must have ridden past you as you came out here.'

'With two armed men to guard them?'

The coroner nodded. 'Arriving like they own the place.'

'Where were they before this?'

'Roland inherited a manor in the White Peak, close to Tideswell. His family made their money from lead mining, but the seam ran out a generation ago. They've probably been up there.'

'How far is it from here, Master?'

Strong pursed his lips and thought. 'Fifteen miles, maybe a little more. Why?'

'I just wondered.' Beyond the name, he didn't know the place. Not too far, a day's walk for a man, no distance at all on horseback. It was one more thing to consider.

'What brings you here, Carpenter? You don't look like a man brimming with answers.'

'We asked around Whittington. None of the goodwives noticed any strangers.'

'This man is clever,' the coroner said with a long, exhausted sigh.

'He knows the area very well. First with Oswald and now this. I don't know what that means, Master.'

'Nor do I.' He ran his palms down his cheeks. 'I was out well into the night. A drowning in the Rother. Nothing to do with this. A child, not even four years old. It's the kind of thing that breaks your heart.'

'I can imagine.'

'What are you going to do now?'

'Talk to Jeffrey.' It was a sudden decision. He didn't even know what good it might do. But he had nothing. Together, they might come up with some plan that didn't involve one of them as bait.

'I'm glad you find him helpful.' Strong smiled. 'He'd be a success if he ever wanted to settle to anything. He'll start something, last a few months and go on to something else.

It's no way to make a life. But the family is wealthy, he doesn't need to work at all.'

No need to work, John chuckled to himself as he left. He couldn't imagine himself in a position like that. A man defined himself by his work. It was how people knew him. He was John the Carpenter. He loved what he did. Even as he thought that, his hands began to itch, missing the feel of wood under his palms.

Today Alan should finish fitting the glazed windows. He needed to make time later to go and inspect the work then make sure the householder paid in full.

He found Jeffrey at the Guildhall, nodding and smiling as he talked to Gilbert the lawyer. He'd come back from London to take over his father's practice two years before, then watched the old man go into a swift decline and die. A lucrative business, perhaps, but one where words and truth seemed to end up in a tangle across the courtroom and nobody grew rich beyond the attorneys.

Jeffrey spotted John, said a few quick words to Gilbert and came hurrying across the room.

'I was about to go searching for you. Come with me, we'll walk out to Whittington.'

'Again? Why?'

'You'll see.' That was all Jeffrey had to say on the matter. As they strode out, he filled the air with inconsequential things, verses from romances, anything to avoid silence.

'That house there.' He pointed towards a neatly-kept cottage close to the bottom of the hill that led up to Whittington.

'What about it?'

'I noticed it yesterday. Anyone going towards the village would pass it, wouldn't they?'

'Of course. And the track doesn't bear off into the woods for what, another quarter of a mile?'

'Not quite so far,' Jeffrey corrected him. 'I paced it off. But yes. I came out here at first light and spoke to the goodwife who lives here. When she'd finished, I said I'd return with you.'

The woman was perhaps ten years older than him, with two young children to help her with the cooking and feeding the chickens. Her husband was a carter, delivering to Derby then on to Nottingham. She noticed all the people who passed. Stuck down here, her curiosity was natural, particularly as few went to or from the village.

Yes, she'd seen the coroner and his men the day before. The gossip had drifted down the hill about poor Adam.

'When I saw you earlier, you told me about a rider,' Jeffrey said.

'That's right,' the woman replied. 'He went by very early, before it was light, going up the hill towards Whittington. I never sleep well while my husband's away, and I wondered who could be passing through at a time like that.' She gestured out of the window. 'I was so curious that I looked. We don't have many go by, and never close to dawn.'

She looked from one man to the other, as if she wanted to be sure they believed her.

'You saw him again, you said.'

'Well, I think it was him.' She hesitated for a moment. 'No, I'm sure it was. As far as I could tell, the horse looked the same, with a white blaze on its chest. Coming back down and heading off towards Chesterfield.'

'When was this?' John asked.

'A while,' she replied, 'but not too long. Still early enough for the dew to be on the ground but full light. He was going quicker this time. Not a gallop, more a canter. But faster than the slow walk up the hill.'

'Did you see what he looked like?' John held his breath and hoped. A good description might give them the killer. But the woman shook her head.

'He was wearing a cloak and he had his hood up. I thought that was strange, because it wasn't a cold morning. I couldn't see his face at all. I'm sorry, Masters.' She lowered her head.

'There's no need to apologise, Mistress,' John said. 'We're grateful to you, you've helped us.'

'Did he murder Adam, do you think?'

'Probably.'

'I liked him. He was a pleasant old man. Him and Oswald. Sometimes he'd give me things he found.' She crossed herself. 'I wish I knew more.'

'That's plenty.' Jeffrey smiled at her, full of charm. 'Thank you.'

'It all helps,' John said as they walked back to town. 'That detail about the horse… I'll talk to the ostlers as soon as we're back in town. They might know who owns an animal with that marking.'

'I'll ask people I know as well.'

'Come to my house at dinner.'

'Are you sure? Won't your wife mind me being there again?'

'Not at all,' John told him with a smile. 'She likes your company. We all do.'

• • •

The ostler leaned on his shovel and frowned. The yard smelled of dung, piled up against one of the stone walls. Soon enough, men would cart it off to the fields, to rot down before it was spread next year.

The man reached into his mouth with a dirty finger and searched for a scrap of something. Finally he spat.

'Blaze on the chest… I know of three horses like that, Master. One of them's old Tom's nag, so you can rule him out. You'd no more ride him than you'd hunt with a lapdog.'

'What about the others?'

'One belongs to my Lord l'Honfleur. I know that because I've had it here once, when he had guests come to stay. Gentle beast, not too big. Not seen it lately, it might be on one of his manors.'

'And the last one?'

'Must be a year since I spotted that one,' he said. 'But it belonged to the Unthank family. The lad, the cousin of the boy who died a day or so back, he was riding it then.' He thought for a moment. 'Mind you, I heard he died, too, months ago.'

The Unthanks. Back to them. He'd dismissed them. But was it possible that they were somehow involved after all?

'No, I don't believe it,' Jeffrey said. They'd eaten, and now they sat in the hall with mugs of ale. Katherine had taken the girls down to the river to help her with a bundle of washing, their linen piled in a wicker basket. Richard was having a bad day, asleep up in the solar. 'I'd take an oath on it.'

'Be careful what you say,' John warned.

'I know, I know.' He ran a hand through his hair, leaving it standing in all directions. 'But I asked them questions myself. I know the family. They wouldn't do this.'

'The ostler said that the other one with a blaze is my lord's property. He's not likely to have done it, is he?'

'We don't even know if the Unthanks still have the horse. Maybe someone else bought it.' He shook his head. 'I don't know. All I can say is that I'm sure this has nothing to do with them.'

'Their fortunes declined after Gertrude preferred the Church to their son.'

'Yes, but... I still won't accept that they're involved.' Jeffrey shook his head.

'Go and find out. You know them. Ask a few questions. Find out where the horse is now.'

'I will.' He stood and tugged down his tunic. Today he was dressed in dark leaf-green, with a matching hood and liripipe that hung down his back almost to the waist. Black hose of fine wool and shoes of carefully-worked leather. No mistaking that he came from money. But he wore it without thought, not parading like a peacock showing its plumage. They were clothes to cover his flesh, nothing more.

The Unthanks, John thought. He didn't want to believe they were responsible. Jeffrey had vouched for them and he didn't want the man to be wrong. But they had a motive, there was no doubt about that. What of Lady Gwendolyn and Sir Roland? So far he'd found nothing to tie them to the murders.

He sighed, then left the house, striding quickly along the street to l'Honfleur's house.

'My lord,' John said when the man was finally willing to receive him. 'You have a horse with a blaze on his chest.'

'I do. But I own several horses. You already know that, Carpenter. What of it?'

'Who's ridden it lately?'

CHAPTER SIXTEEN

'I don't know.' L'Honfleur seemed amused by the question, not affronted. 'The horse has been on my manor in Yorkshire for almost a month. Why do you need to know?'

He explained, although it scarcely seemed worth his breath now. The horse was far away, it hadn't been ridden to Whittington.

'But the Unthanks have one like that?'

'Yes, my lord. They had, at least. Jeffrey of Hardwick is finding out more about that.'

L'Honfleur nodded his approval.

'What do you think about it, Carpenter?'

'I don't know, my lord.' It was an honest answer, the only one he could give.

'It changes everything again, doesn't it?'

'It might, Master. There's always the possibility it's another horse altogether.'

'That's true. Do I take it you're not still pointing your finger at my daughter and her husband?'

'At the moment I don't know enough to accuse anyone, my lord.'

'Then I'll remind you once more: find your evidence. The fair starts very soon.'

He was well aware of that. On his way here he'd seen a group of acrobats arriving, giving a short performance in the market square then passing a hat for coins. Tumbling, climbing on each other, falling and catching, all to the accompaniment of a tabor and rebec. People ran from all over town as soon as they heard the music; he'd spied Katherine with Juliana and Martha, their eyes wide with wonder.

Yes, the fair would open soon. Very soon. And when it happened, his fifty pounds would disappear as certainly as if someone had burned it.

• • •

He paced up and down until Katherine sent him out into the garden.

'If you need something to do, go and dig the soil.' There was an edge to her voice, but kindness in her eyes. Deep down, she wanted the money as much as he did. It would change their lives. They'd be rich beyond anything he could imagine. To men like l'Honfleur or Jeffrey, the amount might be nothing. To a carpenter, though, it was a true fortune.

He started to work, pushing down hard with the spade and turning over the ground. In a curious way, it was comforting. It occupied his body and stretched his muscles. By the time a voice called his name, he was surprised to discover he'd dug over a strip almost as long as a man.

'I'd hoped to be here well before this,' Jeffrey apologised. 'I know time is important.'

'You're doing what you can, I know that. Besides, we both know these people wouldn't speak to me.'

Jeffrey snorted, a mix of anger and frustration. 'It was hard enough to make them speak to me, and I'm kin. After a fashion,' he added, 'although you'd scarcely believe it, the way they treated me today.'

'The horse?' John asked.

'Yes.' He took a breath. 'They sold the animal last year. It was through a horse dealer; they don't know who bought it.'

'Then we're back where we began.'

'Your ostler might not know every horse in Chesterfield with a blaze on its chest.'

That was possible. But it sounded desperate and they both knew it; this was a small town.

'Maybe.'

'There are people arriving all the time for the fair. It could be one of them.'

John cocked his head. 'It wasn't a stranger who went to Whittington and killed Adam, and we both know it.'

Jeffrey nodded. 'True,' he said sadly. 'True.' He put his hand on John's shoulder. 'Don't give up.'

'I won't. I *can't*. But there is something I need to do. Come with me, if you like.'

• • •

Alan was waiting patiently, sitting on the floor and sharpening his chisels with a whetstone before rubbing everything with an oily rag. He looked up, smiling as John entered and began to examine the work.

It didn't take long. He knew everything would be perfect, every joint and fit tight. He tested the glass to be certain it sat firm in the new frames, and that those were squarely seated in the wall. He couldn't have done it any better himself.

A smile for the lad and he turned to the householder.

'I trust you're satisfied, Master.'

'It's good,' the man agreed, before his face hardened. 'But I employed you to do it, not an apprentice.'

'And yet you say it's good?' Jeffrey asked. 'You don't find any fault with the workmanship or the materials?'

'No,' the man replied. 'It's—'

'I taught Alan,' John said. 'He learned from me, he's served his years and his work is the equal of mine. Surely, Master, if it pleases you and you're satisfied, there can't be a problem, can there?'

'I expect the man I hired to be the one doing the work.' He'd lost the argument and he knew it. But he wasn't giving up without a final blow.

'When I came to look at the job, Alan was with me,' John reminded him. 'I told you that we work together.'

'Together! Not him alone.'

'Yes. But the coroner has asked for my assistance, and you're pleased with the work.'

'Perhaps you'd prefer to address your complaint to the coroner,' Jeffrey said. 'I'm sure Sir Mark would listen.'

'No,' the man said quickly. 'No, the work is very good indeed. How much do I owe you?'

He paid without haggling, and after they'd left, John gave Alan the full fee. The boy's hands moved rapidly. Are you sure?

'You did everything. You earned it.'

Thank you. He turned to Jeffrey and the fingers moved once more. A smile and he ran off.

'What did he do?'

'He thanked you. He can't speak. He can hear and he can understand, but his tongue won't work. He uses his hands to speak to his mother, and I learned to understand it.'

'There's more to you than I thought,' Jeffrey said with admiration. 'But it doesn't solve our problem, does it?'

'No.' He glanced up at the sky. It was the very end of the afternoon, shading into evening. Men would still be working. 'We should be able to find the farrier and the blacksmith.'

The smith only knew the horses the ostler had described.

'He's the one who brings them here if they need a shoe or it's shed a nail,' he said with a broad grin. 'Makes sense, doesn't it? Same if they need a new bit or a fitting for the bridle. He brings it here for me to do.'

The farrier kept his business on the far side of the Hipper. It was a small place, just the man hammering out horseshoes, with his son to work the bellows. He put up his hammer and listened as John explained, throwing suspicious glances at Jeffrey in his finery.

'I've seen one or two like that. The Unthanks had one, I know that. But they sold it.'

'Have you seen it since?' John asked.

'A man brought it in earlier in the summer. It had thrown a shoe. Very skittish beast, I remember that. Almost kicked young Harold.' He nodded towards his son, a muscular lad of about thirteen.

'Who owned it?' The man wanted to talk, to tell his story. The only way to find the answer in a hurry was to prod him along.

'Oh.' His eyes widened and for a moment he looked annoyed to be interrupted. 'It belonged to a servant of Sir Roland. You know, the husband of Lady Gwendolyn, my lord's daughter.'

'Yes,' John replied, 'we know who you mean.' His mouth was dry, as if someone had just blown dust into it.

'I had to chase him for two months before his steward paid, mind.' The farrier gave Jeffrey a half-hidden glance. 'I'm sure it's not true of them all, Master, but getting the rich to pay what they owe is a job in itself.'

'Once they have money, they hate to part with it,' John agreed, and hoped he was wrong. To find out, though, he needed to discover the killer. At least it made the farrier smile.

'Back to Gwendolyn and Roland,' Jeffrey said as they walked away. The shadows were growing longer and the nightjars were beginning to call.

'Much good it does us.'

'If we tell my lord, it might convince him to question them, at least.'

'It won't.' He'd seen it in the man's eyes. Unless there was evidence that was as hard as iron, l'Honfleur wouldn't confront his daughter and son-in-law. He wasn't ready to accept that they could kill their own kin. But who would want to face that?

Suddenly John felt weary, as if a weight had fallen on his shoulders. He stifled a yawn with the back of his hand. Sleep, that was what he needed. Hours of it, diving deep and waking rested and alert with his mind working properly.

'In the morning,' he said.

• • •

'The fair begins the day after tomorrow,' Katherine said.

He was lying in the darkness. The promise of sleep had been wonderful. But in the end it proved no more than a tease. After he lay down, it eluded him. Snatches of it, then shuddering awake again. He shifted restlessly as his wife settled beside him.

'I know.' His voice was a whisper. He could almost pin to the hour when the fair would start. The service at the church first to bless the fair, followed by the procession across Chesterfield. Then his time would be done, no more hope of fifty pounds.

There was still time. If he was lucky. But right now, luck seemed like sleep: an illusion. It had turned its smile from him.

'Do you think…' she began, but the rest of the words failed her.

'Maybe.' He turned on to his back and put his arm around her shoulders, drawing her close. Her hair tickled his cheek. The warmth of her body was comforting.

She was a balm of sorts. He did sleep, opening his eyes with Katherine still nestled against his chest. The first hint of light came through the shutters. He rose and dressed, washing his face and hands and brushing his teeth with a willow twig in the buttery. Some bread and a mug of watered ale and he was ready for the day.

• • •

John walked out along the road that passed Roland and Gwendolyn's house. It was still early, not even fully light yet, but already there were people and carts on the road, making their way towards the town. Some looked as though they were part of the fair, others arriving to sell at the weekday market. A trickle of them, all nodding and wishing him a day filled with peace.

But that wasn't what he needed. He wanted things to happen, to find a thread he could tug.

The house was awake, the shutters drawn back. He could see servants hurrying around. A man gathered wood from a pile and carried it inside. A young groom came out of the stable, cleaned off his hands in the trough and vanished into the house.

Early risers, gone to break their fast.

John stopped, studying the land. The stable stood apart, close to the woods at one edge of the property. He should be able to slide through, go in for a moment and make sure they still had a horse with a blaze on its chest.

It was safe, it wouldn't take long.

The air in the woods was dank and heavy. Ferns as tall as a man sprang up between the trees. Good cover as he made his way towards the barn. He crept along, his back to the wall, ears pricked for the smallest sound.

The door was open just far enough for him to squeeze through. He stood for a few seconds to let his eyes adjust to the dimness. Then he went from stall to stall, checking the horses. There it was. A sleek chestnut with the sharp white blaze. It whinnied loudly as he approached and drew back from him.

He hid, quickly ducking into a space behind a bale of hay, and hoped no one had heard the animal. Too late. The groom appeared, stroking the horse's neck and letting his voice soothe the beast.

'Seen something, have you? Must have been a mouse. Or maybe it was a rat. You come on out with me. That'll calm you down.'

The horse was a favourite, that was obvious from the way he treated it, leading gently by the halter and speaking softly the whole time. At the door, the groom glanced around and John held his breath in case the man might spot him.

His heart was thumping in his chest and his forehead was clammy with sweat. Too close, and the danger hadn't vanished yet. He crept to the doorway and cautiously peered out. The groom was standing in the sun and brushing the animal. Not even ten yards away. Hurriedly, he drew back into the shadows and out of sight. There was only one way out of the stable.

He was trapped.

John moved with caution. There were three other horses; he didn't want them to begin making a noise. The space behind the hay bales was close. He could dive back there in a heartbeat if he needed. More than anything, he needed to escape. The longer he remained in here, the greater the danger of someone discovering him, and he didn't want to have to try and explain what had brought him here.

He squatted and glanced out of the door again. The groom had moved away. The horse was between the man and the stable, big enough to block his view. A second quick look. No one else around.

He ran in a crouch, as fast as he could. Then he was around the corner of the stable, standing and dashing off into the woods. He didn't stop until he was a hundred yards or more away, panting hard as he leaned against a tree to catch his breath.

He'd seen his chance and grabbed it. But it might never have come. He could have been escorted out of there at the point of a sword.

A fool? Not quite, he hadn't been that. But neither had he been careful enough. Never enter somewhere unless you already know your way out. He'd heard a man say that once in York. A master thief holding court in an inn, but the words had stuck in his head. It was sensible advice. He'd ignored it and this had happened. Luck had smiled on him once more. He crossed himself and offered up a short prayer.

The coolness and the shade of the trees gave comfort as he made his way back to the King's highway. Still plenty of travellers heading towards Chesterfield. John stood by the road, retying his braies as if nature had called him into the woods, and began to walk back to town. As he passed Roland and Gwendolyn's house he turned his head to take a look up the drive. Just one more man full of curiosity. The groom was still there, walking the horse. No one had seen him; they'd never know he'd been there.

This was the last full day. Tomorrow evening the fair would start. He didn't have the luxury of time anymore. He needed to make things happen, to force them. The person behind the killings was out there, and he needed some way to make them show themselves. More and more everything pointed to

Sir Roland and his wife. He couldn't understand the reason, but did he need that? All he wanted was evidence of what they'd done.

Now all he needed was a plan, one that could be executed quickly and safely.

His boots kicked up the dust. By the time he reached the churchyard, his hose and tunic were coated in it. He took a drink from the well and splashed water on his face and hair. As he shook it off, an amused voice said: 'You look like you've already had a full day, Master.'

'That's because I have,' he told Jeffrey.

The man's eyes were bright and alert, their expression shifting as he listened to John's account. They stopped at the cookshop, ordering pastries filled with meat, and ate as they walked.

No stalls in the marketplace, but a thin stream of people moving to the fairground. By tomorrow it would be packed, even before the townspeople arrived. It grew and grew, but it was this way every year.

'You mentioned a plan,' Jeffrey said as he wiped some dirt off his shoe.

'It came to me just before I saw you in the churchyard. Some inspiration.'

'If God pleases, may it be divine.'

John laid it out. It was quick, a crude sketch of an idea; only to be expected when it came to him so hurriedly. But as he spoke, he started to believe that it could work. The beauty was that it wasn't crammed with detail. Yet it sounded convincing.

'It's possible,' Jeffrey agreed with a frown. 'But it means that people could come after you to try and silence you. You didn't like the plan that exposed me.'

'This one doesn't, though. The coroner will be the one spreading the rumour. He'll be saying he already knows. No one would try to kill him.'

'They tried to attack my Lord l'Honfleur.' Jeffrey's voice was a stark, sober warning. 'Don't forget that.'

It was true. Desperate people did dangerous things, and his plan might push them towards the edge. But he hadn't come up with anything better, and there was no time for refinements.

'We'll go and see the coroner.'

CHAPTER SEVENTEEN

'What do you hope will happen?' Strong asked after he'd heard them out.

'That the people behind Gertrude's killing will act,' John answered. 'Show themselves.'

'They might try to run,' Jeffrey suggested.

The coroner gazed at the ground as he swirled the wine in his mazer. He raised his eyes and stared at John.

'They could come after you,' he said.

'Yes,' he agreed. 'I'll be watching and I know how to defend myself. You've seen that.'

'You said it yourself, the first time we met: you've been lucky. Most men find their luck runs out when it goes up against a sword or an arrow. Are you willing to risk that?'

He tried to push an image of Katherine and the children to the back of his mind.

'I am.'

'That's your choice, although I think it's foolish.' The coroner's voice turned grave. 'But your way puts me in danger, too. More than that, it doesn't make sense. If you've told me who's responsible, why haven't I arrested them for the murder?'

'You haven't done it because you want to talk to my Lord l'Honfleur first and he's away hunting,' Jeffrey said. 'It's true. He left an hour ago and he's not due back until tomorrow evening, just before the start of the fair.'

'It sounds reasonable,' the coroner admitted. 'After all, it was his daughter they killed.' He paused for a moment. 'What happens if no one shows themselves?'

'Then we've lost,' Jeffrey said. 'But at least we'll have tried.'

'These people are clever,' John said. 'They might not believe it. But if they were worried enough to try something as foolish as attacking my lord, then they may well be desperate by now. You have guards, Master. Keep them alert.'

'I shall. Believe me, I shall.' He sighed. 'Tell me honestly, Carpenter, don't you have any better ideas to try? I'll do this if we have to, but I don't like it. The whole thing is so flimsy that a small breath of wind could topple it.'

Sir Mark was right; John knew that. The plan was weak, it was shaky, it didn't hold up to any serious thought. But there was nothing else. And he meant what he'd said. Anyone willing to attack l'Honfleur was already teetering on the edge. They wouldn't take time to examine things too closely. They'd lash out in the hope of saving themselves. The more they did that, the greater the chance that they'd reveal their identities. He hoped it was that way. He was wagering he was correct, and it was a heavy bet. He was gambling with his life and his future. With the fortune that might become his.

'Master, if there was anything else at all, I'd do it.'

'Then we don't have much choice. My lord won't be happy, but I daresay if it works, he won't care.' Another sigh, this one resigned. 'Within the hour I'll see that word leaks out. By later this afternoon most people in Chesterfield should know. Does that satisfy you, Carpenter?'

'Yes, Master. Thank you.'

• • •

'It's done,' Jeffrey said as they stood in the sunshine on the market square. A few high, pale clouds sat over the hills to the west, but otherwise it looked like another glorious day. All around, life would carry on. The fields would be ploughed, cattle would be moved and milked and the sheep would be herded. The simple routines of life.

But for the next day, John's life would alter. He needed to stay aware. To keep himself safe. To keep his family safe.

'John, your mind is miles away,' Jeffrey said.

'I'm just thinking. Planning.'

'I have an idea. Ask Strong for one of his men to watch your wife and children.'

It was a good idea. Simple, easy, and the coroner agreed without a murmur.

'He'll arrive later today and stay in your house until the service begins tomorrow. Keep your family inside. If nothing has happened by the service, they'll be safe enough.'

'Yes, Master. Thank you.'

A final roll of the dice to bring his family the fifty pounds and keep them secure forever. As he walked home, John offered up a prayer.

• • •

'Here?' Katherine said.

'It's only for a day. Until we go to the church tomorrow for the blessing to open the fair.' He tried to make it sound reasonable, to make it seem like nothing at all, but he knew she wouldn't accept it so easily. Maybe he should have married one of those women who took everything her husband said as an order. A woman who obeyed without question.

Even as the thought came, it vanished again. He couldn't have been happy with anyone like that. He needed someone with spirit, someone who could stand up to him and question his ideas. A woman to keep him on his mettle. That was what he had in Katherine, and it was a fine bargain. He was a lucky man. But at times like this he could wish she'd be more compliant.

'Why, husband? Do you think we'll be in danger?'

'No,' he told her. 'But with these people… I'd rather be certain that you were safe. This way you will be, especially if you stay in the house where the guard can keep watch.'

Her eyes flashed, but she said nothing for a moment.

'Who will be guarding you?'

'I can look out for myself.'

'I see. And why don't you stay at home with us?'

'I need to be out there, to draw them—'

'—to be the bait,' she said.

She was right, but he couldn't put it that way.

'To lure them. The coroner's men will be waiting to take them.'

'Do you at least know who they are?' she asked. 'Will you be able to watch for them?'

'I think I do.'

She stared at him, her face giving nothing away.

'And do you believe you're right?'

'I do,' he told her. 'I'd swear it on the Bible in the church.'

'You won't stop and try another way?'

'I can't. There isn't any other way that I can find. I don't know what else to do. And I want an answer. I want that fifty pounds for us so we're not worrying about money every single day.'

She reached out and took both his hands in hers.

'Then may God give us all His grace and protection.'

• • •

He wasn't a man of deep faith, but John walked over to the church. Inside, he let the grandeur of the building rise around him and he prayed he'd be successful. More than that, he asked that he would stay alive and whole.

His words rose, but had they been heard? How many others in the world were praying at this moment? God was everywhere, He knew everything, but how could He be listening to everyone?

John crossed himself and sat in the porch. The sun was on the stones, leaving them pleasantly warm to his touch. The town was noisy. Over his head, men continued to work on the church roof, on the promise of a bonus if it was finished before the service that would open the fair.

The weekday market was winding down, sellers calling out their produce, prices cut and cut so they didn't have to carry it home. The goodwives were all gathered like buzzards to swoop on the bargains in a battle of wimples and wrinkled hands.

The carts were loud as they trundled slowly along the streets with their wheels rumbling and squeaking, so many needing grease or fat on their axles. There was no peace in the world these days. Each year, the volume grew.

It meant there were more people. In those years after the pestilence, England had seemed like an empty place. He remembered walking all day and scarcely seeing a living soul. Smoke from a chimney had felt like a sign of hope. It meant that someone else was alive in the country that God seemed to have forsaken.

Leave it, he told himself. Let the past lie. He needed to keep his mind on the present, to be aware of everything and everyone around.

The sunlight picked out a silhouette in the church doorway and for a moment John began to reach for his knife. Then the figure held up his hands.

'It's me.'

'I couldn't see your face.'

'There's no need to be worried yet, the word won't have spread,' Jeffrey said. 'But better too early than too late.'

'Keep your own knife close,' John told him. 'You're a part of this, too.'

'I'll be safe. No one will think about me.'

'So you hope.'

With a grimace, the man nodded his agreement. 'I do. I'm no man for a battle.'

'It won't come to that. Not for you.'

'And for you?'

'Maybe. But I knew that when I suggested all this.'

'The coroner was right, John. A knife is no match for a sword or an arrow. Take care, my friend.'

'I will.' A movement above caught his eye and he lifted his head. But it was just a formation of geese flying south. Hard to believe on these balmy autumn days, but winter would arrive all too soon.

'What do we do now?' Jeffrey asked.

'We wait and hope something happens.' He guided them towards the alehouse on Low Pavement.

Men looked at them from the corner of their eyes and kept a small distance away. It hadn't taken very long for the rumours to spread, he thought with satisfaction.

They sat, talking about this and that. The weather, business. Nothing personal, nothing that came close to hope or fear. John kept his back to the wall, watching the people who sat at the benches and drank, all those who entered or left. The knife was loose in its sheath, easy to grab and pull. He was ready.

They passed an hour, but he didn't see anyone suspicious. No strangers. Just poor men in mended tunics and hose, with worn-down shoes and endless sorrow in their eyes. Men without work and without a future.

As they left, he took the lead, pausing in the doorway to look around. A flash of movement from the opening on an alley across the street. John pulled back, pushing Jeffrey to the ground.

He heard the dull sound as the knife hit the door frame and the blade buried itself in the wood. Slowly, very slowly, he glanced out. People had stopped to stare. No killer would dare try again with them all watching. He helped Jeffrey to his feet.

The knife had been thrown hard; it took all his strength to wrench it free. Thrown well, far too close for any comfort. He could feel his hand shaking as he held the blade. It was finely balanced, made for throwing. No knifesmith in Chesterfield had produced something like this. Pushing down his fear, John put the weapon into his scrip.

'Are you all right?'

'Yes,' he lied. He'd been ready for an attack, but he hadn't anticipated one like that. There were so many ways to kill a man. It was impossible to anticipate them all.

People had moved on, muttering and talking. Soon it would be all over town. He crossed the road and stared up the alley. Plenty of deep shadows for a man to hide. It led into the warren of streets that made up the Shambles. Not just the home of the butchers; it was where so many of the lawless lived.

There was no sense in even searching; the man would be long gone. All he would do would be put himself in greater danger. Instead, he searched his mind, looking at the fragment of a moment when he'd seen the knife thrower.

What had he looked like?

A dark hood. He was certain of that. It covered the man's hair, and a long liripipe dangled over his shoulder. A mouth set in concentration. Someone who'd waited and waited for the perfect moment. Thick stubble around the chin. Grey, John thought, but as he examined the image in his head, he couldn't be sure.

Black clothes, he thought, but much of him had been hidden in the shadows. It was impossible to be more certain than that. How tall? A little smaller than him. For some reason, he imagined the man was well-muscled, although he hadn't seen enough of him to really know. Try as he might, there was nothing more than that. He could pass the man on the street and never identify him.

'John?' Jeffrey asked.

'I was just thinking.' He tried to sound cheerful, but he knew his voice was brittle and the smile was false.

'How can we keep you safe?'

'You can't. That was the aim, remember? To make me and the coroner into bait to lure them out.'

'Then it's working.' His voice was filled with sorrow. 'But can you survive?'

John glanced back at the alley. 'Let's hope so.'

He'd been quick enough. Lucky enough. God's good grace still shone down on him. For how long, though? At least he knew something about himself now; he considered his life to be worth fifty pounds.

Jeffrey was nervous, terrified. He started at every tiny sound and his eyes darted around, trying to see each little thing. His body seemed to hum with fear.

'Why don't you go and keep Katherine and the children company?' John said as they reached the marketplace. It would be easier without him around. Safer to have Jeffrey out of the way, in a place where he'd feel he was doing something useful.

'Are you sure?' he asked, but he seemed relieved at the question. He could go, be away from the danger, and not feel like a coward who was abandoning his friend.

'Go. I'll feel better knowing you're looking after them.'

He watched Jeffrey hurry away, then glanced around. Plenty of people moving but nobody who looked dangerous.

The knife thrower had left him frightened. But he daren't show that to Jeffrey; the man would have become frantic. He needed calm heads around him. He needed to be ready. They'd come after him sooner than he'd anticipated. They'd failed this time. They'd try again. He could feel that in his bones. And they'd do it soon.

He walked until dinner, his gaze always searching. John knew he was a target, but nobody else came for him. Doubt and fear rippled up his spine, but there was no substance behind the feelings.

Finally, he made his way home. As he came around the screen and into the hall, Jeffrey was standing with a knife in his hand.

'I'm a friend,' John said with a smile. Martha and Juliana ran to him. The older girl was too large to carry now, but he scooped Martha into his arms and swung her until she began to squeal.

'Don't,' Katherine warned. 'She's just eaten. I don't want it ending up on the rushes.'

He sat and gulped down his pottage, watching with pleasure as Jeffrey entertained the children with a story. They were transported by his words, taken to a place of wolves and bears, where men did great deeds. It was a pity the world wasn't as simple as that.

'He told me what happened,' Katherine said quietly as John ate. 'Jeffrey said you saved his life.'

He paused with the spoon halfway to his mouth. 'He did? He's exaggerating. He was never in any danger from the knife.'

She cocked her head. Lines were etched around the corners of her eyes and her mouth. Worry, anguish, all the things that living through each day brought. She glanced towards Jeffrey than back again.

'He said it came very close to your head.'

'Not that close.'

'John…'

'I saw the man who threw it. I was out of the way.'

'We keep going over and over this, husband.' Her voice remained steady, the look of love never left her face. But sorrow ran underneath it all.

'We'll catch them.'

'How can you be so sure?'

The answer was simple: he had to believe that his plan would work. It was all that he had.

'We'll catch them,' he repeated, 'because they're desperate, and that means they'll make mistakes. I'll be ready. The coroner's men will be ready.' He squeezed her hand and tried to reassure her with a smile. 'And we'll have our fifty pounds.'

'I pray you're right. I want to believe you.'

'Just wait. It'll happen.' He looked around the room, seeing the work that needed to be done. 'This will all be the way it looked when Martha was young. Your old house will be fine again.'

'Yes,' she said. She picked up his empty bowl and vanished into the buttery.

He didn't follow. What could he say? What could he do?

In the solar, he changed into his other tunic, the old one from the bottom of the chest. He'd put on weight these last few years and it felt tight on him now, more comfortable unbuttoned across the chest and the belly. It was red, the colour long-faded and dulled. A black hood, the older, short fashion without the liripipe that trailed down the back. It might fool some people who expected him in his other clothes. And just a moment could be all the advantage he'd need.

211

The afternoon was warm, but leaves were falling from the old trees in the churchyard. Autumn was just beginning to tighten its grip.

He walked out to the fairground, out past the market square and West Bar. No one suspicious, nobody paying him too much attention. He was just one more person in the crowd.

The street of booths were all carefully laid out, the field full of sounds, music and shouting, laughter and small explosions of anger. A welter of languages and accent. He kept one hand on the hilt of his knife as he walked, the other on his scrip in case someone tried to cut and steal it. Any small loss was a huge defeat for a poor man.

Up and back, and no one followed him. Then, from the corner of his eye, he noticed a man who seemed to be paying too much attention to the way he put one foot in front of another. He was making a great effort to be sure he walked in a completely straight line. Only drunks did that, and the man didn't have that look about him.

It wasn't the way ordinary people walked. Their footsteps were thoughtless, they wavered from side to side. He'd seen it often enough in all the miles he'd tramped around the North.

Who was the man? Was he following and trying to hide it?

There was only one way to find out. At the corner John turned from the High Street on to Low Shambles. But the man never wavered, walking on and not even turning his head.

He felt his heart beating fast, thumping in his chest. He was seeing danger in everything. Better than reckless, though. A cautious man had a better chance of staying alive.

John walked down the narrow street. The air was thick and greasy with the iron tang of blood from the butchers' shops. Men called out their wares. He hurried by, never looking, turning past the old Knights Templar resting house and sliding through to Packers Row. The streets opened up again and he could take a deep breath of sweet air.

He glanced over his shoulder and saw a pair of men watching. They were big, dangerous. Not wearing any livery, thick leather jerkins over their linen and boots made for marching, not walking around a town.

John started to walk. Quickly, as if he was late to meet someone, but careful not to look as if he was running. He forced himself to go fifty yards before he checked again. They were still there, still coming. Their eyes were fixed on him. A steady, even pace, no rush. No swords, and the knives were still tucked into leather sheaths on their belts.

A quicker pace. Not dashing yet, but moving fast enough to make people stare. There was one place in Chesterfield he'd have the advantage. Somewhere he knew that they wouldn't.

John entered the churchyard, following the path into the porch. A deep breath as he turned the handle of the door. Down the nave, then ducking to the side, out of sight. They hadn't entered yet; he'd have heard the low creak and sigh and the metal of the knob turning.

Very softly, he opened the small door set into the wall and closed it behind him, not making a sound. Then he was climbing the stone steps, a hidden spiral staircase that was set into the wall.

One flight up there was a room set back from the stair, still smelling of wood shavings and oil. He passed it and kept climbing, all the way to the top of the tower. This was the place. He'd worked here for a few days after arriving in Chesterfield. He'd broken his arm in here when a beam came down on it. He's seen the master carpenter's body where a man had killed him.

Looking up, he stared for a moment at the bracing that held the spire in place. There was no pattern to it, as if it had been assembled by guesswork. No matter, it was still standing, with the spire rising full two hundred feet into the air, calling to everyone for miles around. On sunny days the oak tiles on the outside glowed warm and bright.

John moved around, remembering the room. The windlass they'd used to haul wood up from the church was still standing; there had never been a need to take it down. And in the corner, at the top of a ladder, was the door that opened to the tower walk around the spire. Just wide enough for one man, looking down from high over the town.

He let the wind whip through his hair, then crouched below the low stone wall; he didn't need anyone spotting him up here. John rested a wary hand against the spire. The oak tiles were warm under his palm. He was scared to push down hard. The spire was only held in place by its own weight. The people in town called it a miracle. The engineer who'd designed it had always called it science. Whatever the cause, it was a wonder. He could feel it towering over him. From the ground it looked huge; up here, it was overwhelming.

He left the door cracked open. Whatever he did, the men would find him. This way, he had control. Only one could come out at a time. That improved the odds. He'd worked up here before, he remembered exactly what lay where and that tilted it all in his favour. Not much, perhaps, but it was the best he could do. John took the knife from his belt. Now all he could do was listen and wait.

They came, but they took their time. That meant they didn't know the church or the stair; they'd need time to find it and they'd be very careful. Good. Everything worked in his favour. Out of sight, down at the other end of St Mary's, he could hear the workmen still replacing stones.

Patiently, he waited. The pair were slow. But they could afford to take their time. They must know they had him trapped up here. Yet the hunted could so easily become the hunter...

He stirred as he heard the low creak of wood. He knew exactly where they were, standing on the warped board that would never flatten properly. Soon enough they'd discover he wasn't hiding in any corners. They'd see the ladder and the door ajar. With a pinch of luck, they might believe it was a way to escape.

John stood. The door was between him and anyone coming out. They'd be here, already committed, by the time they saw him. The sun was shining in a pale blue sky, and up here the breeze blew steadily, taking away any edge from the heat.

Wait, he thought. Just wait.

The door moved. No more than two inches at first. Someone must have peered out. But he was still hidden. Slowly, it swung wider and then he heard the shuffle of shoes on stone.

Not yet. A moment longer, and another.

He reached out and pushed the door. The wind caught it and it slammed shut. Startled, the man turned.

CHAPTER EIGHTEEN

'Are you looking for me, Master?'

For the first time, John could see the man properly. Not a familiar face, but not a stranger, either; someone he'd seen here or there in town, perhaps, without ever really noticing. He was large, the type who was slowed by his body. His eyes glowed like coals in a brazier.

The man's lips curled into a smile.

'Coming up here like this, you just made it easy for me.'

'Have I? Who sent you?'

The man shook his head. 'It doesn't matter. You'll be dead long before you can use that knowledge.'

'Then it can't hurt to tell me, can it?'

But the man said nothing. He took a pace forward, his knife hand loose, the blade winking and glittering in the sun.

Could he beat a man like this, someone so much bigger and stronger? He'd lured them up here, now he had to find out. Even if he won with this one, there was still another inside.

The man lunged. But he'd shown what he was going to do. Shifting the balance of his feet, looking at the place he hoped to cut, the movements that seemed to take forever.

There was a chance. John retreated. He felt comfortable up so high, moving easily and nimbly along the narrow path. As soon as he turned the corner of the tower, the men replacing stones would be able to see him. No bad thing, he decided.

It might be enough to scare off his attackers. They wouldn't want any witnesses to their murder.

The man was still coming. He looked more confident now, grim and deadly, raking at the air.

John moved backwards. He half-turned his head. Very close to the corner now. This was where it grew dangerous. If he had the mind to do it, the second man could come out and around behind him. A proper trap.

Around the corner. But he only took a small step. Something to tempt the man. It would be right at the edge of his reach, enough to leave him off-balance if he tried.

John watched, ready. The man was going to try.

It all seemed to happen with aching slowness. The arm swung out and down. John shuffled back, grasping the elbow and shoulder after the blade had passed. He used the man's own weight and momentum to force him along. His foot swept out, catching the man's ankle. It was enough to send him crashing against the low wall around the tower, with the top half of his body suspended over the edge and staring down at the ground.

One of the workmen pointed. Others began to shout.

'Happy there, Master?' John asked. He was panting hard, all the fear and anger welling up inside. 'Do you like the view?'

He kept hold of the man by his hood, aware of his smell, so ripe and foul.

'Time for you to answer a few questions, Master. Who sent you?'

The workers were already hurrying down the scaffolding and running towards the church porch. He didn't have long. Still, if he could prise a few words out of the man, then the coroner should be able to have him chattering sweetly.

'Who?' He held his knife to the back of the man's head and let the tip pierce his flesh. A thin line of blood trickled over his skin. 'If you don't tell me, then you'll tell it to someone else, and they'll make sure you suffer before you do.'

But the man said nothing at all. He kept his head turned firmly away.

John heard the footsteps pounding through the room below. Suddenly one of the workmen was out on the tower walkway, another right behind him.

'Around here,' John called.

They came into view, masons with thick hands, covered in dust from their stones. John stepped back from the man, taking the knife from his neck and letting go of his hood.

'Who are you? What are you doing?'

Before he could draw breath to answer, the man he'd been holding leaned further over the wall. John reached out to grab his belt, for anything at all. But it was too late. All he could do was watch him tumble all the way down to the ground.

For a moment, all the words deserted him. The man had killed himself, and in church. A sin magnified over and over. And why? Who had such a hold on him that he'd give his life for them?

He didn't know how much time passed before he stared at the masons. They looked as shocked as he felt.

'There's another like him in the church. You must have passed him as you came up.' He began to move, but powerful arms held him.

'Say what you like, but you're going to wait for the coroner. We saw what happened. He's going to want an explanation from you.'

'I'm working for him.'

'Then it won't hurt you to wait until he arrives and prove it, will it?'

He couldn't win this. They stood between him and the way down.

'Just stop that other man.'

The mason called down to the group gathered around the body below.

'Now just follow us down, Master.' A calming smile. 'You'd best give me that knife.'

He didn't say anything, didn't try to resist. By the time they strode out of the church porch, Sir Mark Strong and his clerk were standing by the body. He wore a pale green surcote over a tunic and hose the colour of dark forest leaves, a pair of riding boots tight on his calves. Two of the labourers were gesturing up at the tower, then turning to point at John as he approached.

'Who is he, Carpenter?'

'I don't know, Master,' he replied. 'He jumped before he could answer my questions.'

'Jumped?' The coroner raised an eyebrow.

'It's true, Master,' one of the masons told him. 'We saw it. This one told us that he works for you.'

'Not quite for me,' Strong replied. 'For my Lord l'Honfleur.'

Under the dust, the men turned pale.

'Did you stop the other man?' John called out.

'He said he was going for help,' one of the men answered.

Too late now. He'd vanished into the streets and they wouldn't find him.

As he waited for his men to arrive, the coroner shouted at the townspeople to keep away from the body. It lay, broken and empty, on the grass.

'What happened, Carpenter?' Strong asked quietly.

John gave him the tale, then the coroner summoned the two masons who'd appeared at the top of the church tower. He listened to their account, glanced up at the spire, then dismissed them.

'Who were they? Have you ever seen them before?'

'I don't know them, Master, but I think I might have seen them in town.' He shrugged. 'I'm not sure. Their faces were ordinary. I might never have seen them before, too.'

'Was either of them the man who threw a knife at you and Jeffrey?'

In his mind, John tried to compare the faces of these two with the fleeting glimpse he'd had of the thrower. It was too short. Impossible to be sure.

'I don't know,' he said again.

'You live a charmed life, Carpenter. Two of them came after you and yet again you emerge without even a scratch.' He shook his head in wonder.

'Have any men come after you, Master?'

Sir Mark shook his head. 'I've been at home.'

The crowd in the churchyard was even larger now, people jostling around for a good view of the corpse.

Strong watched them, then raised his voice. 'Does anyone know the man's name? If you do, say so, by the law of the land.'

He waited, staring out at the people. Finally, one man pushed his way forward. He was older, hair stringy and grey, most of his teeth gone and the ones still in his mouth brown.

'I saw him on the road coming here two days ago.' He nodded down at the body. 'He was with another man. There was something about them, they struck me as a pair of thieves.'

'What did the other man look like?' the coroner asked. He looked at the clerk to be certain he was noting down every word.

'Like this one. Big. A hard face.' He shrugged.

'You said they were coming here.'

'That's right. They were just this side of Unstone. They were carrying packs and wore swords at their belts. They had the look of men who'd been walking a good way.'

'Did you speak to them?'

'I did, Master. They asked about places to stay and I told them they'd be lucky to find anywhere with the fair about to begin.' He turned his head and spat. 'Then they asked about some of the families – l'Honfleur, his daughter and her husband, and the Unthanks. I told them I don't know anything about people like that.' He paused for a moment and thought. 'They looked like men who enjoyed war.'

'What do you make of that, Carpenter?' Strong asked once the man had melted back into the crowd.

'Doesn't tell us anything helpful, Master.'

'The people they were asking about…'

'My lord was in there, too.'

'True,' the coroner agreed. 'But what about the others?'

'They're two other important families in Chesterfield. People know their names.'

Strong nodded. 'You should be a lawyer, may God forbid there are any more of them in the world. But it leaves us no further on.'

'Not quite, Master.' He'd heard something in the old man's speech. 'They had packs. They'd been on the road. That means they must have found somewhere to stay.'

'I can have my men ask. But if they found work as assassins, isn't it likely they'd be staying with the people who employed them? And that could still either be the Unthanks or Roland and Lady Gwendolyn.'

'Whichever one it is, we've worried them.'

'They've gone for you twice in one day. I'll have someone escort you home, Carpenter. We don't want to give them a third chance. You're not immortal.'

'There's not much time left, Master.'

'I know.' The coroner sighed. 'But if you're dead, time won't matter. If they're as panicked as they seem, tomorrow will give you ample chance to catch them. Wait in the church until one of my men comes.'

He came here every Sunday. But standing alone, he realised how large the building was. The biggest church in Derbyshire, he'd been told when they were constructing the spire. He could believe it. When he was here, it was usually filled, people crowded together, all the old goodwives off to the side where they could whisper and gossip. He saw the bench that the old coroner had paid him to make for the choir. Six years ago now. The wood had the smoothness and shine of wear. It was sturdy enough to outlast him; the thought brought a quick prayer that he'd enjoy a long life, to see his children grown and their children born.

'Master?' The voice was soft, carrying and echoing around the high nave. The man from the guard, dressed in the coroner's livery. A sword hung by his side.

'Yes,' John said.

Jeffrey was there in the house, performing conjuring tricks to make the children giggle and laugh. And there was Katherine, hurrying to him and throwing her arms around him before she stood back, holding him at arms' length to be sure he was unhurt.

'I'm fine,' he told her with a smile. 'Not a scratch.'

The guard coughed. 'Master, the coroner ordered me to stay here tonight and make sure nothing happens.'

John looked at his wife. She turned to the guard and said: 'Then we need to look after you. Some ale? Pottage?'

She had her pride. She'd never let anyone else see how poor they really were.

CHAPTER NINETEEN

The morning dawned with a whisper of a cool breeze, the reminder that autumn would arrive all too soon. As he sat up, he remembered what day it was. His last chance to discover a killer and make himself a rich man.

He needed this to be over. He needed that money.

Downstairs, the guard was stretched out, half-dozing on a bench. He stirred, but John waved him back. Nothing had happened during the night. No assault on the house. Jeffrey had returned to his lodgings. All was well.

He poured a mug of small beer and tore off a wedge of bread.

It was still early enough to feel a chill as he sat in the garden. Good, it would keep him alert.

He thought back to where it had begun. Out to Calow and the murder of Gertrude in the anchoress's cell. That was the root, it was where things started. But the branches were tangled as they grew, and the answer lay in them somewhere. Either he'd missed it, or he hadn't understood enough to realise what it was.

He'd followed a trail. Oswald the forager and Adam, his friend and neighbour. Both of them dead to hide a name and keep a secret. That was plain enough. He could trace out the path that led to their deaths.

From there, though, things twisted and turned back on themselves. They became as convoluted as some of the carvings he'd seen in the churches in York. A labyrinth. The more he followed it, the more he felt he was moving away from the truth rather than towards it.

He sat, chewing and sipping, trying to retrace the path, to see what he hadn't seen the first time. To try and understand.

He was still puzzling through it all when he heard the shuffle of footsteps on the dirt and turned, reaching for his knife.

Jeffrey raised his hands.

'The guard let me in. I didn't know if you'd be awake yet, it's so early.'

'I'm trying to make sense of it all. Pour yourself some ale and listen. See if you can understand.'

They were still talking when Juliana ran outside, demanding attention, with Martha following, less sure and steady on her feet. John gathered up his younger daughter and cuddled her on his lap. For a moment he saw the contentment on her face and envied her.

Too young to think about money and all the responsibilities of life. For her, the world was this house and her father's arms to keep her secure. So simple.

A voice interrupted his thoughts.

'You were going to tell me what you've been thinking.'

'Yes.' He sighed. Back here, with the weight of life heavy on his shoulders. 'I was.'

• • •

The sun was higher by the time they'd finished talking. But even between them, they'd discovered nothing. Juliana and Martha had lost interest and wandered off to play near the back of the garden, under the apple tree.

'We should go,' John said. 'We're doing no good sitting here.'

'Go where?'

It was a good question. He didn't know the answer. He had no destination in mind. No need to return to the church and be visited by the image of the dead man crumpled on the ground. But staying at home wasn't going to bring a solution. He'd done all his thinking and it hadn't helped.

He kissed the children and hugged Katherine as if this was an ordinary day. The guard remained at the house, the only sign that anything was different.

'For someone who was almost killed twice yesterday, you're very calm.'

Not calm. He'd pushed the experiences away into a room in his head and locked the door. Later, when there was time, he could examine them. For now, though, only one thing mattered: an answer. The right answer.

He could see the anticipation and excitement of people's faces. Another few hours and the fair would begin. Plenty of strangers mingled with the locals. A long line of people waited at the cookshop while the owner served with a grin on his face. The next week would fill his coffers for a year.

'At least we should be safe in this crowd,' Jeffrey said. 'Chesterfield is too busy for anyone to try and kill you.'

He hoped that was true. He was watching all the faces, but everyone looked innocent, caught up in their own little worlds.

The coroner had a guard outside his house. Interesting, John, thought; had there been an attempt on his life, or was it simply a way of keeping the curious at bay?

Inside, Sir Mark was slowly dictating to his clerk as the young man hurried to keep pace with his words. The coroner held up a finger, wanting John and Jeffrey to wait.

He finished and sent the clerk away to make a fair copy.

'Come with more thoughts about yesterday, Carpenter?'

'No, Master. I just wish we'd been able to catch the other man.'

'So do I.' Strong grimaced. 'But we didn't, so there's nothing we can do about that. He'll be halfway to Derby now if he has a grain of sense. I'm not going to waste time looking for him. Especially not with all those out there.'

'You have a man outside.'

'Safety, nothing more than that. Do you have any proof of who's behind the killing yet?'

'No, Master. Still nothing more than guesses.'

'My lord won't be pleased to hear that.'

'Better the truth than a lie.'

'Maybe.' He cocked his head. 'At the moment, though, a lie might serve you better. It would put that fifty pounds in your scrip.'

'No,' John shook his head. 'I couldn't say anything I couldn't swear on oath.'

'A good man.' He turned to Jeffrey. 'What about you? Do you have any ideas?'

'Nothing, cousin.'

'There was nothing on the body to tell us anything helpful. A knife and a scrip with three coins, that was all. My men are still trying to discover where they were staying. But you can see for yourself, all the people arriving for the fair. Trying to find two is almost impossible.'

'One's gone,' John said.

'People find better lodgings, cheaper places to stay. It doesn't mean a thing. It won't help.'

'Then we're back to where we began. We have possibilities, but no evidence of anything.'

As they came back into the sunlight, he could feel hope beginning to trickle away. He'd risked his life for this reward, and so far it had brought him nothing but attempts on his life. Twelve more hours and the chance would vanish altogether.

He kicked at a pebble and sent it skittering along the ground as they walked.

'Where are we going?' Jeffrey asked.

He didn't know; wherever his feet took him. Out past the churchyard beyond the house where the Unthanks were staying. Servants were busy in the yard, scrubbing down the long table from the hall. He remembered seeing it when he was working there.

'They're having a later supper tonight,' Jeffrey explained. 'Everything is being cleaned. Fresh rushes down on the floor later. Even my lord is invited.' He raised an eyebrow. 'That should show there's no ill will between them.'

'L'Honfleur won't go, will he?' John asked in astonishment. 'Isn't he in mourning for his daughter?'

'There are other considerations. Relations between families. My lord is a powerful man. But power ebbs and flows. Many of his lands are around here, so it's important to keep good relations with others who own manors in the area.'

It was like being on good terms with your neighbours, but on a scale he could hardly imagine, one that covered miles, not just a house on a street.

'Will Sir Roland and Lady Gwendolyn be going, too?'

'I expect so. The Unthanks do this every year and invite everyone important. They've always gone before.'

They strode out a little, along the road towards Newbold. He couldn't see anyone following them when he looked over his shoulder. And there was no prickle of fear rising up his spine. No sense that anything was wrong or danger was close.

'That's where Lady Gwendolyn lives,' Jeffrey said.

'I know. I've been inside. Twice.'

'What? Twice?'

He explained, hurrying over his visit to the stable.

'You were a lucky man. They could have found you.'

'Very fortunate,' he agreed. 'God's good grace was with me.'

They stood, staring down the drive towards the house.

'Do you think they're guilty?' Jeffrey asked.

'My heart says yes,' he answered after a long moment. 'Even if we can't prove it.'

'I can't be so—'

John reached out and placed a hand on his arm. 'Do you see him?'

'The one who just came round from the back of the house? What about him? He's just a servant.'

'No, he's not,' John replied urgently. 'He's one of the men from the church yesterday.'

'Are you sure? Absolutely certain?'

'Yes.' He wasn't likely to mistake that face. 'Run back, tell the coroner, have him bring his men. I'll stay here and make sure he doesn't try to run off.'

'If he does?'

'I'll stop him.'

Jeffrey paused to stare, then turned and hurried back to town.

John found a spot away from the gate. Brambles snagged at the wool of his leggings, and thorns dug into the fabric of his tunic. But he was out of the way, able to observe without being seen.

He loosened the knife in its sheath. If the man hadn't run off yet, it was unlikely he'd go in the next few minutes. Safer to wait until tonight, when the service and the procession began. Then it would be all too easy to slip away; no one would be around to notice.

It all confirmed what he felt inside. Roland and Gwendolyn had been behind the murder of Gertrude. It seemed impossible to believe that any woman would kill her own sister but it had to be true; her blood must run very cold indeed.

Time seemed to crawl. People passed on the road, almost all of them travelling to Chesterfield, eager for the fair to begin. For the first time, he started to believe that something good might happen. That he might find his solution and receive the money.

A man rode out from Roland's house. Wealthily dressed, a silk surcote spread behind him over the horse's flanks, trimmed in fur; rabbit or squirrel, from the look of it, nothing valuable. For a man who was struggling for money, Sir Roland looked comfortable enough. Haughty, as if he owned the world. He glanced around, not even noticing John, tugged on the reins and the horse cantered down the road, away from town. The two men with him followed, spurring their horses and sending walkers scattering to the road's edge.

John was still standing when the coroner arrived, deep in conversation with Jeffrey, with two of his men marching behind.

'Are you certain it was him?'

'On the Bible, Master.'

Sir Mark stood and thought, then nodded to his men.

'In,' he said. 'Make sure no one leaves.' He watched them go, then said: 'You two, come with me.'

No Roland, the steward said; he'd just left, gone riding with some companions. Lady Gwendolyn was visiting. They'd both be back before the service tonight. The coroner was welcome to search. He kept looking at John, knowing the face was familiar, but not quite placing him.

The men were brought out and paraded. He recognised the groom, and two of the others. But the man he'd seen just a short while before wasn't here.

'There was someone else…' he began.

'Only a man delivering for my lady.'

'What did he bring? Where did he go?'

'He walked out,' the steward pointed towards the gate.

'No, he didn't.' He looked at the other men. 'You must have seen him. Who was he?'

Most of them looked too fearful to answer. But one boy, small enough to be a helper in the kitchen, cocked his head.

'He went off into the woods as soon as the men with soldiers came. I saw him.'

'Go after him,' Strong ordered his guards. He turned to the steward. 'You're coming with me. You have questions to answer and you're going to give me the truth.'

'The tide's shifted,' Jeffrey said quietly as they followed the coroner and the steward.

Maybe he was right. Pray God things had changed.

CHAPTER TWENTY

There was nothing to do but wait as the coroner questioned the steward. John found a sheltered, sunny space outside Sir Mark's house and squatted, enjoying the warmth on his face. He could hear raised voices, the sound of a blow, then silence, before it all began again.

Jeffrey paced, unable to settle. At least he didn't want to talk. There was ample noise from the fairground in the distance. All the traders were making their final preparations. Hammering in stakes and tying ropes to keep their booths secure. A low, constant hum of conversation, like hearing a far-off swarm of bees.

He let it all wash over him. Now they knew who was responsible for Gertrude's death. He'd done what Lord l'Honfleur wanted, and with time to spare. He should feel content. If the man kept his word, John had made his family secure for life.

If.

Such a small word, but it carried so much weight.

How long passed? He wasn't sure, but the sun moved in the sky, climbing higher. Somewhere close to dinner time, about ten, maybe a little later. The door opened and the coroner came out. His face was set like stone.

'Master,' John called, and Strong turned.

'Give him some praise for loyalty, at least. He didn't want to betray his master or his mistress.' The coroner shook his head. 'He kept claiming they were innocent. I don't know what they offered him, but he didn't want to say they'd done anything wrong.'

'But?' Jeffrey asked.

'The truth finally came out, cousin.' He gave a grim smile. 'I need to talk to my lord. I saw him ride back from hunting earlier. You'd better come with me, Carpenter. You too, Jeffrey.'

One of the guards marched with them, the same man who'd first come to summon John. Apt that he should be here at the end, in his dark green livery and badge, hand resting on the pommel of his sword.

People watched them from the corner of their eyes then turned away. He could hear the muttering of voices as they passed. Someone made a sign to ward off the evil eye.

They were let into the house without a word, the guard left outside. As they stood in the hall, a servant brought a jug of ale and three mugs. Then the waiting. John walked to the window, tracing his fingertips down the glass. Each pane was thick, distorting the view, leaving it blurred and uncertain. Yet it was beautiful, too, he thought. And warm. No one would freeze in this room when the winter winds blew, and the fire would draw well.

He should feel jubilant. After all, he could afford a glassed window in his own solar now, maybe even one in the hall. Yet he was empty, with a rising sense that all he'd been promised wouldn't happen so easily.

The sound of footsteps pulled him sharply back to the present. L'Honfleur came through from the buttery, holding a mazer of wine. He was dressed for the evening's service and procession, a black velvet jerkin shot through with silver thread and a deep blue surcote that appeared to shimmer in the light of the room. High riding boots of gleaming Spanish leather and leggings made from fine wool. Without even thinking, John bowed, seeing Jeffrey and the coroner do the same.

'I hear you have an answer for me.'

'We do, my lord. John the Carpenter has done what he promised, he's found the people who wanted Gertrude dead and arranged her murder.'

L'Honfleur raised an eyebrow. 'People? There's more than one?'

'Yes, my lord,' Sir Mark continued. 'It's Sir Roland and Lady Gwendolyn.'

His face hardened. 'Are you certain of this? You're accusing my daughter of being responsible for the killing of her sister.'

'It's beyond any doubt, my lord.' There was strength and regret, all tempered by sympathy, in the coroner's voice. 'Their steward has confessed. They were also responsible for the attack on you when you were hunting, and all the attempts on the carpenter's life.'

John said nothing. What could he add?

'I heard about the man at the church tower.' He turned his head. 'But you look whole.'

'I am, my lord. God be praised.'

'The carpenter has done his work on this, my lord. He's the one who discovered the answer.'

John could feel l'Honfleur staring at him and looked down at the thick covering of rushes on the floor.

'Where are my daughter and her husband?'

'He's gone riding, my lord, and Lady Gwendolyn is visiting,' Strong said. 'We don't know where, but they'll be back for this evening.'

'Tell me, Carpenter,' l'Honfleur said. 'Do you feel you've earned your fifty pounds?'

He raised his eyes to look directly at the man. Lord or not, he had a debt to pay. One that had been witnessed.

'Yes, my lord, I do.'

L'Honfleur took another sip from the mazer and stared into the cup for a few moments.

'Bring me my daughter and her husband. Present me with the evidence then. Show me beyond a shadow of a question that they're guilty and the money will be yours. That's my decision.'

'My lord—' Sir Mark began, but the man waved his words away.

'That's my decision and it's the end of the matter. You have proof, don't you?'

'Of course, my lord.'

'Then it should be easy enough for you.'

John didn't take his eyes off l'Honfleur. There was pain on the man's face. He was caught between the two girls he'd fathered. One might have been his favourite, but he still loved the other. To accept she'd killed her sister would be to condemn her. What father could readily do that? He understood everything he saw in the man's expression.

That didn't make it easier for him. He'd dangled the reward. He'd used it as a goad. And now he was pulling it away again.

John clenched his fists, pressing them hard against his legs. He couldn't let himself show anything, daren't say anything. L'Honfleur had power. He was a lord, he knew the people who ran the kingdom. Whatever he chose to do here was law, and no one could gainsay it.

He turned as he felt something pulling at the sleeve of his tunic. Jeffrey, tugging lightly, urging him away. It was better to go now, before he lost control of himself.

'I…' Jeffrey began, once they were outside. The air seemed clean and fresh, but empty of hope. 'I'm sorry, my friend. I expected better of him than that.'

'There's nothing you could do. He made his promise and took it away again. Who's going to care that he cheats a poor man?'

'Be careful if you use that word.'

'What else would you call it? The coroner was there when he made his bargain. He heard the entire thing.'

Jeffrey glanced back at the house. 'My cousin may be speaking for you now. Remember, though, he has to tread carefully here, too. A word to the king from my lord, and we could have a new coroner here.'

Perhaps one who'd leave him alone. His situation would have been no worse if he'd never undertaken all this. But he'd have known exactly where he stood, and there wouldn't have been all these attempts on his life.

They pressed back as the gong cart passed, collecting the dung from the grand houses to spread on the fields. Pulled by a bullock, it moved so slowly, with a thick cloud of flies swarming about it, the stink rising clear to Heaven.

'There is one thing you can do.'

'What?' He couldn't imagine anything.

'Bring in Sir Roland or Lady Gwendolyn. He couldn't deny you then.'

'How?' John asked. 'Even if I see them, I can't pull them from their horses and march them to him.' He shook his head. 'No, it wouldn't work at all.'

'No,' Jeffrey agreed after a moment. 'I don't suppose it would. And Sir Mark will have his men searching for them.'

'I need to go and tell Katherine.' He exhaled slowly. He was filled with sorrow and loss, while all around, faces were bright with anticipation of the fair. Once again, he was out of step with the world. It seemed as if it had been that way since he was young. Surviving the pestilence when so many died. Lost, alone, trying to find his way.

The great fortune God had granted to him was his wife and family. With them he could feel that all might be right in life. But now… now he had to tell Katherine about this.

'Do you want me there?'

'No,' he replied. Kind as the thought might be, some things had to be done alone.

• • •

'He doesn't care about you.' She'd raged and fumed and strode around the kitchen that was set apart from the house. 'He only ever wanted to use you.'

What could he say? It was all true. He'd brought an answer l'Honfleur didn't want to hear. One he couldn't accept. And so he'd chosen to repudiate the offer he made.

They'd gone round and round on it before Katherine pushed her hands down against the table. She'd been kneading dough, and flour dusted her hands and face, turning them white as death.

'There's nothing for it,' she said. 'We'll sell the house on Saltergate. It was always stupid to imagine we could be a family with money and security.'

He placed his hands on her shoulders, stroking the flesh through her gown. He knew what this cost her. She was letting go of the place where she'd grown up, where her memories crowded in every corner. They'd still be in that house if not for Martha. Old Martha, who'd become a part of their family and left them this place.

Martha had been a woman with money. Her husband had been a successful cutler, dead long before John ever arrived in Chesterfield. She'd taken him under her wing, loved Katherine and the children. And in return, they'd looked after her as she grew older and infirm. Maybe their little Martha would have the old woman's spirit and humour.

'If we're paid a fair price it'll help for a few years. Things might be better after that.'

Might. Maybe. That was no way to live, moving from uncertainty to uncertainty. But only those with money had security. It built a wall around them. He'd wanted that for his family. But it wasn't to be. God had been good. He'd given all this bounty. To want more… that was churlish.

But whichever way he tried to think about it, the disappointment tore at him. He felt as if it was hollowing him out. And there was nothing he could do about it.

The hammering on the door stopped him saying more. It was loud enough to hear in the kitchen, even though Juliana came running through to tell them.

It was the man from the coroner's guard. His face was flushed and his eyes glittered.

'Sir Mark sent me to fetch you. We've spotted Sir Roland and his friends. They're coming back towards Chesterfield.'

'Where are they?'

'Someone spotted them out past Calow and came to tell us.'

Calow. Where it had all begun.

'The coroner is going to meet them at the bridge over the Hipper.'

'And then?'

The man's voice hardened. 'We'll take him to my lord and he can answer for what he's done.'

They were marching past the churchyard and down Soutergate, the hill that led to the bridge. The smell of leather filled the air as shoemakers and their apprentices worked hard. The fair meant that the town would be full of people for the next week. They'd have money to spend. New shoes, new boots… it could be a rich time of year for them.

The coroner and two other guards waited by the bridge. They rested at the side of the road, allowing traffic to pass. So many people arriving in Chesterfield. Chattering and full of anticipation. The fairground would be crowded with people tonight.

'I thought you'd want to be here for this, Carpenter.'

'Thank you, Master.' It was Strong's way of apologising for the way l'Honfleur had treated him. A chance to be one of those bringing in Sir Roland. If that happened, it would be impossible for my lord to deny him the reward.

A horseman came galloping, raising a thick plume of dust as he moved along the road. He reined in by the coroner and spoke softly into his ear. Strong frowned as he listened, then nodded. The man rode off again.

'Roland's seen us, or someone's told him we're waiting. He and his friends have ridden off again. They're heading north, as if they're going to Whittington or Unstone. You and you,' – he pointed at two of his men – 'fetch your mounts and follow me. Carpenter… I'm sorry. I'll send word as soon as we have him. You'll be there when we present him to my lord. My word on it, and I hope you believe me.'

He did. The offer was generous.

John trudged back up the hill with the guard who'd escorted him.

'You don't ride?'

The man shook his head. 'They scare me. I tried once; I was so high up I couldn't move. Someone had to help me back down.' He shook his head. 'Foolish, isn't it?'

'No. I think it's very sensible.' He looked up and saw the spire of the church rising high into the sky. 'Tell me, how are you on something solid?'

• • •

'Master,' the guard said, 'how safe are we up here?'

'Very,' John told him. No need to tell him that the spire was only held on by its own weight; that would send him scurrying back to the ground.

They could see so much from the top of the tower. The way the fields spread out, each of them hundreds of acres and divided into wide strips. The roads and tracks dipped and wound along. By rivers, through woods.

The guard pointed as he recognised the coroner's horse, then two others heading away from Chesterfield to find Sir Roland. No sign of him and his companions, though. They could see for miles from the tower, but too much was obscured.

'There, Master, do you see? Off towards the horizon.'

He had to squint. Even then, he could only make out shapes. Three men on horses; he couldn't have been more exact than that. They were riding hard, but that proved nothing at all.

'Is it them?'

'It is. They're putting on quite a pace. If they keep on like that, they'll be in Yorkshire and Sir Mark won't be able to touch them.'

'What?' John asked. 'Why not?'

'They're not wolfsheads, Master, not outlaws. Not yet, at least. He can't pursue them everywhere. His coroner's writ only runs in Derbyshire.'

'Ah.' He'd never known, never needed to think about it. Soon enough they'd be gone from view. 'We should go down.'

'What about Lady Gwendolyn?' John asked as they walked through the nave. 'She'll be back in Chesterfield soon.'

'There's a man at their house, Master. We'll be ready when she returns.'

'What now?'

The guard turned to him. 'We wait.'

CHAPTER TWENTY-ONE

Jeffrey was sitting at the table in the hall teaching the children a game that came from somewhere in his mind. They were caught up in it all, attentive and captured. Even Richard was smiling and happy, and that was something so rare these days.

John and Katherine sat together at the other end. Their heads were close and they spoke softly, only looking up at the laughter and shouts of the children.

'But if he runs off like that, doesn't that mean he's guilty?' she asked.

'I would think so. But I don't know the law, and I can't tell what's in my lord's head.' He grimaced and snorted in disgust. 'After all, I believed he was an honest man.'

She squeezed his hand and he tried to smile. But it was hard when he felt so bitter. To have everything right there, then snatched away on one man's whim, simply because he had that power.

The hours were passing. They should have eaten dinner a long time before, but only the children had appetites. Katherine had fed them. John sipped ale and nibbled pieces of bread. He was alert for any sound, a cheer outside, a knocking at the door. Anything at all that would mean something was happening.

And finally it came. The same guard as before.

'Sir Mark's back. He wants to see you.'

They marched through the town, across the market square and out past West Bar. Chesterfield seemed to grow busier with every moment. Was it like this every year when the fair began? He couldn't remember, but he didn't believe it bustled quite so much.

The coroner's clothes were thick with dust. He strode around his hall drinking thirstily from a mazer, crunching the rushes as he walked.

'We didn't catch him, Carpenter. I had to give up once I knew he was in Yorkshire.'

'What can you do now?'

'An innocent man doesn't flee like that,' Strong said. He put the cup on the table and pushed a hand through his hair. 'I've sent one of my men on to Conisbrough Castle with my seal.' He rubbed the finger where his signet ring had been. 'They'll be able to start searching.'

'I don't understand, Master,' John said. 'Does this mean he's an outlaw now?'

The coroner shook his head. 'Not without a court case. But unless he appears and shows his innocence, it seems inevitable. I want him found and brought back so he has to answer before a jury.'

'Has Lady Gwendolyn returned?'

'Not yet. My men have been asking. No one seems quite certain where she went.'

'What can I do?'

'Nothing.' He exhaled and clapped John on the shoulder. 'It might take time for Sir Roland to be declared a criminal. He's a knight, so he'll have to be tried at the King's Bench. His title demands that. But when it happens, I don't see how my lord can deny you the reward.'

He'd find some way, John thought. But it was safer to nod once and keep his mouth closed. Anything he said might come back to haunt him later.

'I'd like to join the hunt for Lady Gwendolyn.'

'If you want,' the coroner agreed after a moment. 'You can work with my men. I warn you, though, it could be an exercise in frustration. She might have run, too.'

Perhaps she had. But doing something would be better than sitting at home and waiting. Instead he was marching with two other men who wore the coroner's badge and green livery, calling on houses of the wealthy around Chesterfield.

It was a thankless task. They weren't welcome, even at the back doors that the servants used. Three, four, five different places and there was no sign of the woman. Finally, at the sixth, an admission that she'd been there during the morning, before dinner.

'How long did she stay, Mistress?' John asked the housekeeper.

The woman stared down her nose at him and sniffed.

'Long enough, not that it's your business.'

He was happy to ignore the insult. There was a chance to follow her and he was going to take it.

'Please, do you know where she was going from here? Both the coroner and my Lord l'Honfleur want to know. Lady Gwendolyn's father is eager to find her.'

'Then why hasn't he sent his own men?'

'Mistress, he knows we're looking. He has others searching elsewhere.'

A shameless lie, but he didn't care.

'She didn't say. You've had a wasted journey, Masters.'

Maybe it was true. Or perhaps the woman had said and the housekeeper chose not to tell them. Either way, it amounted to the same thing. They didn't know.

Coming out into the light, he glanced across at the stable. A boy was grooming a roan, brushing it with loving care as he talked to the animal.

'Give me a moment,' John said to the guards.

He approached the youth with a smile. 'You like your work.'

No answer, just a nervous nod in reply.

'Do you enjoy horses?'

Another nod, his eyes flickering between John and the guards.

He squatted down so that his face was level with the boys.

'Did you see the woman who was here this morning? She probably looked like she had money. I'll wager she had a good horse.'

'Yes, Master.' The boy broke into a smile. 'A beautiful little mare.'

'Did you talk to her at all?'

'She thanked me for looking after her horse while she was inside.'

'Did you hear where she was going from here?'

A shake of the head. His words had vanished. It had never been more than a distant hope, anyway. He stood and ruffled the lad's hair, then started to walk away. A thought struck him and he turned.

'Did you see which way she turned at the gate?'

The boy pointed to the left. Away from Chesterfield. It didn't tell them much, but it was something.

'Who lives out that way?' John asked one of the guards.

'No one, Master.' He shrugged. 'None of the names Sir Mark gave us. You can travel across the roads and go to Cutthorpe, but that's it. We don't have anywhere else to go.'

They hurried back to town. The spire was always in sight, a beacon. Home. The roads were full. He heard people chattering in different dialects and languages he couldn't understand.

They seemed to sweep him along. But their excitement and eagerness couldn't touch him.

Where had Lady Gwendolyn gone? Had she run? Something in his gut told him she was on the verge of it. But not quite yet. He felt that she was still around somewhere, watching, waiting, wondering how she could help herself.

• • •

'Well?' Sir Mark asked.

John told him the few scraps they'd learned.

'Nothing from the other men, either. I'm going to tell my lord that she's disappeared, just like her husband. For all we know, they have a plan to meet somewhere.'

'Wait, Master. Don't say anything to him just yet.'

'Why not?' The coroner's voice had a hard edge.

'Wait until tonight. Let's see if she's there for the service and the procession to the fairground.'

'All you're doing is giving her a longer start.'

'Master, for now there's no one after her.' All the coroner's men were gathered outside his house, waiting for their orders. 'And she's barely been gone any time at all. On an ordinary day we wouldn't think anything of it.'

'What about Sir Roland?' Strong snapped. 'Are you saying he might be innocent, too?'

'No, Master. He fled. Lady Gwendolyn... we don't know. I think she's guilty. No,' he corrected himself, 'I'm convinced she is.'

'Then why delay, Carpenter?'

'What can we achieve in such a short time, Master?'

'We can talk to my lord. I think he'll believe us now.'

'You said it needs the King's Bench to convict them and have them made outlaw.'

'That's correct,' the coroner agreed.

'And that needs to be done in London?'

'Usually. Not always. My lord could probably arrange a sitting in York or Lincoln.'

'But not done overnight?'

'No. The law moves slowly, Carpenter.' He shook his head. 'All too often, justice comes quicker.' He stood. 'Come on. We're going to talk to my lord.'

'Are you sure you want me with you?' John asked.

'Yes, Carpenter. I definitely want you there.'

• • •

Late afternoon sun came through the window and lit up the stitching on the wall hanging. A scene from the Bible, perhaps, or something out of the imagination. He didn't know, and it didn't matter. It was well done, the figures lifelike, their expressions caught to perfection.

They waited for l'Honfleur to appear. No wine or food put out for them, he noticed; they weren't being treated like honoured guests. Finally he appeared, sweeping down from the solar.

'Well?' he asked.

Sir Mark laid out the situation. Briefly, clearly, and precisely. L'Honfleur listened, head down, face caught in a frown.

'You're certain Roland is running?' he asked. 'Not just hunting or riding?'

'I'm positive, my lord. I went after him myself.'

'Very well,' he said after the coroner explained about sending word to Conisbrough. 'If they catch him, he can come and tell us what he's done. And my daughter?'

Strong hesitated. 'We can't find her, my lord.'

'What do you mean?'

'She's been visiting people, my lord, and we don't know where she might have gone,' John said.

'And what do you intend to do about that?' He turned to the coroner.

'The carpenter suggests we wait and see if she appears for the service this evening.'

L'Honfleur raised an eyebrow.

'Is that correct?'

'Yes, my lord,' John said.

'Tell me, do you feel I've treated you badly in this?'

'My lord?' It was the only answer he could give. He daren't speak the truth.

'When I refused you the reward until we had them, do you feel I was fair?'

'I'm sure you did what you thought was right, my lord.' He could feel a thin, cold trickle of sweat down his back. Fear of the wrong word, a dangerous expression. Anything at all.

'A sensible answer.'

He had no choice. As a man, he had to say it, to let it out, just to be able to live with himself after this.

'But, my lord, you know I had to run for my life when I went out to your manor. The two squires knew who I was. They tried to kill me in the stable and then hunt me down on the moor. I was attacked on the road back from Baslow. Right here, someone tried to kill me by throwing a knife. And I could easily have been then lying dead at the foot of the church tower. I hope you feel I've given you honest, faithful service.'

He looked at Strong. The coroner's face was ashen at his outburst. It was dangerous. Very likely it was reckless to speak that way to a man like l'Honfleur. But John felt better for the outburst. The man needed to be reminded of all that had happened, of the times he'd come close to dying. At the moment he'd done it for the four pennies a day the coroner was paying him. He would never blurt out that my lord had cheated him. But it was there, underneath all he'd just said.

'Then we will hope that my daughter is there this evening. I will want to hear her answers, and I'll know whether they're honest. And,' he added, 'I shall ask her about all that, too.' He stayed silent for several long moments. Would the man's temper boil over? 'I will say this, Carpenter. If she is there and I feel she can be tried on this, I will give you the money.'

A fair, even tone. No sign of anger on his face or in his voice. John began to breathe a little more easily.

'And if she's not in Chesterfield, my lord?' Strong asked quietly.

'Then that will tell me everything,' the man said with sorrow. 'If that's the case, the money will be paid.'

'You heard him,' the coroner said when they were outside. Late afternoon, and people were already gathering in the churchyard.

'I did.'

'I was there as a witness.'

Just as he was out in Calow, he thought, but didn't waste his breath. A rich man's promises were chaff, so easily blown away.

'Yes.'

'You were lucky, Carpenter. I hope you realise that.'

He didn't bother to reply. He knew. But he felt cleansed by it. He'd purged the bitterness that had built up inside. And thanks be to God that l'Honfleur hadn't been furious when he heard it. It was all true, every word, and it had come from his heart. Perhaps the man had been able to see that.

He wanted to believe this new guarantee. But the words didn't reach his soul. After the man had changed his mind once, he couldn't take them seriously. Only actions would change that.

'Prepare yourself for the service, Carpenter,' the coroner said. 'Tonight will be interesting.'

It will, he agreed. It will.

CHAPTER TWENTY-TWO

'You look like a man carrying the world on his shoulders,' Katherine said. They were sitting on the bed, a snatched minute away from the children.

'I feel like it.' He told her how he'd spoken to l'Honfleur. 'Was it foolish?'

She shook her head. 'You stood up for yourself. He cheated you. You know it, the coroner knows it. He knows it, too, if he looks into his heart. He must have, to make this new promise.'

'If he keeps to it. He's broken one oath.'

'There was always one rule for the rich and another for the rest of us.' Her face was set hard. 'And the rule for the rich is very loose.'

She combed her hair, pulling it through until every last, small tangle had gone. Then she used deft strokes of her hands to pile it up, keeping it in place with several small pins. Carefully, she placed the wimple back on her head, feeling around to be certain that all her hair was covered.

'Does that look fine?' she asked. No need to tell her that he'd seen the streaks of grey in her hair and noticed the wrinkles at the corner of her eyes and her mouth. She'd know they were there, in the way women did.

They owned no looking glass. Even Martha hadn't stretched to that. But there was a small piece of polished metal sitting on the chest at the foot of the bed. Katherine examined herself in that, making a few small adjustments with her fingertips before nodding her head with satisfaction.

She ran her fingertips over her dress, smoothing it down. It was simple, homespun cloth, but he thought she wore it like the most expensive silk, something fit for a queen.

He took hold of her hand. There was no lady's smoothness to her skin. The palms were calloused and hard, just like his. But people like them didn't have servants. They worked, not watched. Their labours were part of life. It was how they survived.

'Thank you,' he said.

'For what?' she looked confused.

'For not saying I'm a fool. For loving me. For being my wife.'

'I loved you from the very first day we talked. Do you remember that? You helped to carry my washing up from the river.'

'I remember it well, Mistress.' He smiled. More than ten years ago now. He'd been young, so full of himself when he approached her. She'd seemed little more than a girl. Who could have dreamed then how it would have turned out? That they'd be here today.

A shriek of laughter from the hall. Jeffrey had stayed, happy to entertain the children. In the last two days he seemed to have become a member of the family. Accepted without question, simply there and welcome. John wasn't sure how it had happened, but it pleased him. The young man had become a friend. From a different class, but warm and open, a man who loved life, who liked them for who they were.

John washed his hands and face in the basin. The soap was rough and coarse against his skin. By the time he'd rinsed himself clean, he felt as if his flesh was raw. He looked out of the window, saw no one below, and emptied the bowl into the street.

Down in the hall, the children clustered round, eager and ready to go.

'Soon,' Katherine scolded them. 'Very soon. You can learn a little patience.'

'A word,' Jeffrey said softly to him as he drew him through to the buttery.

'What?' he asked when they were alone.

'We'll be going around the fair tonight.'

'Us and everyone else who's in town. You know that, it's tradition.'

Jeffrey nodded. 'You told me what my lord has promised. It seems to me that you'll end up with your money.'

'Maybe.' He couldn't let himself believe it again, then have his hopes shattered.

'You will. I know you don't have money at the moment. You've been working for the coroner, not at your trade.'

'That's true. But what are you trying to say?'

'The children want their marchpane, their sweetmeats, their swirls of sugar. Ribbons and toys.'

'I daresay they do. Just like every child in town.'

'John.' He stopped and took a breath. 'You know I have money.'

'No.' It was his instinctive answer. Charity was good, if you needed it. But none of this was vital, it wasn't important. A day or two and the children would have forgotten all about it.

'Please. It would give them pleasure,' Jeffrey said. 'More than that, it would give me joy. I like them. Spending time with them, I…' his words faded into a happy smile. 'They enchant me.'

He laughed. The man could weave a web of words. What choice did he have? He had to capitulate.

'One thing each, either a sweet or some tiny item to bring home,' he agreed. 'That's all.'

'And something for us all from the cook stalls,' Jeffrey said. He widened his eyes, looking up like a dog craving affection. 'You know we'll all be hungry, Master.'

Even Katherine would agree to that. He knew it, Jeffrey knew it. He accepted it with a nod of his head.

'Thank you,' Jeffrey said. 'Thank you, my friend.'

• • •

There was still a little warmth in the evening. Dusk was beginning to settle. By the time the service was done and the procession left the church it would be dark, with blazing torches to light the way.

First, though, they squeezed their way through into the churchyard. He was holding Juliana's hand to keep her close, while Katherine had Martha with her. Richard walked beside Jeffrey, their heads bowed in conversation. His son was wrapped up warm against the chill to come. A heavy jerkin over his tunic, his hood up over his head, and thick leggings of coarse wool.

It seemed that every space was filled. Every way he turned he saw faces. They lined the path all the way to the porch and covered the grass.

The tradition was that Chesterfield people had the right to go in first for the service. This was their town, their fair, their church.

He felt on display as he walked with his family, conscious of so many eyes on him, most he couldn't even see. Past the porch and into the nave and he began to feel easier. The church was noisy as neighbours talked and gossiped. The voices rose and echoed off the high roof, filling the place with sound.

More and more people pushed their way inside until everyone was squeezed tight. The heat in the church grew.

Women used their hands to fan their faces and men stood, uncomfortable but uncomplaining.

He kept Juliana close, making sure she had enough air, not stifled by all the bodies around. Katherine had lifted Martha, and the girl looked around with bright curiosity.

Surely all of Derbyshire was in the church, he thought as the priest appeared. The choir rose from the bench he'd designed and built six years before and sang their simple plainsong. The music was slow and moving, filled with grace. It set the mood for the priest's prayers.

The man mumbled, looking down as he intoned the words. Everything was swallowed by the ground and the press of people. All the sense of holiness vanished.

He looked around, spotting the coroner standing over by the wall with his guards. His eyes were flickering as he examined everyone, searching for Lady Gwendolyn. On the other side of the church, l'Honfleur's retainers had positioned themselves to grant him space to breathe.

The priest continued, his voice a low drone. Occasionally he could pick out a word in Latin, with no knowledge of its meaning. The language of God, not meant for people like him.

Nobody in the church seemed dangerous. No gaze fixed on him, no sense of wariness. Everyone looked bored, waiting for this ceremony to be over so they could go outside and into the fresh, cool air.

Finally it was done. The priest raised his head and spoke words John did know. He'd heard them every Sunday, always with happiness in his heart.

'*Gloria Patri, et Filio, et Spiritui Sancto. Sicut erat in principio, et nunc, et semper, et in sæcula sæculorum.* Amen.'

Immediately, those close to the door tried to force their way out through the porch. He could see three men tending to an elderly goodwife who had fainted from the heat and lay on the flagstone floor.

John kept a close grip on Juliana so she wouldn't be pulled away from him. Katherine still cradled Martha. The warmth and the monotone of the priest's voice had put the girl to sleep. Jeffrey and Richard were close.

Gradually, the church began to empty. Breathing was easier. He could move, slowly following everyone else out into the night.

The air was like balm. Dark outside now, with so many stars shining up in the heavens. Just enough of a chill to raise tiny goose pimples on his arms. Katherine's sisters slid through the crowd to talk, then her brother Walter and his family.

'No sign of Lady Gwendolyn, Carpenter.'

He hadn't heard the coroner approach, but now the man was standing beside him.

'In all truth, I never believed she'd be here, Master.'

'Neither did I,' Sir Mark admitted. 'I don't know that my lord did. He hoped it. Prayed for it, maybe. But her absence says everything. He has no choice now, and I think he accepts it. Imagine what you like, but don't be too hard on him. He's lost one daughter and now he has to condemn the other for killing her. That's hard for any man to take.'

It was true. Perhaps that was the reason behind his reluctance to hand him the reward, not a lack of honour.

'He'll pay you now, Carpenter. I'll make sure of it.' He pushed his lips together in a sad smile. 'It's the least I can do.'

He should have been happy. He should have felt jubilant. But John had no sense of victory as he began to walk through the churchyard to join the procession out to the fairground. He was going to be a rich man; all his cares should have vanished. But they stayed perched on his shoulder.

All the dead still needed their justice. Gertrude, Oswald the forager, Cuthbert Unthank, old Adam. Their souls, their lives, deserved that. He could hear their voices softly praying.

John knew that he'd done all he could. He'd found those responsible for the deaths. They'd run. It was out of his hands. He wasn't the man to go in pursuit and catch them now. That was for others with horses and weapons.

'Husband?' Katherine gave him a questioning look.

'I'm fine,' he told her. 'The coroner said he'd make sure my lord paid as he promised.'

Her smile lit up the night. It was her joy at the money and what it all meant. This was over, and now their lives could return to normal. He could be a carpenter again, and she didn't need to worry for his life every time he left the house. Their children would have a father who'd arrive home every evening.

They were part of the procession, following others out of the churchyard and shuffling slowly along. But there was no hurry. He could enjoy the evening, take pleasure in having his wife and his family with him, even the company of a new friend.

'It's done, then?' Jeffrey asked.

'That's what Sir Mark promised.'

'Then it's settled. He'll make certain of that.' He grinned. 'How does it feel to know you have money?'

'Strange,' John answered after thinking for a moment. 'I'm not ready to believe it yet. It won't be real until my lord gives it to me. Until then it's just words and they can mean whatever the person saying them chooses.'

'That makes sense, I suppose. It's the safe way to see it.' He turned to Richard. 'But you'll have a comfortable life. You won't want for anything.'

The boy said nothing; how could he really understand? And he would want for one thing: life. Soon enough, another few weeks or months, and he'd be dead. He wouldn't live to see his sisters grow or the way the world changed as you became an adult.

John felt the wave of sorrow sweep up and engulf him. It came when he least expected it. What was the point of money if it couldn't buy life? Just another reminder that all the things man valued so much were nothing to God. He watched over the world and made His decisions. They may hurt, they may seem to make no sense, but they were His.

All around them, people were talking and smiling. They were happy, looking forward to the fair. He should be, too. He had a great deal to celebrate. Yet he felt that it didn't touch him, as if one of those glass windows separated him from the world and left him outside looking in.

They were moving across the market square, part of a line that snaked further than he could see. Torches burned in high sconces on the walls to keep everything bright. So different from most nights. Shadows flickered and danced and moved around in the darkness.

He felt a hand rub against his and looked down. Katherine. Smiling, relieved. He took hold of her fingers and squeezed them lightly. She was content. Surely that meant more than anything else.

The moment settled, then shattered as a woman screamed. He looked around in panic, trying to see what was happening. But people were too close for him to make out anything at all. He tightened his grip on Katherine, trying to keep her close, while his other hand kept close hold of Juliana.

A glance over his shoulder. Richard was with Jeffrey. His family was safe.

Another scream, closer this time, and then he saw.

He'd only had a single glimpse of the woman when she rode away from her house that morning. But he had no doubt. It was Lady Gwendolyn. The crowd parted before her. She carried a knife, with something dark and dripping from the blade.

Before Katherine could do anything, the woman had snatched Martha from her arms. She turned and hurried away while the girl wailed and held out her arms.

He didn't need to think. He pushed Juliana in front of Jeffrey.

'Look after them,' he ordered. Stunned, the man nodded.

John plunged after Gwendolyn. She was easy to follow. People saw the knife and the madness in her eyes and pushed back to give her space. He heard feet and looked over his shoulder. Katherine was keeping pace with him.

'Go back,' he said.

'No,' she answered, and he heard an entire world in that single word.

Gwendolyn was quick. Even with Martha in her arms, she was running fast, close to the fairground. John pushed down hard. He'd just begun to close the distance when she entered the fair.

The light came from the stalls and booths, standing like small islands in the darkness. He had to stand for a moment to try and see where Gwendolyn had gone.

Katherine was behind him. He could hear her feet pounding on the ground as she ran.

Then a woman cried out, and he darted towards it, following the noise. He was breathing hard, and fear prickled all through his body.

What did she want? What was she going to do to Martha? How could he stop her?

He couldn't see her. But he could hear. A thin, drawn-out wail from his daughter spurred him along a row, knocking people aside. He didn't care. He wanted Martha back, safe and sound.

The fairground seemed to stretch out forever. He knew full well it was a large space of land. Tonight, though, it rolled out for miles ahead of him. No matter how fast he ran, he felt he would never reach the far edge.

The crowds thinned. Most hadn't come this far. A woman behind one of the stalls looked at him then pointed dumbly. He followed. The panic was rising inside. If she hurt Martha…

Suddenly, there was no noise to guide him. He was lost. Still on the fairground; he could see the stalls all around and the low lights. But he felt as if everyone was holding their breath, waiting for something to happen.

John whirled around, as if he expected an attack. He had his knife in his fist, although he had no idea how it got there; he couldn't recall pulling it from the sheath on his belt.

Finally, a piercing call, close to thirty yards away, just down the slope. He charged along, calling out Martha's name. He wanted to let the girl know he was coming. Katherine would hear it too. It would be a beacon for her.

He was close. He could sense it. He wasn't just a figure careering blindly through the dark. Gwendolyn was nearby. She was there, and his daughter was with her.

'Martha!' He raised his head and shouted out her name. Then he heard the sound. Muffled, as if she had a hand over her mouth. No more than ten yards distant, caught in the deep shadows.

A lantern sat in one of the booths. He snatched it up and held it in front of him. Enough light to pierce a short way into the night, but it didn't go far enough.

He heard Martha sob. The sound caught at his heart. He couldn't let that happen. He couldn't let Gwendolyn hurt her.

His heart hammered in his chest, thudding against his ribs. He could hardly breathe, gasping for air.

Why was Gwendolyn doing this? How had she known who he was? How had she known about his family? Was this her revenge?

He tried to push the ideas away. He had to think about the here and now, not reasons that would make no sense. The woman had lost her mind. It couldn't be anything more than that.

Yet he couldn't find any pity for her in his heart.

Slowly, very cautiously, John moved forward. He held the lantern in one hand, his knife in the other. He'd never struck a woman in his life, never hurt one. But he would kill Gwendolyn without a moment's regret if it would save Martha.

A flash of the light on metal and he could pick her out. Standing, facing him, with Martha trying not to squirm in her arms. Her knife was close to the side of the girl's neck. The smallest slip and she'd slice through the flesh.

His daughter was terrified, staring at him with begging eyes. But there was nothing he could do. As long as Gwendolyn had the girl, she had the power.

'Let her go,' he said. He tried to sound calm, in control, but the words tumbled out sharp and scared. 'Please, let her go. She's done nothing.'

The woman didn't speak. She didn't need to; her eyes said everything. They glistened. They seemed luminous, more animal than human.

He raised his hands.

'What do you want? Tell me, Mistress.'

But still she didn't reply. He took a step closer, then stopped as she tightened her grip on the knife and brought it closer to Martha's neck.

'If you blame me, you can have your revenge on me.' He held his arms higher in the air. 'Let her go. Kill me instead if you feel I've caused you all this pain.'

Gwendolyn said nothing. Her mouth moved but no sound came out.

He watched her, searching for any sign, for anything at all that he could use to save his daughter. His palms were slick with sweat, the knife hilt sliding around in his grasp.

'Come on. Kill me and let her go. She's never hurt you. She doesn't even know who you are.'

That made the woman blink. The world seemed to have shrunk. He knew there were people all around, but they might as well not have existed. There was only Martha, Gwendolyn, and himself. No one else was real, they were shapes at the edge of his sight. He'd dreamed them.

He had to stop this. For his daughter. For himself. For his wife. He knew Katherine was here, even though he couldn't see her.

'Mistress, what do you want? Tell me, I'll listen to you. Just let my daughter go and we can talk. Do that and I won't hurt you, I give my oath on it.'

Her eyes moved towards him. Studying him as if she was seeing him properly for the first time. Her mouth opened and she snarled. An animal sound right next to Martha's ear.

The girl couldn't help herself. She began to struggle. She needed to be free, to be safe. Gwendolyn tried to press the girl close against her body. But as she did, her mouth opened and the snarl became a squeal of pain.

She dropped Martha, trying to whirl around. John hurried forward, scooped up the girl and moved back out of reach.

As the woman turned, he could see the small, sharp knife sticking out of her back. And beyond her, Katherine, staring with absolute hatred.

Gwendolyn pulled her arm back to lunge at Katherine. Before she could, a sword came out of the night and took her in the belly. She stared at it in disbelief for a moment as her eyes widened. Suddenly she seemed all too human and fragile. She started to crumple. Her knees gave way and she tumbled on to the floor, hands pushing at her stomach, trying to keep the life inside her body.

It was a hopeless task. He could see that. She must know it herself. He pulled Martha against his body so she didn't have to watch.

'It's fine,' he whispered in her ear. 'You're safe now.'

The coroner stepped from behind Katherine, still holding his sword.

'My Lady,' he said quietly. 'You left me no choice.'

CHAPTER TWENTY-THREE

'Gently,' John said as he eased the new window frame into place. Along the top he'd shaped the wood to fit the settling in the house since it had been built. Snug and perfect as he brought his face close to check. 'How is it down there?'

He glanced at Alan. The young man grinned with satisfaction.

Good. Now all they needed to do was fix it into place, then put in the glazed windows with their catches and leather hinges that would allow them to open, close and lock. With luck, the job would be completed today.

The sound of hammers and nails filled the solar of the house on Knifesmithgate. Then he stood back and studied the work.

'I'd say we've done well with that,' he told Alan. 'Now, you've fitted windows with glass before. Show me the right way to do it.'

The mute young man led him through, step by step. It was exactly the method he'd have chosen himself. It made sense, it was simple, and one man could do it on his own.

'Good, good.' He tousled the lad's hair. 'Let's get started and I'll sleep warm tonight.' Between the glass and the heavy shutters, they should never be cold in the solar again.

September had become October and the nights had turned chill. The fair was nothing more than a memory. Soon enough they'd have the full bitterness of winter.

This had been Katherine's only request after l'Honfleur had paid him. The only extravagance she needed. And it did cost in the purse, there was no doubt. But he didn't begrudge it. Maybe it would bring Richard a few more comfortable months of life.

The job didn't take the rest of the afternoon; soon enough they'd swept up the room and sat wiping their tools with oily rags before putting them away in their leather satchels. John counted out four pennies from his scrip and placed them in Alan's hand.

'You've earned it. Remember, we have an early start tomorrow. Out to Dronfield to repair the barn at the manor house. I'll call for you at dawn.'

Alone, he stared at the window, not hearing the soft footsteps on the stair or realising anyone was there until he felt the arms circling his chest.

'It's beautiful, husband.' There was a kind of awe in her voice, a reverence. The glass was thick, the panes wavy. But it let in the light and kept out the wind and the cold. Something for the wealthy, but he had it here.

He was a man of means now. Fifty pounds had changed it all. The roof was fixed. No more drips of water with every storm. All the work that needed to be done immediately was complete. The same with their other house on Saltergate.

And while it had dented that sum he possessed, even with the money spent, there was still plenty left. More than he could have imagined owning in his life.

His life had changed. He knew the reward would alter everything. But he hadn't anticipated the effect it would have.

People wanted to hire the services of the carpenter who'd found Gertrude's killer. He didn't understand how greatly people had held the anchoress in their affection. But his part in it all had quickly become known and people wanted him for large jobs, small jobs, anything at all. He was already booked to the end of November, and still people were asking if he could do this or that. He was making good wages as a carpenter, the best money he'd earned since he'd arrived in Chesterfield. There was plenty to keep Alan occupied and earning, too.

John had forced himself to leave today free to put the window and its new frame into his own house.

He felt content with life. His son was dying, but there was nothing he could do to stop that. Day by day, Richard inched away. At least he wasn't in pain. It was God's will. All they could do was love him and make sure he stayed comfortable.

The girls loved everything. Playing, learning. Jeffrey visited every day, a part of the family now, and he taught the alphabet and simple sums to Richard and the girls.

'You don't have to do it,' John told him.

'I enjoy it, my friend.' He smiled with the pleasure of it all. 'I like being with them.'

The pressure of Katherine's hand on his arm pulled him away from all his idle thoughts.

'One of the coroner's guard was here while you were banging away.'

'What did he want?' He was suspicious. More work for the coroner. It was the last thing he needed when business was so good.

'It's nothing like that.' She smiled. 'I asked him outright. Sir Mark would like you to go to his house when you have the chance. He has news.'

News? That could only mean he'd heard something about Sir Roland.

Gwendolyn was dead. She taken her last breath at the fairground, her life slipping away through the wound in her stomach. She'd said nothing. No regrets, no apology.

The priest from the church had administered the last rites. By then, though, she was already slipping beyond knowing, caught in the space between now and eternity.

The coroner had faced no court for what he'd done. Even l'Honfleur had given him the kiss of peace as they stood over the body, before my lord took her to be buried.

For days after, Martha rode the night mare in her sleep, even as they soothed her. But it had faded now; just once in the last week.

He still didn't know *why* Gwendolyn had done it. Not only snatching his daughter, but all the way back to killing her sister. He could make guesses, but what use were they? He'd never know the real reason behind it all, he thought as he washed the wood chips and sawdust from his hands and face and combed his hair with his fingers.

• • •

Chesterfield smelt of autumn. There was a tang in the air, a crispness against his skin as he crossed the market square. He could see smoke rising and caught the scent of apple wood on the air.

The fair had long since departed. By now there was no sign it had ever been here. Even the bloodstain on the earth had been washed away by the rains. Nothing remained.

He and Katherine had tried to talk about it the night after it happened. But neither of them could find the words to fit. In time, perhaps. Or maybe it was simpler to let it lie, to gradually mound the dirt over it and bury it, try to forget that it had happened.

A servant ushered him through to the hall of the coroner's house. The heat of the fire was warm and welcoming, the cup of small beer tasty on his tongue.

'Carpenter.' Sir Mark came through from the buttery, carrying a goblet of wine.

'You wanted to see me, Master.'

'Yes. Two messengers arrived today. One of them was from London.'

He waited for Strong to continue. The man had plenty to say, he could read it in his face. Better to let him do it at his own pace.

'Sir Roland has been declared outlaw by the King's Bench. Anyone can kill him with impunity now.'

'That's good news,' John agreed. 'But it was what you expected, wasn't it?'

'It was,' he agreed. 'The better news came with the other messenger, from Carlisle. They captured Roland last week.' He shrugged. 'He might be dead now, for all I know. But he did speak when they dragged him before the sheriff.'

'Oh?' Now he was interested. Finally, they might understand it all. 'What did he have to say?'

'It's money,' the coroner told him with disgust. 'Nothing more than money.'

'How?'

'Gertrude belonged to a convent. We know that. My lord intended to leave much of his money to it. He'd never made a secret of that; it was in his will. Lady Gwendolyn thought that if her sister was dead, her father would increase the share of the fortune he left her. He might even give her most of it, and she could borrow against it while he was still alive. She and Roland had spent everything they owned. The bankers had granted credit for what they expected in the future and they'd run through that. There was nothing left. They hoped that with Gertrude dead and the promise of a greater inheritance, the bankers would offer more credit.'

'Greed,' John said and Sir Mark nodded.

'Pure and simple. They knew you'd exposed them. They decided to leave on the day of the service and the procession to the fair. Roland told the sheriff that they left separately, thinking no one would suspect. They intended to meet in Scotland and make their way to France, away from justice here.'

What would they do there without money, he wondered, but he said nothing. It was a question that would never have an answer.

'But she never went.'

'No.' He let the word stay there, alone, for a moment. 'He cried when he heard his wife had died. At least give him some honour for that.'

He'd never cried for the others who'd been killed, John thought. Or perhaps they barely counted in Roland's mind.

'Did he know why she stayed?'

'He didn't. He wondered if she'd lost her mind, but he couldn't say.' The coroner sighed. 'I thought you'd like to know it all.'

'Thank you, Master.' He bowed and started to leave.

'One final thing, Carpenter.' He smiled. 'You're safe. I don't intend to ask for your services. Unless there's a time I really need them, of course.'

Outside, he stood and breathed deeply.

To know it all… that was impossible. No man could look into another's heart and see everything that was there. Not even a priest. But he had an explanation of some fashion now, and it left him filled with sorrow.

A young woman who'd given her life to God had to die to satisfy her sister's appetites. All the others who had been murdered… they were the debris gathered along the way. He could have been one of them. So could his daughter. He'd shed no tears for Gwendolyn, said no prayer for her soul. He'd feel no regret when he heard that Roland had been hung.

Slowly, he ambled home. All this had changed his life. It had come close to ending it. But he was still here, with God's good grace. He had his wife, his family. His life. A fortune and a future.

Katherine raised an eyebrow as he entered the hall.

'What did he want? Was it anything important?'

'No,' he replied after a small pause. 'Nothing important at all.'

ABOUT THE AUTHOR

As well as penning the John the Carpenter mysteries, CHRIS NICKSON is also the author of the Dan Markham mysteries and the Lottie Armstrong series (both for The Mystery Press). Chris is a well-known music journalist, and he lives in Leeds.

Also by the Author

The Crooked Spire
The Saltergate Psalter
The Holywell Dead

★

Dark Briggate Blues: A Dan Markham Mystery
The New Eastgate Swing: A Dan Markham Mystery

★

Modern Crimes: A WPC Lottie Armstrong Mystery
The Year of the Gun: A WAPC Lottie Armstrong Mystery

www.chrisnickson.co.uk

Praise for